A WOMAN'S GAME

PAULA McCOY-PINDERHUGHES

Designed by Vince Pannullo
Printed in the United States of America by RJ Communications.

ISBN: 978-0-578-13063-7

CONTENTS

DEDICATION

This book is dedicated to the memory of my sister, Dottie. Your lifelong inspiration and unwavering belief in me is in large part the reason I write stories.

To my sons, Christopher and Justin, whose love and support always keeps me moving in the right direction through this journey of writing.

"His name is Matthew Conyers, and I plan to share the rest of my life with him." His deep brown eyes washed across her horror-stricken face. "Sonya," he continued, almost apologetically, "I hope we can work out an amicable arrangement so I can spend time with Ary and Marcus, I'm still their father." His family stared in disbelief, wondering what else he would need to say, especially after the touching Thanksgiving blessing he'd given just moments before his revelation.

"You all know I love you very much, but I've chosen to start a new life with someone I unexpectedly fell in love with." Bruce Alexander rose slowly from his chair at the head of the dining room table and turned to speak directly to his wife of 18 years.

His tone was at first sincere, but as he continued it became peppered with the legalese that had become second nature after more than twenty years as an international business attorney. It was cold and tempered as he continued the speech he'd been preparing for months. "I've left a folder on the desk in the den outlining a financial settlement for the dissolution of this marriage. I'm sure it'll be enough to take care of the children, and you, until you can get on your feet. I know you'll be able to consult with an attorney who'll agree that the settlement is fair. I've also left the address and phone number of where I'll be living, in San Diego."

San Diego, dissolution of marriage, attorney, share my life with him was all that Sonya could comprehend. It had to be a dream, a nightmare. He must have been talking about another business trip. He must have meant 'her' name was something or other, a 'her' she might be able to compete with, talk him out of, and explain that it was a mid-life crisis, a terrible mistake.

Bruce reassured his children a final time that he loved them and that he cared for the well-being of their mother. But at that very moment, everything he'd stood for in the eyes of his family ceased to exist.

Sonya, Ary, and Marcus sat motionless, in shock. Their eyes followed him as he walked through the front door, stopping for a final, *'Goodbye,'* and into a waiting limousine.

CHAPTER 1

SONYA'S nagging suspicions had finally come to light. She'd accepted long ago that her once cherished relationship with her husband was on a permanent decline. But she'd purposely chosen not to upset the delicate balance of a family life she'd worked so hard to cultivate and maintain.

It was shortly after the family returned from a Hawaiian vacation that hints of an extramarital affair grew more apparent. Bruce began spending long hours at the office and taking frequent business trips to the West Coast.

It was in Hawaii that Bruce discovered what had been missing from his once storybook life— Matthew Conyers, a six foot-two inch, physically fit, Esquire handsome attorney in his mid-thirties.

On one brisk October morning Matthew decided to move away from his hometown of Rockport, Maine, a small, winter retreat community where idle gossip was considered the main form of entertainment among its long-time residents. He'd packed his bags and moved as far away from the sleepy New England hamlet as he could. Far away to the beautiful Naval City of San Diego.

Hoping to spare his wife of four years any embarrassment, he'd told family and friends that his inability to father children was the reason for the divorce. The actual truth was that he'd grown tired of living a heterosexual lie.

Matthew hung his legal shingle along the San Diego bay and focused mainly on rebuilding a lucrative practice. Little energy was spent on crafting a new social life until the day he met Bruce Alexander.

CHAPTER 2

THE men met on the Hawaiian shoreline. Bruce prepared for a surfing lesson while Matthew talked of tackling the notorious forty-foot waves off Waimea Bay with the instructor. Intrigued, Bruce struck up a casual conversation and found they had more in common than an interest in surfing. Both men admitted to having a penchant for trying new things. Matthew was also in Hawaii to experience, up close, the illuminating volcanoes. Bruce, an avid sportsman, admitted having tried just about every water sport except surfing. And on this trip he'd made a promise to himself to give it try.

Prior to Hawaii, Bruce and Sonya still slept in the same bed, enjoying each other's conversations about work, the kids, and weekend plans. Sex, on the other hand, had ended years before. Shortly after Hawaii, his entire demeanor changed. Communication with Sonya grew sparse and social get-togethers were lost in the past. Bruce planned business trips so often that he rarely made even a late showing at his son or daughter's parent/teacher school conferences or extra-curricular activities. Still, Sonya insisted that he make it home for birthdays and holidays, joining the family for what had become an Alexander tradition of specially prepared dinners in their well-appointed dining room.

At night, Bruce waited until the children had gone to bed and Sonya had fallen asleep before retiring to the guest bedroom, strengthening his resolve to leave. As time went on, knowing that her husband was in the arms of a stranger, Sonya looked for other ways to comfort herself—summoning energy from an even higher source to be able to chauffeur the kids to activities all around town, volunteer three times a week at the local art gallery and squeeze any time left over for lunch and shopping with close friends.

Given time, she prayed, Bruce would admit his infidelity and they would move past this. But what she couldn't have imagined was the tragic imprint his Thanksgiving announcement would leave on all their lives.

CHAPTER 3

"**I**'VE already explained everything mama, I'm leaving—
I've made up my mind. And yes, I know the money is
good where I am and I'm sure the quote-unquote 'glowing
opportunities' would have eventually come, but I've received
an offer of a lifetime and I'm not going to pass it up."

Ary was glad she'd decided to have this conversation over
the phone. She didn't want to risk seeing her mother's facial
expressions at the news.

"Isn't that what you and daddy always taught us—to take
chances?" she pleaded. "Well, I'm taking a *huge* chance now
mama. The time is right, I can feel it."

There was nothing more Sonya could say to dissuade her
now twenty-seven year old, headstrong daughter from leaving
a job that paid well, promoted women to meaningful management positions, offered excellent health benefits, and had more
than just a sprinkling of successful black men rising in the
company's ranks. And why, Sonya wondered, did Ary always
remind her of what she *and* Bruce had taught their children.
Why, for that matter, would she even mention the word '*daddy*'
after what he'd done to the family?

"Ary, honey, believe me, I would never discourage you
from seeking a better opportunity. But you yourself brought
up the fact that this new firm is practically lily white from what
you could tell at the interview. And why would *you* want to be

17

the one who adds color to the mix, or face any unnecessary obstacles for that matter?" Sonya grasped for any possible last straws. "What about the commute? Do you actually want to take the Long Island Railroad five days a week into New York City? The crowds, the noise Ary, and the time factor alone! You wouldn't get home until God-knows what hour! Please think carefully about this before giving them an answer, sweetheart."

"Mama, I *have* thought carefully about all of that, and besides," she said, almost under her breath, "I've already accepted the position."

Sonya sat further back in her favorite chair in the tastefully decorated, spacious family room. She swept a gaze around the walls adorned with a mixture of ethnic paintings and provocative abstract art, which had at one time, inspired lively conversations during the many dinner parties she'd hosted with her husband.

"Mama listen, neither the New York crowds, noise, time nor commute will bother me. And my commute won't be so bad because I've already found a place right across the George Washington Bridge—in Fort Lee."

"New Jersey!" Sonya blurted, waving her slender hand toward the fresco-domed ceiling. "Lord, give me strength," she mumbled. "What, pray tell, is wrong with living in Hillsdale? You have a lovely townhouse that's fifteen minutes away from your job and twenty-five minutes away from our home in Brookstone. Anyone else would kill for such convenience. Honey, Long Island is safe, spacious, and quiet."

"Ma-ma…" Ary trailed.

"Ary, I don't ordinarily interfere in your decisions. I understand that you're a grown woman capable of accomplishing whatever you set your mind to, but please tell me that you've

carefully and rationally considered this career move *and* the
sudden relocation to New Jersey!"

"Mama, I told you. I have. I've thought long *and* hard about
it. But I can't be 100 percent certain that it's gonna work out for
me there, or if it would even continue working out for me here.
No one can be 100 percent sure about anything, mama. You of
all people should understand that."

Her last statement wasn't meant to sting, it was only said to
strengthen her argument. Sonya fell silent.

"Mama, I love a challenge. And given the reputation
of National Petroleum Inc., as a predominately male, hard
numbers, driven organization, it makes the challenge all the
more appealing. And besides, Mr. Burton told me in my exit
interview that if things don't work out for me over at my new
job, I could always come back and work for him…for less
pay," she laughed, hoping to induce at least a chuckle from her
mother.

"Mama, I've been here for four years, and I'm ready for
something different."

She tried enticing her mother with a change in tone. "You
know mama, the signing bonus at the new firm 'ain't too shabby.
And with my new, even more generous salary, I can treat us to
a Saturday afternoon of mother-daughter beauty at the new
spa, Metamorphosis in the city. Maybe a little shopping on 5th
Avenue? French dining at Daniel Boulud's? A Broadway show?
A night at the 'W' New York? Need I go on?" Sonya was still
unable to respond.

"I know you worry about me mama, and I love you for
caring, but I'll be fine. I'm sure I'll meet other people and I'll
keep in contact with my old friends. No matter what, I have to
be true to myself, right?" Sonya recognized her daughter's last

statement as one of the fundamental principles she and Bruce had instilled in their children.

She finally conceded, "You're right, Ariel," using her daughter's full name whenever she felt the argument was lost. "I know you must have gone over this decision more than once in your head, and I'm sure everything will work out fine. But let me just say that I only want what's best for you and your brother, more than what I was able to hold onto…" Her words lingering as she stared out the family room rear wall of windows, looking out onto the once inspiring backyard landscape, which in the past had lifted her out of her darkest moods.

"Mama please don't say that," she begged, knowing what could come next.

"I'm sorry Ary. I don't want to ruin your news."

"Hey," she continued, trying hard to lift her own spirits, "Remember this. I'll miss you—your surprise noon-time stop-byes and our impromptu dinner dates."

"Lord mama! It's not like I'm moving to another country! Fort Lee is an hour and a half away at most, and last I heard, they did have phones, the Internet, and e-mail up and running in New Jersey. Look at it this way mama, you'll have another reason for going into New York aside from visiting the art galleries. What do you say?"

Without acknowledging her daughter's offer, Sonya dug deeper inside to muster a final sincerity. "Sweetheart, I believe in you and I know you'll be successful at whatever you choose to do."

CHAPTER 4

UNOFFICIALLY, he represented the role model for any aspiring Marketing Vice President in the company—tall, blond, and brilliant. Officially, Joseph Larsen had been Senior VP of Marketing at National Petroleum Inc., for seven years and conquering a competitor was never far from his thoughts.

"What time is she coming, G?" he asked, slightly grinning.

"Well, taking into consideration the seven-thirty breakfast meeting I had over at HJL, which, as you know, notoriously runs late, I told her to plan on being here at nine o'clock." John G. Gicardi was NPI's President and CEO. Handsome, powerful and well respected throughout the industry, he was known simply as 'G' by his staff and those close to him.

With his brow heightened, Joseph responded. "You had a breakfast meeting with HJL that didn't include me? Oh man, I must be slipping," he said, only half joking.

"Listen Joseph, get hold of Chris Sanders. I want him to meet with her after I'm done—I'm thinking I should probably pair them up as a team."

"No, wait," he hesitated. "On second thought, don't bother. Maybe she should begin as a direct report to Dwayne Hargis. Yeah, that might work out even better." G was known for making swift decisions that more than 90 percent of the time, turned out to be the right one.

"Alright G. I'll catch you later. I'll be in my office going over the Kendall Oil strategy. And by the way, I wasn't here when she interviewed, so I never got the chance to look over her, 'qualifications.'"

G shook his head and grinned as he'd done so many times before at Joseph's chauvinistic remarks. They walked in opposite directions down the dimly lit corridor adorned with Victorian wall sconces and elaborate 18th century European paintings.

CHAPTER 5

ARY awoke before the alarm clock could do its job. She'd set it for six, but for more than half an hour, she lay in bed reflecting on her decision to work at National Petroleum Inc., one last time. It'd seemed that all her life she'd looked for ways to prove to herself and others that anything was possible—walking at ten months old, reading by the age of three, and at seventeen, graduating at the top of her high school class. And, she'd successfully filed away her father's exit as a torn photo in the Alexander family album.

Captivated initially at her first interview by the aggressive goals of the company, she was ready to make her mark and eager to be able to use her foreign language skills with NPI's overseas clients. But at the same time, she was well aware of the long hours and personal sacrifices she'd have to make. There would be little time for hanging out with old friends after work or stealing away for a lunchtime mani-pedi, or a too-good-to-pass-up sale at Saks. Still, she thought, the potential financial rewards would be well worth the sacrifices. And with the additional income, she'd easily be able to afford the high cost of her Hudson Riverfront condo, complete the payments on her new BMW 535i ahead of schedule and have more than enough left over to treat herself to a fabulous weekend getaway in the Caribbean, a weeklong summer share on Martha's Vineyard or the Greek vacation she'd planned more than a year ago.

'It's six a.m. commuters, and time for some of y'all to put on your TGIF workface,' the soulful radio announcer crooned. Ary stretched, tossed her jade colored, down-filled comforter aside, and fumbled for her warm, faux, fur-lined slippers. *'Unfortunately, the weatherman says to expect scattered showers today through Sunday evening. But not to worry, the skies will clear out Monday morning, just in time to do it all over again.'*

Arrrgh… she moaned, making her way to the bathroom, piling her thick, shoulder length tresses on top of her head. *Why today, of all days?* She thought. *I need my hair to look good today.* She pinned it up with the three bobby pins lying on the bathroom countertop and reached for the flowered shower cap, which had seen better days, hanging on the back of the doorknob.

All the women in Sonya's family had thick, luscious, full heads of hair, ranging from kinky to wavy to silky curls and Ary had thanked God more times than she could remember for blessing her with her mother's family hair genes. Sonya had long ago introduced Ary to her favorite hair salon in New York's Harlem, 'Ricky's Beauty Studio,' one of a long line of stable fixtures in the famous community, home to Sylvia's Soul Food Restaurant and the Apollo Theater. Each time she visited Ricky, he reminded her as he did all of his female customers, to sleep on a satin pillowcase or wrap their heads with a silk scarf before going to bed. This ritual was meant to protect the natural oils in the hair and extend the 'do' until the next appointment.

'Hey girlfriend,' Ary remembered him saying recently, 'I kaint believe you switching jobs and fixin' to work wit us in the Big Apple. But I guess don't nobody stay too long nowhere these days, either by choice or by force, huh?' Ary smiled as she remembered the conversation. 'So you go on young lady and show them oil people what a smart, beautiful, black woman wit mo' degrees than I can count, can do. And child, don't wait, go on in there and kick some butt right away.' She remembered how Ricky could make even the most bourgeois sister smile.

Unwilling to risk an expensive hairstyle on any lingering bathroom humidity, Ary stepped out of the tub quickly, wrapped her lean body inside an oversized, plush cotton towel, and dried off as she made her way down the narrow hallway to the bedroom. She slid open the middle drawer of her armoire and retrieved the recently purchased champagne colored satin bra and panties. In the top drawer were unopened packages of expensive pantyhose. Not wanting to chance a snag, she carefully slid a light-gray pair up one leg and cautiously stepped into the other.

One side of the tiny walk-in closet hung conservative business suits. On the opposite side was casual attire. A two-tiered wooden rack held neatly lined rows of heels, sandals, boots, and sneakers. Ary had amassed an impressive shoe inventory.

Satisfied with her choice of a dark gray wool blend suit and a rose-colored cashmere sweater, the one with the scooped neckline, she stopped to observe her image in the floor length mirror leaning against a wall. Ary shook her head from side to side, just enough to give her hair the lift and bounce it needed. *I think I've managed to pull together an unforgettable first impression,* she thought.

CHAPTER 6

DRIVING around the massive parking facility a couple of times before noticing a car backing out of a space that didn't read 'reserved' near the elevator entryway, Ary sped up to beat anyone else with a similar thought. She quickly exited her car and raced to beat the closing elevator doors. Seconds later, she arrived inside the sprawling atrium. The shimmering green marble floor inlaid with octagonal designs appeared to have been recently buffed and waxed. Massive columns of white granite in each corner of the atrium looked as though they were the sole beams holding up the thirty-five-story building. The acoustics made every conversation sound as if the voices were in concert, emanating from a nearby symphony hall. She stood still for a moment, fixing her eyes on the splendor of every corner. She could appreciate the artistic quality of the structure. This was a lot different from the five-story, office building she'd worked in on Long Island.

She approached the security desk, gave her name to a rather large, expressionless man, and mentioned that she was a new employee at National Petroleum, Inc. But before issuing her a temporary employee pass, and without uttering a word, the guard's eyes seemed to question her, as if wondering why, out of all the other businesses that made up this office tower, she would choose to work for NPI. His callused finger traversed several lines down a computer screen before finally stopping at

'Alexander.' And in a voice coated with sternness, requested a picture identification.

"Sure. Would a driver's license be okay?"

"That's fine," he answered, his brusque tone rippling through her diminutive chest.

Ary stretched opened her grey Prada tote handbag.

"Step aside please," he said, continuing to monitor incoming employees.

"I know I have it," she mumbled, never looking up. "I always carry it in my wallet. Damn, I hope I didn't leave it on the table when I changed purses. Oh! Here it is."

The guard matched the tiny license portrait with the person standing in front of him and scribbled her name on a 4x4-inch pass.

"Take the middle bank of elevators to the eleventh floor."

As she moved through the turnstile, she glanced back at him for what seemed like more than an unexplained minute.

Upstairs, Ary introduced herself to the receptionist and waited patiently in a silk striped, Queen Anne chair—one of two facing a wall of tinted glass windows peeking out onto the neighboring cityscape.

"Mr. Gicardi, your guest is in the reception area," she announced in a mellifluous voice. It was eight forty-five.

CHAPTER 7

GICARDI, *Gicardi,* Ary rehearsed silently—hoping not to mispronounce it once he appeared.

"Welcome to NPI, Ary," G offered from behind her chair.

She stood up quickly after recognizing the sonorous voice of the forty-something year old man, turning to face him. This time, she was able to concentrate more on his looks and not on every word he'd said during the interview. He seemed to be of Southern Italian descent. His hair was thick, wavy, and almost jet-black except at the temples, which revealed streaks of gray, aptly adding to the refined character of his chiseled face. His dark blue suit served to compliment his tanned skin tone and emphasized his six-foot, three-inch frame. And although his feet were noticeably large, they served to sanction his masculinity. G offered her his hand.

"Glad you didn't change your mind," he joked. "How was your commute?" Stunned at first by his regal appearance, not recalling how handsome he was when she was introduced almost two weeks before, she managed to quickly pull herself together to accept his gesture.

"Thank you, Mr. Gicardi and no, I didn't change my mind," she grinned. "And the commute was fine, no problem at all." Her voice was steady even though inwardly, her nerves rattled her core.

"Were you able to get a decent spot in the garage? How about the security guards downstairs—they didn't give you any trouble did they?" he asked, jovially.

"Oh, no! I found a great space and the guard in the lobby was extremely helpful."

"*Extremely helpful*, huh? Well Ary, if the guards were that cooperative, then I know I've made the right decision. They're a tough crowd to please."

She smiled and felt the tension waning.

"Come. Can my assistant get you something to drink before we settle down? Coffee, tea, juice?"

"I'm fine, thank you."

"Well, if not now, I promise, you'll have time for…."

Halted in mid-sentence, a hastily approaching woman interrupted before his sentence was complete.

"G, when you get a moment I'd like to discuss the Rumsen account."

He cleared his throat before answering. "Of course Marguerite, we'll do that in say, thirty or forty minutes. I want to get Ary settled in first."

"Of course," she replied almost sarcastically, before extending a feather-light handshake to Ary.

"Welcome to NPI."

Ary wondered why some women practiced that prudish and seemingly insincere fingers-only handshake. *Were they afraid of catching something or did they consider it a sign of femininity?*

Managing to keep a smile on her lips, she responded "Thank you very much Ms….?"

Marguerite smiled curtly and said, "Ms. Armstead, Vice President of Customer Relations," before turning her attention toward the handsome CEO.

"So in thirty or forty G? I'll meet you in your office."

"Yes Marguerite, in my office, in forty minutes," He answered wearily.

She took only a few steps before curving back to look towards the new employee.

Suddenly she felt an instinctive need to protect the man she'd fought so hard to keep.

CHAPTER 8

JOHN G. Gicardi and Marguerite Armstead worked for competing firms in the oil industry. Although they rarely saw each other in the field, they always managed a flirtatious exchange when they did.

"Ms. Armstead, you are an *ambitious* and *exciting* business woman who carefully targets her prey, then capriciously uses all of her assets to reel them in."

"Well, Mr. Gicardi, when I see something I want, I go after it, lock, stock and barrel. It's difficult for me to hold back."

They were clearly attracted to one another, but never dared cross the implied, business/personal relationship line. She knew he was married, and he was very aware of her involvement with a competitor in the industry. But all of this changed on the day of a heavy spring rainstorm when both were trying to hail a NYC taxi.

"Mr. Gicardi, is that you?" she asked, standing just off the curbside, using her hands to protect her face from the pounding rain.

"Hello Ms. Armstead," he shouted over the roar of thunder. "You know, your beauty is even more captivating when you're wet." She managed a smile through the downpour.

A medallion taxi pulled up, splashing the waiting couple, neither of whom was equipped with a hat, umbrella or raincoat.

"I've been waiting for a while," she yelled over the howling wind and forging rain. "And on a day like this, you know every-body in the City is hailing a cab. So, why don't we share?"

"That would be very much appreciated," he returned.

"Sixteenth and fifth," she said to the cab driver as they climbed in from the unrelenting storm.

"So, Mr. Gicardi, you live near me don't you?"

"Well, I did until my recent divorce. Now I'm uptown on eighty-sixth and Broadway."

Marguerite looked surprised. "I didn't know. I'm sorry to hear that."

"Don't be. I'm not. But I am soaked to the bone," he confessed—his body shivering.

"Looks like we both are," she said, pointing to her soggy dress. They talked mostly of business during the twenty-minute ride and laughed about him having to turn around and head back uptown.

"East or West side?" the driver asked.

"West corner," she answered curtly. And just before the cabbie pulled to the west side of the street, Marguerite said, "G, you're welcomed to come up for a few minutes and dry off, unless of course, you're in a hurry to get home."

"Nothing waiting at home for me but work," he joked. G looked over the front seat at the taxi meter, paid the fare, including a generous tip before exiting the cab. He then offered a chivalrous hand to Marguerite, who after willingly accepting, dashed towards her building.

"Evening Ms. Armstead, nasty weather out there," the doorman said, as he pried open the heavy glass door of the three-story brownstone.

"Hello Manny. You're absolutely right," she answered, racing quickly into the waiting elevator. G nodded a friendly hello to the doorman, following closely behind his astonishing host. Marguerite pressed the number 3 on the panel and the doors slowly shut.

Staring at her guest, she tilted her head and shook her body from head to toe, as if stricken with a sudden chill before breaking the awkward silence. "Whew, home finally. That was quite an ordeal." Without answering, he found himself gazing at her. He felt his body temperature rising and tried to imagine what she looked like underneath the dampened dress whose fabric now clung to her petite frame. She seemed different from the strong, assertive, aloof person she portrayed to the business world.

He wondered if this would be the opportunity to finally seduce her. Could it be that that's what she wanted too?

Once inside, G noticed the eclectic décor as they entered her apartment. African facemasks and framed Baroque art from 17th Century Europe hung from the rich, cranberry painted walls that were met by taupe, crown molding at the ceiling. Two windows facing the front of the building were draped in luxurious red fabric, accented with gold piping along each side. A Birchwood coffee table separated the Scandinavian beige leather sofa and matching loveseat, which were situated strategically in the middle of the living room. But it was the white carpeting that caused him to pause at the foyer, causing an instinctive reaction to remove his shoes.

"Oh, the carpet, I'm sorry. It's just my personal reminder that the outside world may be a jungle, but once I enter my home, it all vanishes into an atmosphere of pristine elegance," she said, smiling impishly.

"Listen, why don't you change into something dry, and

comfortable. There's a robe in the guest bedroom closet, just down the hallway to the right. I think it'll fit.

G walked down the tiny corridor into the bedroom and freed himself from his wet suit. He found a black satin, ankle length robe hanging near the front of the closet. It looked new, as if it had never been worn. He emerged into the living room while still tying the robe with the gold sash. Marguerite entered from the master bedroom, donning a sleek feminine version of the same. She walked barefoot past him, across the white carpet and took two wine goblets from the top shelf of a lighted break-front. With her back to him, she asked, "Can I offer you red or white libations tonight, Mr. Gicardi?" G noticed the feminine curves of her silhouetted body as she stretched to reach the glasses. He walked up closely behind her, and with both arms, reached around her diminutive waist, taking the goblets from her hands and putting them back in their original place. He pointed toward two long stemmed lilac crystal flutes.

"I think the color, style and shape of those more closely reflects your own beauty," he whispered in her ear. She turned slowly towards him, staring into his piercing green eyes.

"You're blushing," he said. "I didn't mean to make you uncomfortable." His eyes studied her face with a fiery intensity.

She didn't answer. She knew then that he held the key to secrets only the right moment could unlock. Gently, he pulled her curvaceous body into his virile frame. Exploring her anatomy with the strength of a man and the gentleness of an experienced lover, he began kissing her lightly on her brow, then down to her eyelids and the tip of her nose before reaching her full, rose colored lips. They kissed and embraced with the passion of lovers separated by time. The intensity height-ened as he reached her slender neck. With her eyes closed, she remembered dreaming of him before this, but dared not risk telling him or betraying her own lover. But now, she didn't care; this was not the time to care.

G carefully opened her robe and began the heat intensifying ritual of kissing and caressing her breasts, sucking gently on her hardened nipples. Slowly, she pushed the robe down from his broad shoulders, stroking his physique with her manicured nails. Their burning flesh began to weaken from extreme desire.

Still standing, Marguerite's hand found the sash that would unlock the treasure she longed to have. She traced her inner thighs with his stiffened manhood, grasping tighter as it swelled to perfection in her hand. He held her tighter, wanting to taste her, every inch of her body. She needed to have him. Sweeping her up into his arms, he took her not to the bedroom as she expected, but instead, laid her glistening body down upon the chaste carpet. She felt the heat of their bodies igniting into flames of lust. His wet tongue followed an imaginary line from the cradle of her breasts to her throbbing femininity. G's mouth became the guardian of her genitalia. Not even she could escape his sentry.

He rose up and down to meet her dancing flesh—pressing his well-toned body firmly upon hers. She pleaded for him to enter her and begged him to thrust deeper and harder—he willfully obliged, again and again, urging her to surrender, moaning in ecstasy as she screamed with pleasure. Any evidence of their tryst would remain hidden in the fibers of her once virginal carpet.

Chapter 9

G and Ary walked past the reception area when a man in an obvious hurry burst out from a well-concealed bathroom. He was Dwayne Hargis, one of NPI's senior marketing analysts.

"Whoa…. slow down man! I realize time is money, but I also value the safety of my employees!"

"Oh! Sorry G. But I've got places to go—people to convince—money to make."

Ary detected a waning southern accent.

"That's what I like to hear!" G laughed. "But before you go, I'd like you to meet Ary Alexander, our latest marketing apprentice."

Dwayne offered a firm handshake.

"Ary, hello. I'm Dwayne Hargis, nice to meet you and welcome to NPI."

Feeling a sense of comfort in his strong grip, Ary thought how nice it was to see another black face.

"Thank you, Mr. Hargis."

"G, I have a nine-thirty appointment uptown and I don't want to be late. I'll be out until around noon. I've already alerted Joseph, but if you need to reach me, just call, text or email my BlackBerry. And please Ary, call me Dwayne." She smiled.

"Hey, thanks for the heads up guy. And let me know if I can be of any help."

Dwayne nodded, smiled and disappeared through the glass doors.

G stared as the elevator doors closed behind the handsome analyst.

"He's one of our best."

Dwayne was tall, dark and extremely handsome. Ary wondered about his personal story. Was he married, gay, living with someone or into women with porcelain skin? But before her racing thoughts continued, they'd reached G's office.

"Finally!" he said, pretending to be exhausted. "We're here. I didn't think we'd ever make it," he finished with a slight grin. "Connie, no calls or interruptions for the next twenty minutes please," he instructed his executive assistant.

Chapter 10

G chose to sit at the small, round, cherry wooden table in the middle of the office instead of behind the enormous mahogany desk where he made multi-million dollar deals, and invited her to join him.

"Ary, maybe you've noticed already that everyone around here calls me G, and I'd like you to do the same."

"Of course, G."

"Now, as you probably saw during your interview a few weeks back, we move at a frenetic pace around here, so I'll ask our VP of Marketing, Joseph Larsen, to explain in detail how the department operates, get you up to speed on a few of the accounts that have already been assigned to you, and possibly even introduce you to a client today or tomorrow, depending on his schedule." Ary nodded in agreement.

"And now that I've had a moment or two to think it over," he said, tapping his index finger to his temple, "Dwayne Hargis, the young man you just met in the hallway will be the person you'll directly report to. Now, all I have to do is tell *him* he has even *more* responsibility. So this will be our little secret until I can get hold of him later on today, ok?" They both laughed.

At first Ary didn't know whether to be relieved that she would be reporting to an African American, or whether to take this as an overt sign of narrow-mindedness. No matter, she was pleased, Dwayne seemed personable enough.

"Do you have any questions for me?"

"Actually, I think I bombarded you with most of my questions during the interview. So now I'm just anxious to get started with Mr. Larsen."

"Please Ary, call him Joseph. NPI is your new extended family. We're all on a first-name basis, well, everybody except for me. I'm the only one who goes by a middle initial. It's one of the perks of being CEO," he playfully winked. "But all joking aside, we look out for one another in this office and in the field. We get close to the competition, but only to strengthen our objectives. Whatever means one uses to cut a deal is perfectly acceptable, as long as it's *perceived* as legal! And by the way Ary, that last statement was said just to gauge your reaction." She wondered what her expression must have shown and quickly summoned a smile from the corners of her mouth.

"Of course Mr. Gicardi! I'm sorry. I meant to say G."

"No problem. I realize it'll take a few hours to get used too. I'll have Connie get you settled in and I'm sure Joseph will send for you shortly."

G stood up and walked her towards the door, finding it difficult to turn his eyes from the sandy haired beauty. He extended his hand.

"Welcome aboard, Ary. I know you'll be successful here. And if there's ever anything I can do for you, you know where my office is."

"Thank you, G."

Ary walked through the looming doors and noticed a short stack of files with her name emblazoned on a white sticker across the top sitting in a chair near the busy executive assistant's desk. She picked them up, looked at Connie for approval that they were indeed hers to take and found the way to her cubicle after Connie pointed her in the right direction. For the next several hours, Ary immersed herself in client and company information.

CHAPTER 11

"**E**XCUSE me, Ary, I've just been informed that you'll be reporting directly to me."

"Oh, Dwayne hello. I'm sorry, I didn't notice you there," she said, somewhat startled. "I've been totally engrossed in the reading materials."

He leaned against the portable wall. Just an hour earlier, G had called him to his office—first telling him that the promotion to management he'd sought six months ago would be effective immediately, and secondly, that promotion meant having people responsibility—namely, Ary and a former intern recently brought on board.

"No problem. Listen, have you spoken with Joseph Larsen yet?"

"No, I haven't. But G said that Joseph might be able to introduce me to a client either today or tomorrow."

"Oh, okay," Dwayne said, tilting his head to one side. "Then why don't we spend a few minutes together so I can get you up to speed on how our company operates, unless of course G wanted Joseph to do that."

Ary sensed a change in tone, but didn't understand why.

"No, no, I don't think so."

"Okay then, my office is down the hallway. Just keep curving to the right. I'm the second door on the left. Let's meet in about fifteen minutes. That'll give me enough time to return a call or two."

"Ok, I'll see you then."

Her eyes followed him as he rounded the corner—taking note of the confidence in his stride. Her mind reminded her to concentrate on her work, not his swagger.

In what seemed like no more than five minutes of concentration, every phone started to ring, including hers. She wondered if she should answer. Who could be calling for her.

"Ary Alexander, how can I help you?" she answered.

"Hello Ary, this is Joseph Larsen, Vice President of Marketing. We haven't formally met yet but I wanted to take a moment to welcome you to the company."

"Thank you, Mr. Larsen."

"Call me Joseph."

"I keep forgetting. Joseph, of course."

"Hey listen, I'm off to meet with a client, but when I return at about one-thirty or two o'clock, I'd like to take you out for lunch and acquaint you with at least one of the accounts you'll be responsible for."

"Sounds great," she answered enthusiastically.

"I'll stop by your cubicle and pick you up."

Ary turned her attention to the clock on the wall behind her chair. It was almost noon. She got up and began walking towards Dwayne's office, but suddenly realized she'd forgotten the leather-bound notepad she'd brought from home.

As she reached inside her small briefcase, which leaned alongside her desk, her phone rang. Her initial reaction was to ignore it—she didn't want to risk being late. It rang again, demanding a response.

"Good afternoon, this is Ary Alexander, how may I help you?"

"Ary, it's Dwayne Hargis."

"Dwayne, I…"

"Did you get lost?"

"Of course not. Joseph called and I…I'm on my way."

She grabbed the notepad and headed towards his office.

Dwayne's scantily clad space was equipped with a nondescript black metal desk, a matching credenza and a tiny window whose only treatment consisted of gray mini-blinds. Two black cotton fabric chairs faced him. It paled in comparison to the opulence found in G's suite. Dwayne got up and extended his hand over a desk full of open client files.

"Please, have a seat."

Ary chose the chair closest to the wall. An inexplicable urge to feel protected came over her and the stark white pictureless walls provided that assurance for the moment.

"Ary, as I'm sure you're aware, the oil industry is a very 'old-school' network. And if I may be frank with you, there aren't very many people of color or women for that matter playing the game."

"I am aware."

"Good. You have to be able to stay ahead of the next guy at every turn. There's little room for mistakes. You almost have to be a mind reader, which is something you'll understand better as you become acquainted with your clients and the competition. I've always been fascinated by the industry and the money to be made from it. And once you're accepted as a player by both sides, the only thing that matters is how many dollars it adds to the company's bottom line and in turn, your own financial portfolio, not necessarily what you did to cut the deal."

"So long as it's perceived as legal, right?"

"Absolutely. You're a quick learner. I hope what I'm saying isn't making you uncomfortable. I wouldn't want you to start having second thoughts about your decision to join the firm."

"May I be frank with you?"

"Please, go ahead."

"Well, as a woman of color I've faced challenges for the better part of my professional life and have come through them all intact. I did my research before considering what industry I wanted to work in and for what company. I knew that the white, male-dominated, oil environment in the States would present obstacles, but at the same time provide generous rewards for being able to clear crucial hurdles. NPI is a new company that has proven itself a strong contender among its more established competition in a short period of time. And for that reason, I wanted to be a part of it."

Dwayne was impressed, but chose to continue his introduction without acknowledging her. Ary was mesmerized by the presence of a strong African American male in a position of power. Her mind drifted as she remembered how proud she'd felt seeing her father interact with powerful men and women of different races and cultures whenever he took her to his office or abroad on a business trip. However, up until now, she'd managed to suppress those thoughts, keeping him out of her head during the better part of her young adult life. She hadn't heard much of Dwayne's latter conversation.

"Bastard!" she mumbled.

"I beg your pardon?"

"Oh my God, I wasn't, I didn't mean you, I..."

"Well then, you must have already had the pleasure," he surmised, thinking she was referring to Joseph. "That was my first impression when I first met him too. But I never said anything. I guess there was no one here to say it to that would understand—if you know what I mean."

"Yes, I think I do," she replied, without really understanding what he meant.

"Anyway, I think we're all finished here for now. Any questions?"

"No. You've been very helpful. Thank you."

He watched her leaving his office—staring at the doorway long after she'd gone, knowing that at NPI, beauty and brains was more of a curse than a blessing.

Ary checked her watch. It was 1:15pm. After a few minutes of twisting in her chair to find the right comfort spot, and leveraging the handle underneath the seat up and down, she settled in with her elbows resting on either side of the padded armrests and her back comfortably molded into the ergonomic frame. She continued reading the customer files. By the time she looked at her watch again, it was 2:30pm, with no sign of Joseph.

Now her stomach sang an awkward tune of discontent.

"Sounds like somebody didn't have enough to eat for lunch," Dwayne joked, as he neared her cubicle.

She sat up straight.

"Oh hi, Dwayne. Actually, I haven't eaten yet. I was waiting for Joseph."

"I'm sure something must have come up." Dwayne was accustomed to the ritual of covering for his boss. "Can I get you anything? I'm heading down to the cafe in the atrium."

She wanted to accept his invitation, but politely declined.

"Oh, thank you. But I think I can wait a few more minutes."

"Alright then. See you later." He walked away, picking up the pace to catch up with a colleague.

Ary leaned back into the groove of her chair wondering if she'd made the right decision.

CHAPTER 12

"JOSEPH, one day we're not going to be so lucky. We'll literally be caught with our pants down!"

Her name was Morgan Reynolds. She was the wife of the President and CEO of SKG, a major competitor of NPI. But Morgan was obviously more fond of the competition.

She spoke bluntly but softly to Joseph, whose office was locked to the outside world, but always opened to beautiful women.

"Sweetheart, stop your worrying," he whispered. "I knew when I started working for this company seven years ago, and set my sights on this corner office that the walls were sound-proof and the door, solid oak!" Joseph reassured Morgan in his customary way, of squeezing her firm buttocks and kissing her pencil thin lips.

"Come on honey, let me show you out."

"When will I see you again Joseph? It's getting harder and harder to go for more than a week without seeing you." He curved his arm around her waist.

"Don't worry, sweetheart. I have a business trip planned to the West Coast next Monday, and both you and I know how I *hate* traveling alone." His gray eyes gazed into her ocean blues. She found in Joseph a passion she'd missed during her six-year marriage to Brian Reynolds. His eyes told her to prepare for more stolen days and nights filled with unbridled sex.

As he reluctantly ushered her towards the door, Morgan turned and confided that she was running out of excuses for her husband. "I'm starting to really worry that he suspects something."

"Darling, you're a successful, sensuous, beautiful, career woman in your own right, who happens to be managing the most profitable account in your husband's company's history. You and I both know it's not by accident that he's entrusted you with BP. It's the golden egg," he said, convincingly. "He knows you have the professional and personal skills to keep the clients happy. So stop your worrying and tell your little hubby that you have to go out West and take care of business. Brian *suspects* nothing—he only *expects* that you keep performing...and so do I." They smiled reassuringly at each other as she walked through the door. "Have your assistant email mine with the flight details," she whispered, just as the door was closing.

Chapter 13

JOSEPH grew up in the wealthy town of Darien, Connecticut. 'A poor little rich kid from a wealthy, snobbish, community,' is how he liked to describe his upbringing. But because of his mother's scandalous divorce from a domineering, abusive husband, Joseph had to grow up quickly, standing in as her protector during verbal and physical assaults by his father in their 10,000 square foot estate, and as his mother's 12-year old date for opening night events in New York and Connecticut when her other suitors were unavailable. Through it all, Joseph never found it within himself to hate his father as most children would have at seeing their mother mistreated. In fact, as he grew older, and without his mother's knowledge, the two of them would meet at least twice a week near the Stock Exchange on Wall Street in downtown New York, near the elder Larsen's office to learn the lessons of capitalism first hand. They never spoke of the earlier abuse, only of ways to increase lasting fortune.

CHAPTER 14

JOSEPH looked at his Rolex watch. "Damn, lunch with Ary. Morgan's right. One of these days…"

He went into his private bathroom, straightened his narrow blue tie and combed his blond mane away from his face.

Fidgeting in front of the mirror and pondering over the many excuses he'd conjured up when it came to appeasing women, Joseph decided to use an old tried and true alibi. *Let's see. The meeting with the client took longer than I expected and I'd like to make it up over dinner.* Reasoning that no new NPI employee would ever challenge the validity of a VP's assertion, he ran a hand through his hair and smirked. "It is certainly not my intention to alienate the female new hires so quickly."

As he started down the corridor towards Ary's cubicle, he turned around suddenly and headed back towards his assistant.

"Michelle, call Ary Alexander and apologize for me. My meeting took longer than expected. Ask her if she'd be available for a 7p.m. business dinner at Aureole. I'll meet her there."

"Yes, Mr. Larsen."

Joseph filled the remainder of his afternoon with teleconferences, conference calls, and reviewing a proposal with Dwayne for a potential hundred-million dollar client.

CHAPTER 15

"I hope you approve of my restaurant choice?"

"Yes, it's lovely," she said, smiling while straightening out the cloth napkin on her lap. Aureole's was actually a restaurant she'd hoped to experience while on a date.

He glanced at his watch. "I apologize for being a bit late."

She noticed the diamond face of his Rolex.

"I only arrived a minute or two ahead of you."

"Wonderful. Well, this dinner is more of a welcome to this great company of ours." He raised his water glass in a toast. She followed suit.

"I hope Michelle further expressed my apologies for not being able to have lunch with you on your first day. I know how overwhelming first days can seem."

"Yes, she did. And I appreciate that you even offered to take me to lunch today. As a VP, I know you're busy. I also grabbed a quick bite at my desk once I realized that you were tied up," she lied.

"Well, I appreciate your forgiveness," he teased. "Now, let's see," he continued as he looked around the room and summoned a waiter. A tall, thin man, dressed in black pants, a white shirt and a long white apron appeared almost immediately. Strewn over his right arm was a neatly folded white cloth.

"Sir, Madam. Welcome to Aureole. May I offer you our wine list?"

"That won't be necessary," Joseph assured him. "I'll have a martini, extra dry, two olives. Ary, what's your pleasure?" She looked first at Joseph, then turned to the waiter.

"I'll have a ginger ale...on the rocks, please."

"Are you sure? It's all right you know. Business hours *have* officially ended."

"I'm sure, thank you." The waiter tipped his head to Ary then turned his full attention to Joseph.

"Thank you, sir."

"I guess then you're not much of a drinker?" Joseph asked, sitting further back in his chair.

"It's not that. I enjoy a glass of wine in the evening or champagne on special occasions."

"That's certainly good to hear young lady."

"And why is that?" she smiled.

"Because you'll find that most of our clients are pure, unadulterated lushes." They laughed in unison.

"Well, I guess that would mean that at least one of us should remain alert. I mean, how else would I get that mega-million dollar contract signed?"

"Touché!" he fired back. "So tell me *Miss* Alexander, or is it *Mrs.*?"

"I prefer Ms."

"Ok, '*Ms*' Alexander," he said, stretching out the one syllable salutation, "what schools did you attend?"

"I received my BA in Art History at Columbia University and my Masters in International Business Affairs from Harvard."

"International affairs huh? So I guess that means you've traveled abroad?"

"Many times. My family and I traveled extensively

throughout Europe, Africa and South America. I'm fascinated by different cultures. My father is an attorney specializing in international business law, and so he traveled frequently. My mother is an artist and she loves traveling the country and the world meeting new artists while discovering new artistic works as well as little known museums. My brother and I were very aware of how fortunate we were to be able to travel with them."

"I'm captivated. Do you have an interest in traveling internationally, for business?"

"Actually, that's one of the reasons I chose to work for NPI. I'd love to get the opportunity to represent the company abroad. I know that you have clients in France, Germany and England as well as Saudi Arabia. I'm fluent in French and my German just needs a little polishing. And although I know it'll be a challenge, I intend to learn Arabic."

Joseph couldn't force his eyes away from her.

"I had no idea what a gem G had hired when he brought you on board. I'm impressed already and I'm sure I've yet to discover the most intriguing qualities about you."

"Your drinks, sir, madam."

CHAPTER 16

"I know what you must be thinking, Ary—'*two weeks on the job and all they have me doing so far is reading.*'"

"No, of course not. I've managed to keep myself busy with industry information. So I don't feel bad—I'm a big girl, I can handle being left alone," she laughed.

"Alright then big girl, today's the day."

"What day?"

"Today's the day I introduce you to your client."

"Really. But I thought…"

"You thought Joseph was going to do it? That was last week. Ary listen, you'll need to learn this sooner rather than later. Joseph Larsen is an extremely busy, very hands on VP. He tends to get involved in every aspect of NPI's business, not just marketing. Although I can understand wanting to know *some* details about certain things as a Marketing VP, but I myself would concentrate more on matters like buying up smaller firms to expand our market share."

Dwayne's statement was laden with derision towards Joseph, yet it seemed, at the moment, to be directed at her. There was definitely something brewing in his head. One minute he was congenial, the next, arrogant and demanding.

"So you really think I'm ready?" she asked, softly.

"Ready?" he questioned, staring into her eager eyes.

"Ready to tackle the client."

"Let me put it to you this way. I'd say that if you weren't ready, then maybe you should reconsider your career choice here at NPI."

What an ass, she thought.

"Dwayne, I didn't actually mean that I wasn't prepared in the literal sense. What I meant to say was…"

"I'll meet you in the lobby in five minutes," he said, interrupting her mid-sentence. "The meeting will go like this: I'll make the initial introduction and then you'll have the floor. You'll talk about our recent successes and how that can translate into theirs. You'll have 15 minutes to impress the first time out—there are no second chances and no room for slip-ups. I'll see you in five."

"Dwayne," she called, catching him as he walked away. "I have two accounts—which one are we seeing today?"

His dark brown eyes tightened, and with a voice deeper than usual he turned and answered, "Be prepared for both."

Ary countered with as much authority as she could assemble. "I am."

She reached across the desk for her purse, laptop, and customer portfolio and with a quick swipe of lipstick and a swift fingering of her hair, headed for the elevator.

I really think this man would find a way to fire me if I were late to my own funeral, she mumbled. While she felt his attitude was quickly crossing the 'royal pain' line, she found herself oddly attracted to him. Maybe it was because in some ways he reminded her of Bruce, but he also mirrored a male version of herself. She found his cockiness and confidence sexy.

CHAPTER 17

ARY and Dwayne shared a cab back to the office.

"So, Mr. Hargis. Would you say I was ready?"

"Ms. Alexander, you literally stopped the show. After the first seven minutes of your presentation they were completely engrossed! They couldn't believe that a black woman..." he stopped, catching his verbal thoughts before causing any further damage.

"A black woman?" she asked, shocked at his statement.

"Ary look, these people don't have many dealings with women and especially African American women or women of color in general for that matter. Hell, I don't think they've ever gotten used to dealing with a black man when it comes to the oil business in the States. And I've worked damned long and hard to gain their trust and confidence and nothing or no one is gonna come in here and destroy it. Call it paranoia or call it astute, I don't really care, but I'll tell you this, I'm not willing to put a pretty face, no matter what color she is, who doesn't know what the hell is going on, in front of any NPI client. Hell no, not at the risk of making me look incompetent."

Ary was stunned at his candor. She leaned back against the vinyl taxi seat, not sure of how to respond.

"See, I didn't come from a privileged background where everything was just handed over to me. I'm from the hills of

West Virginia and I understood early on that to make it in this world as a successful black man, you might first have to dance to the white man's music. My folks had to work two jobs each just to put crumbs on the table. I don't ever remember eating breakfast at home when I was a child. My mother would get my two brothers and me ready for school every morning before she headed out to job number one, and walk us to the church a mile away, just to eat breakfast. And if it weren't for the school lunch programs, we would've had to wait until eight o'clock at night before we ate anything else. My Dad spent most of his time in Richmond working in the Navy yards. He made it home when he could. Most times that meant four or five times a month. And when he did manage to get time off, he worked in the coal mines during the heavy season." Dwayne pursed his lips and turned away from her.

"Why am I telling you this? Because I'm hoping that as a black person you can understand how hard it is, especially growing up with little more than the hopes and dreams inside your heart."

Ary didn't say a word. She'd never experienced poverty and had only sustained a few racist battle scars—but she wanted Dwayne to know she was empathetic. What would he think if he knew about her family? God forbid this machismo man find out about Bruce and Matthew.

She wondered why he would just assume that every African American knows or has experienced what it's like to be poor. So she pretended. "Dwayne, I understand what you're saying, I do. But I'm not a recent college graduate and my prior professional accomplishments aren't lost on NPI. And believe me, I crave success just as much as you and I'm not about to jeopardize it in any way, especially by not being prepared."

They reached their destination, saving him from all but a cool stare.

CHAPTER 18

"IT'S Air France mama, flight 1227. I'll arrive at 9 p.m. their time, so 3p.m. yours on Thursday and return home Sunday night at 11pm." Ary secretly wished she was telling a boyfriend or husband what her itinerary was instead of her mother.

"Honey, I do remember that France has a six hour time difference," Sonya shot back. "What hotel will you be staying at? Will you be on the Champs Elysees?"

"No mama, I won't. I'll be at hôtel Pierre on Rue Cartier and I'll give you a call after I arrive and get settled. Don't worry mama, I have been to France several times and I do speak the language."

"I know, Ariel Marie, I paid for your lessons. But it's still a mother's prerogative to worry none the less."

"Yes, mama, I know and I am grateful to you and daddy for making me take those private French lessons, even though I took French throughout junior high and high school."

"You know, Ary, I can't say that I do remember much gratitude coming from you when it came to taking *any* lessons outside of school—ballet, tap, voice."

"Mama!"

"Piano, flute, not to mention African drumming, and ballroom dancing."

"Ok mama, you've made your point." Both women laughed.

"Well Sonya Alexander, I *am* grateful to you for pulling me in seventy-five different directions and exposing me to other cultures and artistic interpretations. I am very fortunate and I love you for that."

"Aw honey, I love you too. And I was only teasing."

Sonya had never changed her last name after the divorce. In fact, she was still comfortable with being called Mrs. Alexander by people who didn't know any better. She'd held that title for eighteen years, and even now, more than twelve years after the break up, it was hard to relinquish.

"And while we're on the subject of love mama, what's going on with Marcus and the mystery woman? Whenever we see each other or speak on the phone he doesn't even mention her name to me."

"I don't know Ary, I've never met her. I only know that he leaves and says he's going out and won't be back most nights. I really think he's just searching for someone to call his own. Maybe he's still looking to replace the love he felt he'd missed from his father or maybe I didn't give him what he needed…."

"Don't say that mama. You tried your best. I guess being a male, Marcus needed daddy so much more than I did. I think this woman might be providing the cure for a void of emptiness you or I can't fill. And you know, I don't buy for one minute what the 'professionals' say when they talk about how boys without a father in the home can be just as well adjusted as the ones who do, as long as they have positive male role models."

"Ary, your father's choice did nothing to help Marcus! He suffered so much in school with the kids speculating about why his father suddenly left. But I don't think Bruce's staying would have made it any better. After less than a year of therapy, it was decided that Marcus was ready to move on with his life. Although honestly, I was never fully convinced."

"Mama, sometimes I think having a gay father in the house *can* be a positive role model."

"Honey, when Bruce called three months after being gone, wanting to come back into your lives, confusion would have come walking through the same door it had previously walked out of. He'd changed and so had we. He thought he could pick up the pieces and be a father again. Well, I'm sorry. A parent doesn't have the luxury of taking time off from his children. They're not clients. He couldn't just put our feelings on hold until he'd worked out the kinks in his lifestyle."

"Mama this conversation seems to be leaning towards your feelings of daddy, not Marcus."

"Ary, hold on for a second, I have another call." But before Ary could respond, Sonya had switched the line.

Whenever she 'stepped over the line,' hitting too deep when it came to Sonya and Bruce, there was always another call or someone at the door. This time however, Ary was certain the call waiting signal never beeped.

"I'm back honey. What were we talking about? Oh yes, the trip."

"Yes mama, the trip. Anyway, it's getting late and I still have a few things to pack."

"Okay baby. Have a safe flight and I'll see you….ah, when you return."

Ary knew that pause. The 'you're too busy to even come and visit your own mother like you'd promised,' pause.

"Alright mama. Good night. And listen, when I get back from Paris, why don't we meet in the city for dinner one night. Or, better yet, I'll cook for you…at my place."

Pleased at her daughter's attempt as a chef, Sonya recovered with, "Okay sweetheart. I'd like that."

"I love you mama."

"I love you too."

CHAPTER 19

SONYA held the phone until she was certain Ary had hung up. She'd always adored her children and felt that she was placed on earth to be a loving wife and nurturing mother and that her artistic talents were thrown in as a bonus from God. As the kids grew into adulthood, that adoration blossomed into pride. Ary and Marcus had come a long way since Bruce left—much further than she had—and she'd envied their emotional maturity and personal achievements. But she worried, like all parents when it came to their children's wellbeing, no matter how old they were. Ary and Marcus were all she had now and she wanted to hold on to them for as long as possible.

She reached across the bed and turned off the light.

Ary walked over to the recliner near her bedroom window, sinking down into the comfortable cushions, tucking her feet under her buttocks and looking out among the star filled night sky. *I should do more for both of them,* she thought, *like plan a fabulous weekend getaway for the three of us or at least try and make it out to Long Island to visit more than I do.*

She quieted her thoughts, dismissing them as nothing more than self-inflicted guilt trips—reminded that it was Bruce who tore his family apart, not her. According to Sonya, he'd ruined her life. But what she could never understand was why her mother hadn't found someone to replace him with or at the very least someone to take her mind off the past.

Sonya was an attractive, very young looking fifty-two year old woman, and her daughter had been urging her for years to cross the color line if her own hadn't shown any interest. *"Mama,"* she'd say, *"it's as if some black men are telling us, once the package has been opened, the goods are spoiled."*

But Sonya preferred them dark. Ary had joked during a few futile phone conversations that she would introduce her mother to Dwayne. *"He would cure your insatiable taste for black men with his supercilious personality."* But then again, she thought to herself, he'd probably remind her too much of the man she'd married and once loved.

Ary had dated white, black and brown men. And unlike her mother, she'd made the decision long ago that if some of her own were not available because they preferred blondes, then she would stretch her hazel eyes far beyond a distant horizon.

She walked over to the closet, opened the door and contemplated what clothes she'd need to pack. Two suites, two pair of casual pants, a couple of shirts, cashmere sweaters and a blazer were laid out on the bed. The black Christian Louboutin peep-toe pumps and plum colored Repetto Mary Janes would match her outfits perfectly. She packed everything carefully into a red leather garment bag. Underwear and toiletries would be tossed into a carry-on in the morning. It was late and her eyes were heavy and ready to close to the outside world.

CHAPTER 20

EVERYONE else had gone, taking with them the bound packets of information and NPI contracts. Ary walked around the conference room table gathering the extra packets on the table near the large French double doors.

"I was so surprised to see you here, Joseph. I had no idea you were coming."

"I hope I didn't make you nervous?" He watched her as she moved around the room pushing the chairs back in place.

"A little," she admitted.

"Well, I couldn't tell. You seemed at ease. But I guess that comes from knowing the language and understanding the culture."

"It does work to your advantage. I was actually expecting to see Dwayne, hoping he would have the opportunity to see me in action on the other side of the ocean. Did something come up?"

Joseph's reddened face couldn't conceal his irritation.

"Everything's fine with Dwayne. He's babysitting the domestic leg of Durand Enterprises this week, and after our meeting the other day, assured me you could handle the first phase of the client on your own. He said you were a 'quick study.'"

"I appreciate his vote of confidence. But I'm guessing that you wanted to see for yourself?" she laughed.

"Something like that," he answered with a smirk.

"Well, I'm sure by dinner tonight the client will have had an opportunity to go over the fine points in the contract with their attorneys and be ready to sign early next week." She pushed the last chair as close to the table's edge as it would go.

"You're that sure are you?"

"I am."

"You *were* convincing, Ms. Alexander," he said, staring intensely into her eyes.

"What time did you schedule dinner tonight?

"Seven o'clock, Café Broüchard."

She was hoping that by some miracle of business, he wouldn't be joining the group tonight. He had in fact made her extremely nervous. His impeccable good looks, his stature, composure and awkward intelligence were all very appealing. How would she concentrate tonight? She needed to remain focused and professional. It was different when she met him at *Aureole's* in New York. That was a business dinner. But this was intended as a pre-celebratory gathering. This was Paris after all, and there would be lots of drinking.

To not drink would be misconstrued as rude. But all night she would have to remain mindful that her boss' boss sat only a few feet away.

Ary and Joseph walked down the hallway of the eighteenth century office building. She managed to keep a safe distance from the man whose unexpected appearance was unsettling at best.

"Ary, how's your room at the Pierre?"

"It's beautiful, and yours at the..."

"St. Regis," he answered, not giving her the chance to complete her sentence. "It's on the Champs-Élysées and it's always outstanding. So listen, how well do you know the City of Light?"

"Very well. I managed to squeeze in a trip out here without my parent's knowledge during spring break of my junior year of college. A couple of girlfriends and I went to all the forbidden places a parent would cringe at if they knew about it."

"Is that so?" he laughed. "Well, do you think an old guy like me would be interested in going to any of those places?"

"I don't know," she answered, playfully, "but I'll make a deal with you. If you'd escort me to the Louvre this afternoon, I just might be willing to share at least one of those taboo places with you." He leaned against an ornately decorated wall. Her charm was infectious.

"My car will be waiting in front of your hotel at one o'clock. We'll grab a bite to eat and afterwards meet with Lady Mona Lisa and some of the boys of the Renaissance period."

"Sounds wonderful," she said, chuckling at his lame attempt at humor. "I'll see you at one."

Joseph walked away, leaving her holding the extra client folders close to her chest.

CHAPTER 21

BACK at his hotel, Joseph asked the concierge to make reservations at Café Jade, across the River Seine, on the left bank —a hangout for existentialist writers. Jean-Paul Sartre, Gabriel Marcel, Beauvior and later Hemingway and Picasso all frequented the haunt. And now it was a hangout for the local chic.

"I've been here a few times," he bragged, "and the food is exceptional, the wine superior and the scenery magnificently inspiring," he finished, kissing the tips of his fingers.

"You've convinced me," she laughed.

"May I order for you?"

"Please."

Joseph brushed off his French, ordering carefully to the patient waiter.

"L'Agneau de Champs Elyséen rôtis, les pommes de terre boulangeres, la ciboule, avec jus naturel." (*Roasted Elysian Fields Lamb, potatoes boulangeres, scallion, with natural juices*).

"I couldn't be any more impressed than if I were out with a native," she teased.

The weather was unusually warm for mid-November with temperatures hovering between fifty-five and sixty degrees. Ary gazed into the sky. Observing the slow moving clouds she thought, *what a contrast to the hustle and bustle of commuters, tourists and traffic in New York.* The sound and rhythmic flow of the river provided not only a picturesque backdrop, but also a sense of calm, a needed refuge so far away from home. As she wiped her wind-blown hair away from her face, Joseph reflected on how sensuous she looked at that moment.

"No matter how many times I've gone to the Louvre," she said, "I always manage to see the same painting in a different way. It's amazing you know, art really is a brilliant form of expression."

"Is that so?" he asked, innocently.

"My God, yes! I grew up in a house where at every turn there was a sculpture, a painting or a work in progress, opening up my world in ways that would be difficult to imagine without them. My sense of who I am is grounded in some of my mother's paintings. And my father's love for literature exposed my brother and me to great writers, poets and playwrights." Ary looked up to see the Eiffel Tower raised boldly against the Parisian sky. "See the Tower? When I was a kid on vacation with my family, I thought it was just a heap of metal and concrete. Not until I was in my late teens did I understand its true beauty and significance. My parents always introduced my brother and me to a myriad of things, but they encouraged us to find the meaning of those things on our own. When we were young, they took us to African and African American Museums up in Harlem where some of my mother's own works hung and to the unassuming museums and galleries in the East Village in New York. They'd tell us to go and explore and interpret what we saw."

Joseph listened as Ary revealed herself to him, layer by layer.

"While some of my friends talked about the dresses they wanted to buy or have made for senior Prom, and what guy they prayed would ask them, I dreamed of wearing the native garb of the Edo and one day maybe even living among the people. I guess I was kind of weird, huh?" she asked laughing.

Realizing she'd done all the talking, she stopped to give him time to respond. "I'm sorry. I'm sure you'd rather be discussing business instead of hearing me reminisce about my life growing up."

In fact, he was captivated. He could have listened to her all night. Although he'd had little contact with African Americans outside of professional acquaintances, Joseph, unlike some of his colleagues in the industry, didn't harbor any outward prejudices.

"On the contrary. I find it fascinating. And on one level, I can identify with you."

"Really?"

"Yeah. Where I grew up, in Darien, Connecticut, it would have been unheard of not to discuss your exotic summer travels when school was back in session. But unlike you, I was *forced* to go to museums, plays and operas. As a child, I found it absolutely revolting, but there was no way my divorced, high society mother would be seen going to the Metropolitan Opera House at Lincoln Center on opening night alone!"

"Well, how could she?" she questioned with a playful air of arrogance, chuckling in her cloth napkin.

"But when she remarried, she no longer forced me to go to the opera or the museums, she'd only ask if I *wanted* to go with the two of them, to which I promptly refused," his slender Irish nose wrinkling at the memory.

"But now, when I look back on it, maybe it was because I wanted to hurt her for bringing a new man into our home, which only solidified the fact that my dad wasn't ever coming back. But I appreciate everything she exposed me to. Even trying to step in to fill the shoes of my absent father."

"That sounds so sad."

"Enough of going down memory lane."

"Hey," he said, changing the tone of the conversation. "I was really disappointed that your little secret place was now a Starbucks."

She raised an empty glass. "Here's to capitalism, alive and well."

They both laughed.

They continued sharing stories of thrilling foreign travel and amusing city tales in New York. Neither wanted lunch to end.

That night, at dinner, Joseph fielded some of the tougher inquiries from the clients. Ary hadn't expected them to have so many objections to the proposal, it wasn't apparent in the earlier meeting. She wasn't sure whether they were trying to stump her in front of her VP or if their concerns were valid. She appreciated him having come to Paris after all. But when the time came to fielding any last minute hurdles, Ary sprinted past the finish line. Joseph was impressed, she was satisfied with the outcome, and the Frenchmen were anxious to begin the celebration. They toasted the deal with a bottle of Dom Perignon, 1967, and reveled for several more hours into the Parisian moonlit night.

Joseph offered Ary a ride back to her hotel, and as a gentleman, walked her through the lobby doors.

"There, safely back at your residence. I trust you'll be okay tonight, seeing as though we've all behaved like Bohemians!"

"Je suis d'accord monsieur ! (*I'll be fine, sir!*) I think I'll read over a few notes before going to…"

Before she could finish, Joseph kissed her supple lips for a modest moment that instead, felt more like a priceless minute. He stared deeply into her hazel eyes before rushing out through the revolving door. She stood in silent, frozen thought, watching as his black Mercedes sped away deep into the night.

An hour had passed when she knocked lightly on his hotel room door—her mind drifting in opposing directions, nervously waiting. The door opened slowly. Joseph stood in the entryway, his hairy chest peeking through a partially unbuttoned shirt. Ary hesitated before going in until he reached for her uncertain hand. The warmth of his smile and tone of his voice helped to reassure her decision. "I've been waiting," he whispered.

CHAPTER 22

TOSSING the clothes from her garment bag onto a convenient chair, she screamed, *What have I done?* The fact was, she was keenly aware that she'd slept with the handsome VP and wondered what would happen if he mentioned it to G?

Okay Ary, grow up. You're an adult and so is he. I won't mention it to anyone of course and I sure hope he doesn't. Her thoughts quickly faded to that romantic night in room 2542. Joseph had been gentle, yet strong, daring, yet cautious, a leader who was willing to follow. Oddly, her thoughts turned unexpectedly to Dwayne, but vanished just as quickly, realizing he'd shown little or no interest in her outside of work.

She looked towards the bright green digital clock on her nightstand, recalling the promise to call her mother once she'd returned from her trip.

"It's late. But she's probably up worrying about whether I made it home safely." She pressed the number 2 on the receiver, speed dialing her childhood home.

"Mama?"

Sonya wearily fumbled for the phone, obviously awakened from a sound sleep.

"Ary, honey, are you okay? What time is it? Where are you?"

"I'm fine and I'm home. It's twelve forty-five in the morning. Mama I apologize for calling so late—but I need to talk to you."

"What's the matter?"

"Nothing, mama, everything is fine. In fact, everything is wonderful."

Sonya sat up, blindly fumbling for the switch on the table lamp sitting atop the South African imported nightstand.

"Honey, did you close the deal?"

"Yes, but that wasn't the most interesting part of the trip."

"What do you mean, Ary?"

"I met the most wonderful man."

"In three days?"

"Mama please, just listen. It was all so amazing."

Ary explained how she and Joseph spent the afternoon together and how different he was away from the office.

"He stood firmly by my proposal when the clients tried to renegotiate on some of the points I'd made earlier at the meeting."

Sonya was surprised at how irrational her usually grounded daughter sounded. She'd seen Ary in love before, in college, but she'd always remained level headed and focused on her studies. And after going away to Harvard, she broke off a New York University relationship because, as she told her boyfriend, 'long distance romances yield short term memories.'

"Ary, isn't it Joseph's *job* to support you? I mean, you told me this account was important to the firm. Isn't it worth, what, ten million dollars?"

"Yes, that's right mama," she answered, sounding annoyed.

"So baby, what else happened? What about Dwayne? Wasn't he supportive too?"

"He didn't come."

"Why not? Wasn't he supposed to be there?"

"I don't know. There was something about a domestic account issue. Mama, I think I might be falling in love!"

"What? With Joseph? The Vice President?"

"Uh huh. I know it sounds illogical, but I only know what I'm feeling."

Sonya demanded to know what happened as diplomatically as she could, knowing that her daughter was also an adult.

Without going into great detail, Ary told her mother that she and Joseph had been intimate and that she hadn't felt this connected to anyone in years.

"Oh honey, it was only a night and I don't want to see you hurt. How old is he anyway? Ary, what does he say about what happened?"

"I haven't spoken to him yet."

"He hasn't called you?"

"No mama, not yet. It's only been a day. And he's thirty-nine years old, not that it makes any difference."

"Ary, listen to me. Joseph goes off to Paris—the City of Lust."

"Mama, please."

"And ends up in bed with a beautiful, young, smart, *black* employee—way over there. Baby, he's a VP at a very conservative and very visible oil company. I don't think he'd want to jeopardize his job or his reputation by..."

"By what, mama? What are you saying? That it wouldn't have happened on American soil? Because I'm black? This is the 21st century and *he* wasn't the first white man I've slept with."

"Ary, I'm sure he wasn't. But with Joseph you have more to lose. Honey, listen, you've just started a promising new job with an enviable income and you're clearly on the road to success.

You've always sought challenges, and with a company like NPI, I have no doubt that you'll face plenty. Baby, this position is what you say you've always wanted—don't let a man's raging hormones in a romantic country get in the way and destroy your dream."

"Are you saying that I don't know how to control my own feelings!" she screamed. "I have always kept my emotions in check!"

Sonya remembered how on several occasions Ary's judgment in men had been questionable. But she'd said nothing, reasoning that her daughter had to experience life's disappointments in order to grow.

"We have so much in common," she countered defensively. "I've waited for someone like him for a long time, and unlike Dwayne, he doesn't have to attack me just to prove he's the boss. Mama he marvels at everything I do and say."

"And why is that? Is it because it doesn't seem possible that a woman, or dare I say, a black woman could be so cultured, intelligent *and* beautiful, all at the same time?"

"You obviously don't understand what I'm saying to you, mama and I'm sorry I woke you up for such nonsense. I have to get up early tomorrow and so do you."

"Ary, wait."

"I'm sorry you can't be happy for me mama," she said, her voice quivering. "And I'm sorry you haven't realized that I'm not immune to loneliness. I need someone to hold me once in a while mama, someone to tell *me* it's okay." She took a deep breath to compose herself. "I have to go. I'll talk to you later."

Sonya held the cordless up to her ear, wondering if she'd said too much. She didn't want to see her daughter hurt or her career or name ruined. Neither had she fully recognized Ary's loneliness—she was too immersed in her own. Sonya would never purposely alienate her daughter, but at this moment, she was unsure of how to protect her. She turned off the light and lay awake, deep in thought, searching the dark room for elusive answers.

CHAPTER 23

ARY sat in her cubicle trying hard to concentrate on a proposal she was scheduled to present to Dwayne that afternoon. The elation over last week's success in Paris still lingered freshly in her mind and yesterday's arrival of the client's electronically signed contract over the company's intranet served as testimony to her business acumen.

All at once, the office phones rang in unison. She snatched hers from its base.

"NPI, Ary Alexander, speaking."

"Hello sis."

"Marcus?"

"Well how many brothers do you have?"

"Marcus, how are you? I've missed you little brother."

"I've missed you too, big sister. I'm okay, I guess."

"What do you mean 'you guess?' C'mon Marcus, what's wrong?" she asked, reverting back to her role as the protective older sibling.

"Ary I'm gonna be in the City this afternoon around two o'clock. Do you think you have time, I mean, can you meet me at…"

"Where should we meet?" she interrupted. "Do you want to come here? Or do you want to just walk around? We can go to a nice restaurant, my treat. Whatever you want."

"I'll meet you at your office at 2 o'clock? Maybe we can walk to the park? I just need to, just need to talk to you Ary," he stuttered.

"Sure Marcus. Two o'clock is fine. Come to the 11th floor of the Philips building on 5th Avenue and 53rd."

"Okay. See you then."

Ary began to worry. What was so wrong in Marcus' life that it was worth a trip to the City, a place, as he'd gotten older, he didn't particularly care to go anymore? After his father left, Marcus developed several eccentricities. The most noticeable being a fear of crowded places.

Ary hadn't spoken to Marcus in almost three weeks and now this unexpected meeting. She wondered if it had anything to do with his new girlfriend. *Was she pregnant? Did he have a fight with Sonya about it?* Now her concentration was really broken, and it was only eleven o'clock. Her thoughts switched from worry to panic.

When Bruce left, Ary had become extremely protective of her brother, fielding questions at school about Marcus' own sexuality. She'd told two close girlfriends about Bruce and swore them to lifelong secrecy. When whisperings about how Bruce left crept out in their school, she blamed it on the school counselor after Sonya confided in her in hopes of getting help for Marcus' depression.

Marcus' grades suffered and he'd begun acting out in school—getting into fistfights and stealing school supplies from his classmates and classrooms. Rather than put him in special education classes, which was the recommendation of his school counselor, Sonya instead cashed in CD's, Money Market funds and various other savings and investments to defray the cost of a hefty prep school tuition bill. She also took the advice of a close friend in the medical field and took Marcus to a child psychologist—two towns away.

"Oh shit! My presentation to Dwayne is at two o'clock today. Damn!" She considered calling Marcus to ask if they could postpone their meeting, but hastily decided against it. This was her family and he'd seemed adamant about seeing her today. She paced around her cramped quarters with one hand on her hip and the other planted firmly on her forehead, searching for an excuse not to meet with her boss.

She took the long way around the corridor down to his office hoping to summon a convincing explanation.

"I'll say one of my client's called and wants to see me at 2. That's sounds reasonable."

Confident in her story, but still replaying the words in her head, Joseph's office came into view. The door was closed. She hadn't spoken to him since returning from France, but reasoned that his head must have been filled with more important figures than her own. She was partially right. Joseph was in measured negotiations with a 34-26-34 figured green eyed blond and had instructed his assistant not to disturb him with phone calls or uninvited guests for the next thirty minutes. Ary walked on.

She noticed Dwayne's partially opened office door. Spying cautiously inside, she found no sign of him.

Shit, now what? She walked over to an empty cube and dialed the operator.

"National Petroleum Inc., This is Ann, How may I direct your call?"

"Hi Ann, it's Ary."

"Yes Ary."

"Ann, I'm looking for Dwayne."

"Let me check the system log. He's at a customer location and won't return until one forty-five this afternoon."

"Perfect. Thank you."

"You're welcome."

Ary placed the phone back in its cradle and walked back to her desk. She began typing an email message:

Dwayne: Mr. Olsen from Waxman Partners called and requested a brief meeting this afternoon. I'll call you later with an update.

Ary

Satisfied, she went to the corporate library on the fourteenth floor to work on a proposal until Marcus arrived. Once she read through the first few pages, her mind was focused more on why Joseph hadn't called or stopped by her desk than on a solution to the customer's problems.

Had mama been right? No, she couldn't have been. How would she know anything about men, really? She'd lost hers years ago.

Her heart pounded erratically as she briefly contemplated confronting him for an explanation—but just as quickly changed her mind. *"I'll let him make the next move. And besides, I'd like to keep my job. Right now I need to focus on Marcus."*

"Mr. Larsen," Michelle called, "I have G on the line."

"Thanks. Give me a second."

"Yes sir."

"Fuck!"

"Again Joseph?"

"Oh baby, I didn't mean you. Well, not now anyway. Get

your things together and see yourself out. I'll call you later." He pushed the button for speakerphone.

"Hey G, what's up?"

"Joseph, were you in the middle of something?"

"I was," he confessed, glancing at his playmate as she slowly and seductively dressed for him. "But it can wait."

"Hey, what happened in Paris with Ary?"

"What do you mean?" he asked, defensively.

"I mean, I heard from Dwayne that she blew them away with her presentation and that she overcame some last minute obstacles with the skill of a seasoned NPI professional. Is this true?"

"Yeah, yeah, didn't I tell you?"

"No, you didn't."

"Forgive me, G. You were away and I've been extremely busy. You know how it is this time of year. So, yeah, she was awesome, poised, never losing her composure, clearly in control of both meetings."

"Both meetings?"

"Ary suggested a dinner meeting that evening. She's impressively knowledgeable when it comes to how the French conduct business. I think they were all amazed, and so was I."

"So the deal is sealed?"

"Ten million dollars over three years. She's..."

"Only been here for a short while and already understands our philosophy of getting things done quickly," G interrupted. "I feel like she'll have a long and prosperous future with us here."

Joseph took that as a warning not to drive her away with a broken heart as he'd done with a couple of other female recruits.

"Ok, just wanted to touch base with you on that. I've been so busy with meeting after meeting and trying to avoid a take-over of my baby by those corporate giants that I haven't had time to celebrate her first win. I really think she's going to do very well here Joseph, don't you agree?"

"Yep, I certainly do."

It was one thirty when Ary decided to go back downstairs to her office. As she exited the elevator into the reception area, she noticed a well-dressed man sitting in the same chair she'd sat in on her first day. She walked over and bent down beside him.

"Hello there, handsome!"

"Hey sis," he said, standing up to greet her. "How are you? I know I'm kinda early. They called your extension but you weren't there."

"I know, I was upstairs in the library. How long have you been waiting?"

"Maybe ten minutes at most. You ready? You'll need your coat. It's freezing out there."

She kissed him on his frigid cheek.

"I can tell!"

"Do you need to make a pit-stop first?"

"Geez Marcus, a pit stop?" she laughed. "Actually, yeah, I do. I'll just be a minute."

"Take your time. Handle your business," he joked.

As Ary entered the ladies room, Dwayne emerged from the elevator rushing through the reception doors, intent upon getting to his office to return calls from clients who'd emailed him while he was tied up in other meetings. But his attention was drawn to the lean, nervous looking man standing next to the Victorian chair. Not accustomed to seeing many visiting black faces, he decided to stop and greet the stranger. He thought maybe this could have been a new recruit.

"Hey man, how are you?" he asked, offering a handshake.

Marcus turned around to accept the gesture. "I'm fine man, how 'bout yourself?"

"Doing good. Hey, you being helped?"

Ann wrinkled her forehead, wondering why Dwayne assumed she would have left a visitor waiting without acknowledging his presence.

"Yeah, yeah I am, thanks."

"Great. I'm Dwayne Hargis, one of the marketing managers here at NPI."

"Dwayne, it's nice to meet you. I'm Marcus Alexander."

"Alexander? Any relation to Ary Alexander?" he asked, surprisingly.

"I'm her brother."

"I didn't even know she had a brother."

"Yeah, she does. I'm the baby brother and apparently, the well-kept secret. Maybe it's because I gave her such a tough time when we were kids. But isn't that what little brothers are supposed to do?"

They laughed.

"Yeah, I suppose you're right. Hey man, it was good meeting you."

"Same here."

As he walked to his office, Dwayne glanced at his watch. It was one fifty-five.

Ary sighted her boss as she came out of the ladies room and pushed back against the wall. She decided to take the short cut, breaking into a trot on the way back to her desk to retrieve her purse and coat.

"Ready Marcus?" she asked, almost out of breath.

"Wow, that was fast. You did remember to wipe, right?" She curled her arm into his and led him to the elevator.

CHAPTER 24

ARY and Marcus left the Philips building and walked up 5th Avenue toward Central Park. They spoke very little, strolling arm and arm, admiring the Christmas and Hanukkah decorations hanging from the street lamps and shop windows. The scenes were beautiful.

Her mind wandered—thinking about how she'd had to grow up faster than she was prepared for. Sonya and Marcus needed her. Whenever Marcus had a musical or theatrical performance, Ary would leave field hockey practice or a match, even if she had to feign an illness or an injury to be able to attend with her mother, whom she felt needed her support. She'd often stayed up late into the night, providing a shoulder for Sonya to cry on. She'd made certain her grades were perfect in school in hopes of winning a four-year academic scholarship. Whatever money her mother could spare, she felt, should be used to help pay the mounting household expenses and supplement Marcus' private education.

The wind had become noticeably stronger and colder. Marcus buttoned his coat and raised his collar. He pulled the black Bismarck Fedora firmly down on his head then turned abruptly, stopping in front of his sister, causing her to halt suddenly in her tracks. Although she was already wearing a cashmere cap, he pulled the hood from her oversized Shearling coat over her head and wrapped the loosely hanging winter scarf snuggly around her neck.

"Is that better?"

"Much better," she smiled with gratitude. "And you?"

"I'm fine. Hungry yet?"

"A little. I could go for something quick and light."

"I think I've just spotted the perfect food."

"Marcus, that doesn't sound good."

"I haven't said anything."

"You've *spotted* our food? Out here? That could only mean one thing Marcus Alexander," she said, pointing to the busy hot dog and falafel vendor on a nearby corner.

"Well, you said quick and light."

"I get the quick part. But those dirty water dogs are hardly light on the stomach."

"Actually, they are. But that doesn't occur until about an hour or two after you've eaten them."

"Ugh, Marcus. C'mon, I know a little place near the Park."

"Suit yourself," he laughed.

Watching the Handsome Carriages filled with tourists gallop by in Central Park, reminded them how as children, their parents would bring them to the City during the holidays. How exciting it was. They'd start with a carriage ride through the Park, then walk over to the world famous FAO Schwartz toy store. Sonya followed Ary through the doll sections as Bruce chased Marcus, each child pointing out the toys Santa would deliver on Christmas day.

An afternoon matinee of 'A Christmas Carol,' at Radio City Music Hall would help to kick off the holiday season followed by an erratic New York City taxi ride uptown to visit a small art gallery, lavishly decorated with Slave Quilts, African Kente

Cloths and red, black and green candles, beckoning its visitors to celebrate the meaning of Kwanzaa. The children couldn't wait to feast their tiny eyes on Sonya's paintings and sculptures. They appreciated their mother's works even more during this time of year. And finally, dinner always called for a special treat at Sylvia's Soul Food restaurant, where by now, tourists from Alabama to Asia crowded the landmark for a historical taste of Harlem. The Alexander family's holiday excursion ended with a visit to where Sonya's childhood home once stood, but what was now part of a row of pricey boutiques, signaling the revitalization and gentrification of Harlem. Nevertheless, the children enjoyed listening to their mother tell tales of the struggles and ultimate triumphs of her own family.

"Your table is ready, please follow me," the host instructed.

Marcus made a sweeping motion for Ary to go first.

She followed the host through a narrow aisle to a small table for two. Although lunch hour would technically be over for workers in another city or town, New Yorker's never adhered to the status quo. The restaurant was crowded with businessmen and women, city and suburban shoppers and the sound of foreign languages spoken at every turn. The host offered Ary a chair and informed them that a waiter would be over shortly.

Ary worried if the atmosphere would be overwhelming for Marcus. "Is this place okay with you? I guess I underestimated the holiday crowds and I know how you feel about…"

"Ary, it's fine, don't worry, I've gotten better with that over the years."

"Are you sure? Because we can go to…" Before she could finish her sentence, or Marcus could object, a waiter appeared at their table offering menus.

"May I start you off with something to drink?"

"I'll have a ginger ale."

"Make it a double," Marcus quipped.

"So Ary, who's the brother I met at your office? Dwayne… somebody?"

"You met him?"

"Yeah, while I waited for you. He seems like a cool dude."

"Well, that 'cool dude' happens to be my boss and believe me, he's no *brother* of mine. I can think of several compound words that would accurately describe Dwayne Hargis, all of which end with the word 'hole.'"

"Whoa, sis. Do I sense some hostility brewing towards the brotha?"

"If Dwayne were my '*brotha*,' she gestured, using air quotes, "I would have begged mom and dad to auction him off on *eBay* or just put him up for adoption."

"O-K. I'm gonna leave that alone."

"Marcus, why is it that some professional black men always have something to prove? And usually at the expense of a black woman?"

"What are you talking about? Not all of us have something to prove. And for the few who do—who are you suggesting they're proving something to?"

"Marcus, don't pretend to be naïve. Some professional black men are rude and downright mean to their own women. Speaking in offensive tones, and ego tripping. And respect? Well, let's just say that it's not a familiar custom. But don't let a white or Latina female sashé their little butt's in front of them. They're bound to lose all sense of reason."

"First of all Ary, I don't think the Latinas would take kindly to your description of their butt's as 'little.'"

"Marcus!"

"I'm kidding. No I'm not," he whispered, under his breath.

"Seriously, Ary, you can't speak for the majority of black men out there. We adore our women and there would be no pedestal high enough that we wouldn't try to put them on. Maybe your boss is tough on you because there aren't a lot of, well, pigmented people running around your company, including you sis. Now don't throw anything at me!" he laughed, ducking to the left side of the table at her harsh stare. "Give him a chance. Talk to him. Maybe he just wants to make sure you learn the business and prove to the white boys that we can do just as well as they can, given equal opportunity."

"What the hell are you talking about Marcus? Am I supposed to be the 'great black experiment' to help him prove his management skills to the white establishment?"

"Ary listen, I really don't want to talk about Dwayne what's his name. Can we call a truce and save that for another day?"

Ary realized she was taking her frustrations with Dwayne, and subconsciously, Joseph, out on her brother.

"I'm sorry. You didn't come here to listen to me bitch about my boss, and truthfully, he's not that bad."

"Your drinks," the waiter interrupted. "Have you decided on your meals?"

"Gee, I've been so busy talking I haven't had a chance to even look at the menu." She skimmed it over quickly. "Let's see, I'll have the smoked salmon with brown rice and steamed vegetables, please."

"And you, sir."

"I'll have the veal marsala with portabello mushrooms, a side of Fettuccini Alfredo and the cheese and tomato baked Italian bread," he rattled off, patting his stomach. "See, I don't have to watch my weight, I have the ladies do the watching for me."

"I can't say that I blame you sir," the waiter admitted.

Ary laughed.

"Did I tell you how much I've missed you, Marcus? Your humor got us through the hard times back then. We shouldn't stay away from each other so long, no matter how busy we are. And we should call each other at least once a week, don't you agree?" Ary looked into her brother's eyes for his answer. "It's been three or four weeks since we've talked on the phone and I haven't seen you in almost three months!"

"It hasn't been that long Ary, but you're right and I agree. We're all we have." He looked at her as if searching for evasive answers in her face.

"What's the matter, Marcus? Why did you *need* to talk to me?"

"I don't know where to begin," he said, looking down at the dark wooden floor before facing his sister. "Well, for starters, you've never met Caroline."

"Who? Oh, is that the mystery woman?"

"She's not a 'mystery woman,' Ary. She's beautiful, ambitious and fun loving."

"Then why haven't you introduced her to me or mama?"

"We're not engaged! We've only been dating for maybe two months now."

"Two months? Marcus. Why are you keeping her a secret? Is there more to it than you're telling me? What's the…"

"Ary," he bellowed, "can you stop with the third degree and pause long enough for me to answer your first question…if I so choose?" He noticed three waiters turning to stare and realized how loud he must have sounded—he cleared his throat.

"Listen. Caroline is in her last year of law school. We met in Southampton."

"Southampton? Who do we know in Southampton?"

"We," he said, pointing to himself and his sister, "didn't know anyone in Southampton until I met Caroline...or so I thought. Come to find out, her uncle has a house in East Hampton."

"I'm lost. Southampton, East Hampton? Why were you in East Hampton?"

"I wasn't in East Hampton. Hold on a minute and let me explain. I've been attending law school at Columbia University since September."

"Are you kidding me? You? In New York? With all the crowds? I thought you hated coming to the City and what about your CPA career?"

"I never said I *hated* the City, I just *prefer* working in the burbs. And I'm not a CPA, I'm an accountant. But now I want to try my hand at law."

"Like daddy?"

"No, not like him, like me. I'm doing it for *me*. I think I can make more of a difference in law than I can keeping somebody out of hot water 'cause they added one too many zeroes to their bottom line," he said, with a hint of cynicism.

"Anyway, I met this woman on campus one night and we hit it off pretty well and I asked her out. After a couple of dates, she invited me to a weekend party out in the Hamptons, and I accepted the invitation. That's where I met Caroline. The party was at a private club for her uncle."

"Caroline's uncle or the other woman?"

"Caroline's. Meghan, the woman I was dating knew Caroline from hanging out in the Hamptons during summers.

After she introduced me to Caroline, I felt sort of a heated rush all over my body. I found out she was also at Columbia Law and we ended up talking for most of the night."

"Marcus, by now I'm guessing that both these women are white?"

"Ary, it just happened. I didn't seek them out, I truly didn't. And you know mom and dad never raised us to be prejudiced."

"Neither did they raise us to be fools. They taught us to be proud of who we are."

"What is that supposed to mean? I know for a fact you've dated white guys, so why are you getting on my case?"

"Marcus, it's not that I'm chastising you. You have a right to date whomever you want. But what about us? What about all of the other black women out there looking for *good* black men? What are they supposed to do? Cross the color line too?" Ary was speaking not only for her African American sisters, she was speaking mainly for herself. She knew she couldn't tell Marcus about Joseph today...especially not knowing if there was really anything to tell.

"Ary, I've always dated my own women and I'll probably get the chance to date them again, seeing as though I don't know what's going to happen between me and Caroline."

"Wait a minute, you just said you liked this woman and now you don't know what's going to happen? Did I miss something here?"

Marcus took a long sip of his ginger ale and then let out a lengthy sigh.

"Meghan detected the chemistry between me and Caroline and suggested that she catch a ride home after the party with some friends."

"Oh, is that how my white sisters keep our guys—pass 'em on down the line when they're through?"

"Should I continue?"

"Sorry."

"Maybe I should order you a drink first."

"Why?"

"Waiter! A glass of Merlot for the lady and a Tangueray with a twist of lime for me."

"Mar-cus?" she asked, dragging out his name. "What's going on?"

"The party," he continued, "turned out to be a surprise birthday gig for Caroline's uncle who was in town for some R&R. We were still enjoying our conversation when someone said, 'he's here!' I wasn't paying much attention because frankly, I couldn't keep my eyes off of her."

"Uh huh," Ary said, annoyingly.

"Then she said she wanted to introduce me to him. I said sure, why not. I did just crash the guy's party. Ary, when we were introduced, I nearly passed out."

"Why? Who was he?"

"Matthew Conyers."

"Daddy's lover!" she screamed, causing every diner in the restaurant to turn in their direction.

"Oh my God, Marcus, oh Lord! Where the hell is that waiter with my wine?"

"Waiter," she called, grabbing the glass out of his hand as he attempted to put it on the table. "Just bring the goddamn bottle!"

"Yes, Ma'am."

"Ary, are you okay? Ary?"

"You haven't told mama, have you?" she said, swallowing hard.

"Are you crazy? Why the hell would I do something I know would kill her?"

"It damn near just killed me." She finished her wine in two sips. "My brother is dating the niece of our father's lover, partner or whatever. Oh Marcus, was he there? Was daddy there?"

"He hadn't arrived yet. But then Matthew looked at me and said, 'Did she say your name was Marcus *Alexander?*' I said, 'yep, yes-she-did.' He stared at me for a second, then at Caroline, then slapped me on the shoulder and said, 'It's nice to meet you Marcus. Thanks for being a part of my…surprise.' Then he walked into a crowd of people in the middle of the room. Caroline looked confused and asked if we knew each other. I panicked, said no, then made an excuse to leave. I told her I had to study for a test on Monday and that I'd call her. I didn't call for two weeks. She kept calling and leaving messages on my voicemail at work, my BlackBerry and at home."

"Why did you give her your home number? You live at home…with mama!"

"That was before I knew who the guest of honor was and I do have my own phone line, Ary."

"Does mama ever answer it?"

"No. But what if she did? What do you think Caroline would say, 'Oh, hello Mrs. Alexander, we haven't met yet but my name is Caroline Grant and my uncle is porkin your ex-husband. May I please speak to Marcus?'"

"I can't believe you're actually sitting here making jokes about such a serious matter. What are your plans, Marcus? What do you intend to do about this?"

"Well, after giving it some thought, I got up the nerve to call Caroline back and explain the situation and apologized for not returning her calls."

"So, she hadn't figured out who you were?"

"Apparently she never knew about dad. But after he got there and began fraternizing with all the friends and relatives, her antennae went up; Bruce *Alexander*, Marcus *Alexander*—both African American, tall, handsome, some facial resemblance and one of them hastily leaves the party as the other pulls in. Yeah, I think she had a clue."

"So, is *she* okay with all of this, Marcus?"

"Oh yeah. But I'm sure in the back of her mind she's wondering when *I* might stumble out of the closet and leave *her* for one of her other uncles. Once again dad has fucked up my life."

"Marcus, the fact that he's gay shouldn't be a factor in fucking up your love life. It has nothing to do with it. The other thing is, how often does she even see daddy and Matthew? I mean—they do live on the West Coast."

"Yeah, that's true. But Matthew apparently has this wonderful house on the beach overlooking the ocean and you know how dad loves the water. And that to me big sister, is a little too close for comfort. The other problem is, I can't introduce Caroline to mom and I'd like to. I know she'd love her."

"Oh yeah? Don't be so sure about that baby brother. But I agree with you, I don't think you should make any sudden introductions just yet. No matter what she says, she's never totally gotten over daddy."

"I know. And lately she's been talking about him a lot and I'm the lucky one who gets to hear it in the evening when I come home—which is the real reason I decided to go to law school, at night, in the City."

"You're bad Marcus," she said, smiling. "Seriously though, I really think you need your own place, especially in light of what's going on. Can you afford to move?"

"Have you been listening to me? I just started law school. I certainly can't move now."

"I'd be more than happy to loan you some money or maybe you should ask daddy?"

"Have *you* lost *your* mind? I don't want his money and I don't need yours, Ary."

"Okay, tough guy, put the daggers away, let's think this through. Where does Caroline live?"

"In the city and she clerks part time with a new firm uptown."

"Uptown?"

"Yeah, uptown. Haven't you noticed, Harlem's integrated. So now you know why I've kept her away from you and mama. It was for your own good."

"Oh sure! For *our* own good, huh? Just keep her away from mama's house Marcus. How serious are you about this woman, anyway?"

"Let's just say I'm not interested in seeing anyone else."

"After just two months? For once I'd like to see a young, professional, available black guy get *that* serious about a sister."

"Here we go again."

"Alright. I won't mention a word about this to mama, I promise. In the meantime I think you're gonna have to talk to daddy. Tell him how you feel. When was the last time the two of you spoke?"

"I'm not sure, maybe three or four months ago when I called to ask him some questions about law."

"Was it a pleasant conversation?"

"Are you kidding? It started out fine until I heard Matthew saying in the background, 'Honey, I'm home!' That did it for me. Why can't he keep that part of his life separate? I don't need to hear that shit. I'm not the least bit interested."

"Well, I hate to break the news to you 'lil brother, but daddy's 'lifestyle' is not going away and neither is Matthew. Listen, I don't know if I'll ever be able to fully embrace it either. But my love for him, or who he was, is greater than the sum of his parts, pardon the pun."

Marcus smiled, then took a slow sip of gin, closed his eyes and savored the aftertaste. He placed the glass down carefully, making space on the crowded table to prop up both elbows, letting out a long sigh as he remembered what he'd kept from Sonya and Ary for so many years. What they didn't know was that he'd suspected his father's homosexuality long before Bruce made his irrevocable announcement. It was late one April evening. Marcus had gone down to the kitchen to sneak another piece of the peach cobbler Sonya made for Bruce on his return home from a three-day European business trip. After quietly opening the refrigerator, he heard his father's muffled voice coming from the den. Panicking, he turned to go upstairs, but suddenly had a change of mind and tiptoed down the darkened hallway, crouching behind a concealing wall. Bruce spoke softly on the telephone, assuring the person on the other end that it wouldn't be much longer before they'd be together, for good—that he too was tired of all the posturing. Marcus' heart raced, unsure of what to think. Maybe he'd misheard his father's conversation—but by the end of the ten-minute dialogue, any doubts were alleviated and his father was left exposed. He'd heard Bruce call his lover by name and confess his love.

Marcus was devastated. Feelings of confusion, betrayal and

anger rushed through his twelve-year old mind. He needed to confront his father, demand an explanation—but he'd never stood up to Bruce before, and he was unsure of how to do it now. He'd prayed it was all a misinterpretation. It was, after all, very late and the door to the den was closed, all but for a slight crack. He prayed that it had been a bad dream. But as the days went on, his troubling emotions refused to subside. Still, he was too afraid to share his discovery with the people he trusted most.

"Ary, you've always been there for me," he acknowledged, looking deep into his sister's eyes. "And it seems I've always turned to you for advice. I trust and respect your judgment and I thank you for meeting me today."

They toasted each other, finished their meals and stayed a while longer. She'd forgotten all about her two o'clock presentation.

CHAPTER 25

ARY left Marcus at the restaurant. He'd wanted to sit and brood over his predicament alone for a while. She explained that she needed to get back to the office and prepare for tomorrow's meeting. They hugged a lingering goodbye. She kissed him on the cheek then maneuvered her way through the aisle towards the bustling doorway.

Outside her office building, she noticed a man in a gray uniform standing in the cold. He stood near the entrance puffing hard on a cigarette. She realized it was the guard she'd met on her first day at NPI and wondered why he wasn't wearing a coat.

"Aren't you cold?"

He took the cigarette out of his mouth and blew a cloud of smoke into the frosty air. "Naw, not really. This'll keep me warm."

She'd never asked his name, and each day as she came to work, she purposely swiped her badge at the turnstile away from his post. He'd always worn such a serious face. No one should be that serious at eight o'clock in the morning, she'd thought.

"Well maybe I should start smoking too because, I'm freezing."

He managed a reluctant grin.

"Naw, don't go doing that. It's an expensive and deadly habit. Besides, someone as pretty as you don't need to go puttin' years on her face."

"What do you mean, 'putting years on my face?'"

"Smokin' dries out your skin, especially in your face. And after a lot of years, makes it look and feel leathery."

"Then why do it?" she asked, with an air of concern.

"I been doin it so long, I guess I don't know no better," he laughed, showing a rare display of emotion. "By the way, how's it goin up at NPI? You been there for what, three or four months now?"

"It's great—never a dull moment, so far."

"Are you reportin' directly to the big guy?"

Ary was getting colder but wondered where the curiosity about her job was stemming from. She decided to forgo comfort and continue the conversation.

"By the way, my name is Ary Alexander."

"I already know that. I signed you in on your first day? You couldn't find your I.D.…."

"I do remember," she interrupted. "But I never got your name. I was in such a hurry to get upstairs. I guess I had 'first day jitters.' I apologize."

"No need for that. I'm Robert Miller." He pointed to the silver badge pinned to his uniform breast pocket. "Everybody calls me Bob, well, everybody 'cept my sister, she still calls me Robert."

Ary smiled.

She took off her glove and offered him her slender, bare hand. "Bob it's nice to meet you." He looked surprised that she would go through the trouble. Her soft flesh felt warm. His unprotected hand was cold and rough.

"Everybody that comes and goes from that company always seem to be in such a hurry."

The wind was beginning to pick up. Her body shivered.

"Bob, I'm sure I'll see you later. Hey, don't stay out too long, it's flu season."

He dragged hard on his cigarette and panned his head around as she walked through the gold plated doors. Somehow, the chill of the winter wind felt slightly more forgiving.

CHAPTER 26

"**A**NN, has Ary called?"

"No, Mr. Hargis, I haven't spoken with her."

"Thank you." Dwayne hung up the phone and looked at the digital clock on his desk. The blue numbers glared 5:45p.m.

Pounding a fist on the desk, causing papers to scatter, he cursed, "I guess she forgot about our meeting. Well, she sure the hell better not forget about being at the client's office in the morning." He decided a phone call to her tonight was more than warranted because, he felt, financial opportunities like the one's he'd experienced in just a few short years were few and far between for many men and women of color in the U.S. oil industry. Even his friends on Wall Street told him they envied his rapid rise to success.

Dwayne knew outside of NPI, the old oil barons were still amazed every time he'd scored a multi-million dollar deal. In his early days of presenting proposals to potential clients, he'd witnessed more astonished looks than he'd care to remember. *How was it possible that a young black man knew so much about this close-knit society of the very wealthy?* He was intelligent, knowledgeable and articulate. It was irrelevant what college or university he'd come out of or how many advanced degrees he'd earned— he was in the constant mode of proving himself. There were those he felt, even at NPI who questioned his abilities. Joseph, he thought, would rather have hired someone, anyone with a lesser tan, and Marguerite—she walked around the office as if she were NPI's officially designated Queen Bee, speaking to him only when she needed something, and seemingly busting a blood vessel before the conversation could end. Nevertheless, he had G in his corner and as long as G was calling the shots and Dwayne continued bringing in the money, there was nothing to worry about.

It was six o'clock. "I'm not hanging around here any longer tonight. I'll go over the account from home."

As Dwayne hurriedly packed up his things to leave, Ary casually strolled in.

"Hi Ann."

"Oh Ary, Mr. Hargis was looking for you. He called about fifteen minutes ago."

"Thanks Ann," she whispered, rushing to her desk.

"Shit. The presentation!" She knew he'd be more than a little angry, but decided to deal with his passion in the morning. She grabbed the briefcase off her desk and headed toward the elevator.

As Dwayne stepped over the threshold of his office door, his phone rang, causing an awkward stumble.

"Damn!" He waited for a second ring then turned to pick it up.

"Dwayne Hargis."

"Mr. Hargis, it's Michelle, I'm glad I caught you. Mr. Larsen would like to see you in his office in ten minutes."

"Any ideas as to what it's about?"

"No sir."

Dwayne wanted to slam the phone down but restrained himself.

"Tell him I'm on my way."

Why did he always manage to need something at the end of the day.

"Maybe if he'd take care of real business during business hours there would be less stress on everyone around here."

"Goodnight Ann."

"Goodnight Ary and I'm right behind you."

Traffic was heavy across the bridge. The smooth sounds of Wynton Mansalis' jazz trumpet took her mind off her day. After driving for forty-minutes, she finally arrived home, pulling into the underground garage and into her reserved parking space. Walking inside the small lobby, she stopped to retrieve the mail, leafing through it as she made her way toward the elevator. There she waited patiently beside two women and exchanged a friendly smile.

Fort Lee provided a convenient and scenic retreat from the hectic pace of working in the City, and her 24th floor apartment, a lucky, end of summer find listed in the Sunday New York Times by owners who'd initially planned to sell but decided against it when the market took a dive, provided a welcomed change.

Ary exited the elevator and trekked around the corridor, anxiously unlocking the door to solitude. She placed the mail on the foyer table, kicked off her shoes and tiptoed across the carpeted living room floor to open the vertical blinds, revealing a picturesque view of the George Washington Bridge. Bright lights radiated from surrounding condos and modern glass office towers. But the sparkling green glimmer from the bridge provided the most spectacular show. It was even more dazzling during the dark winter nights.

She tossed her briefcase down beside a small writing desk in her bedroom and decided that after the shocking news from Marcus, a warm, relaxing, herbal bath would help to put her mind at ease.

A jar of lavender, salt-water crystals on the bathroom countertop seemed inviting as she poured the fragrant grains under the running warm water and carefully stepped in. The aroma quickly enveloped the tiny space and returned her thoughts to the night she shared with Joseph in Paris. The 5 foot 8 inch, one hundred-fifteen pound, vanilla-skinned beauty remembered how he undressed her, slowly. He was tender and attentive, wanting to please her, without her having to ask. He seemed to know exactly what she needed. As the perfumed bath water crossed over her body, she closed her eyes, languidly sliding her hands along the sides of her lithe frame. Joseph didn't want much from her that night—his aim was to please. She fondled her supple breasts, remembering how he swept her up into his powerful arms. He gently laid her onto his inviting bed, took a cube of ice from a glass that only minutes before held an imported scotch, and placed it between his teeth, guiding it down the center of her well-toned abdomen. The stimulating foreplay continued as he expertly directed the melting cube onto her womanhood before sensually crunching and swallowing it. She moaned in ecstasy, guilty of being lost in a sensuous moment.

Now, with her head held back, she ran her fingers through the strands of hair that had escaped her hair clip and gently lay across her shoulders. Her body rose and fell to the rhythmic beat of her orgasm.

An hour had drifted by when her stomach growled a reminder to end her fantasy and eat before settling down to business. Quickly drying off, she made her way to the kitchen, peering inside the refrigerator and deciding on leftover seafood salad as tonight's meal. After dinner, she felt relaxed and drained and laid down for a quick nap before reviewing the material for tomorrow's presentation. She tossed all but two of her many pillows towards the foot of the bed and tucked herself under the warm down-filled comforter, drifting into a welcomed sleep.

Buzzzzzzzzz! The alarm clock was unrelenting, startling her as she abruptly sat up.

"Oh shit, it's 9:30! I've overslept." Jumping out of bed, she raced to the bathroom, turned on the cold water faucet and began brushing her teeth.

"The meeting!" she screamed, spitting out the foam. "This job is everything I've always wanted. What the hell am I supposed to tell Dwayne? I can't believe this shit is happening. How could I have screwed up like this?" She caught a glance of her tussled hair in the mirror, quickly brushed it back into a bun using brown bobby pins and a hairclip to secure it in place.

She sprinted back to her bedroom, shuffled the clothes in her closet and pulled out a beige suit. "This'll have to do." Her attention was drawn to the window where she thought she'd heard raindrops. Only after pulling back the curtains did she find the night sky filled with bright stars and a full moon.

"What the hell? It's still night? What time is it?" After remotely turning on the 26-inch flat screen on the wall opposite her bed, she realized the actual time. According to the TV Guide channel, it was 9:47pm.

"What's wrong with this stupid ass clock?" she scowled.

"You all but caused me to have a friggin heart attack. You've taken on a mind of your own!"

The phone suddenly rang sending her into an orbit of disbelief.

"Holy Jesus! What now? Hello!"

"Ary, it's Dwayne Hargis. I know it's late."

"Dwayne! No, It's ok. I was up… going over my notes for tomorrow," she fibbed. She plopped down onto the bed and asked, "What's up?" stealing a needed breath before he could respond.

"Listen, weren't we scheduled to go over the presentation today?"

"Didn't you get my message," she asked, almost defensively. "It said I was going to the customer's location?"

"Yeah, and I assumed you were coming back to the office later in the evening. I guess I'm used to our new folks working a little harder and a lot later."

"I apologize for the confusion. I do plan on coming in at seven o'clock tomorrow morning. Can we meet as soon as you get in?"

"I'd prefer to go over it tonight."

"Tonight!"

"Over the telephone, Ary."

"Of course, sure, just give me a minute to pull everything together.

"Take your time."

Ary couldn't believe her luck. Tired and confused, she ran to the kitchen, grabbed a bottle of water from the refrigerator, ran back to the bedroom, and pulled the client's folder out of her briefcase."

"I'm back," she said, silencing an untimely yawn.

"You sound out of breath. Is everything okay?"

"Everything's fine," she lied.

Dwayne was unsympathetic. They talked until almost midnight. Ary's eyelids were heavy and her neck was tense. She was exhausted.

"I think we're all set for tomorrow then."

There was no response.

"Are you still there?"

"Yes," she answered, only half conscious. "I feel confident about tomorrow's meeting."

"I'll meet you in the lobby at 8:30 tomorrow morning. We'll grab a cab and head over together."

"Good night, Dwayne."

"Good night Ary, and, thanks."

"Anytime."

After she'd hung up, she realized she'd had no idea what his last words were. She fell asleep on top of the customer file which, by now was strewn across the bed. The faint sound of car tires treading over wet roads lured her back to sleep.

Dwayne leaned back into the black Italian leather loveseat in his living room. After the conversation, he changed into his blue silk boxers and turned on an old war documentary on the History channel. Fifteen minutes into the program his interest faded, and he pushed the mute button.

He went over the call in his mind. *I really should give her more credit,* he thought, *especially after seeing her perform under pressure.* But she had only been on board a few months and he could never be too cautious. He recalled the words of his father: *Dwayne, never put your faith in another human being. Put your faith in God. People always manage to screw things up for you, but not God, not the Almighty.*

He lived by that edict and was now reassured of having done right by calling her. *She was sharp,* he thought, even at night. And her willingness to calm his fears by rehearsing the entire presentation showed true commitment. There *was* something special about her, something he couldn't quite put his finger on. He'd hoped they would make a good team or at the very least, a tolerable one. And they would, he figured, as long as she understood where *he* was coming from. He'd hoped Ary was aware of the pressures of blacks in corporate America, although he'd already deemed her one shade away from passing.

Dwayne switched the channel to MSNBC, and his thoughts to Joseph, who, admittedly, he'd learned a lot from, but who also, at their last working lunch with Ary, had gazed at her as though she were the main course. And no matter how G felt about Joseph's womanizing—he'd always turned a blind eye because of the millions he'd made for the company. He too would also have turned a blind eye, were it not for the fact that Joseph had seduced a woman he'd been dating from another firm. That, he thought, was some *fucked up shit*.

He considered warning Ary about his boss' exploits, but just as quickly changed his mind.

No, I won't. I won't get involved. She's a grown woman. But the truth was, he'd become involved the first day he'd shaken her hand.

Joseph laid in his king-sized, bed, tossing and turning for more than an hour. He couldn't seem to close his eyes for more than a few minutes. Ary kept creeping into his thoughts. He'd already admitted to himself after their Parisian tryst that she was sexy, sweet, young and…black! At thirty-nine, he'd never experienced the pleasures of any other woman besides a Caucasian.

But now, he couldn't keep his mind off her and no female had ever kept him awake at night, when it didn't involve sex.

"Joseph H. Larsen, leave that alone," he demanded.

There were too many other fish in the sea waiting to be caught by his magic reel and none of whom had ever stayed on his hook for very long.

But Ary was obviously the cause of his vexing thoughts tonight and he was uncomfortable thinking of how she might impact his ego, reputation or future plans. Positioning himself in the center of his bed, he placed his hands behind his head and stared at the ceiling. Sleep would prove to be a formidable opponent tonight.

CHAPTER 27

G finished his weekly briefing with senior management in the Executive boardroom. Marguerite sat at the far end of the fifteen-foot boardroom table, directly opposite him. Joseph came in during the latter half of the meeting using damage control at a customer site as his excuse. As always, G pretended to buy his story. In reality, Joseph was tired from lack of sleep the night before—and decided on his way to work, that it was time for another Bi-coastal trip. He needed to be away from Ary, Morgan and all the others whose names escaped him at that moment.

"Joseph, I'm glad you could make it. I hope you weren't too inconvenienced by our *scheduled* weekly meeting." Everyone in the room laughed.

"G, haven't you figured out by now that I always schedule customer problems on Friday mornings." G chuckled.

"Marguerite and Chris will bring you up to speed later. Oh, and I need those notes on our favorite rival, SKG. They're going after the BP account. Who do we have working on that? I suggest either Dwayne or Mike Castellano. What's your feeling Joseph?"

"If I might interrupt," Marguerite said, surreptitiously, "I would strongly suggest Castellano for this one."

Joseph looked around the room full of men before asking, "And why is that?"

"I'm not saying that Dwayne isn't up to task, I'm sure he is, but we do need to groom some of these other guys too."

Joseph knew she'd never been fond of Dwayne and she hadn't held any deference for his abilities, crediting his fortuitous career at NPI mostly on luck, having the right accounts and having Joseph in the background to make things happen.

"Grooming guys? What the hell are you talking about? This isn't a zoo!" Joseph blasted.

"Well, I certainly don't see you having any trouble *grooming* the new female rep for high profile accounts. Annie, that's her name right?" she asked, looking directly at G.

"It's Ary, Marguerite. And I understand she's quite proficient, right Joseph?"

"*Extremely* proficient," Joseph directed at Marguerite. "She has a rapport with the clients like I haven't seen in a while. And let's not forget how quickly she closed the Paris deal. As a matter of fact G, I'm so confident in her that I insisted she present to ChemCo this morning with Dwayne."

"You did what?" Marguerite exploded. "ChemCo? That's *my* former account. They're a tough nut to crack. Are you certain she's the best choice, Joseph? Why didn't you consult with me?"

Joseph glared down the table at her.

"I wasn't aware that the Senior Vice President of Marketing had to consult with the VP of Customer Relations before making any *marketing* decisions, especially when it comes to accounts he alone is ultimately responsible for."

G looked at Marguerite, then at Joseph, tired of the growing friction between them. He couldn't have the NPI family falling apart. It wasn't good for business.

"Marguerite, what are your concerns with Ary? She's

Harvard trained, fluent in several languages, amiable and attractive, which, as you know, doesn't hurt when you're in a dead heat proposal situation." The rest of the group shook their heads in agreement, amused by their leader's candor and lightheartedness.

For the moment, Ary seemed to have a monopoly on being admired.

Marguerite was furious.

"Joseph, I am in no way suggesting that you have to *consult* with me on anything you don't want to. And, as you say, I'm just a VP. My only concern is that the ChemCo players are a very finicky bunch. It took me a good year to get that signature, which brought in more than a quarter of a billion dollars to my old firm and I'd hate to see us lose that kind of revenue because of a rookie's inexperience."

She canvassed the room for reactions.

"Look, all I'm saying is that we need to be sure."

With still no support from the group, she continued her initial plea. "As far as the BP account goes, I stick by my choice of Castellano. Look, he worked for American Oil Trust for two years before coming to us. And as I'm sure you're all aware, they're one of the smaller companies BP recently acquired. His connection with them gives us a distinct advantage. I know he has firm relationships established there and his familiarity with company policy would only serve as a positive force in our favor."

G thought for a moment. "I see your point, Marguerite."

"I don't mean to be dogmatic G," Joseph insisted, "or belittle your *past* accomplishments Marguerite, but Dwayne is the man for the BP account. He's worked tirelessly on gathering research on the management style of the company, especially in light of the fact that they've acquired *two* smaller oil companies and some of the titles and decision makers have all changed now. Dwayne wines, dines and damn near adopts their work ethic when he's there just to make them feel comfortable. That man knows everybody and their birthdays, from the secretaries to the Executives at BP and their subsidiaries, and his negotiating skills rival mine. And let us not forget he seriously dated a former successful BP marketing analyst for a while, giving him an insight into the thinking process of the department. G, this account doesn't need a marketing analyst in the grooming stage, it requires one seasoned enough to guide it from initial to final phase. And lastly, with that type of carrot dangling in front of him and the money he stands to make from it, I honestly don't see Dwayne letting anything, anyone or any other company get in his way."

"Then it's settled. Dwayne will oversee the BP account strategy."

Marguerite was seething. Her face turned beet red. There was total silence in the room after G's decision.

"We're all done here. Gentlemen, thank you. Marguerite, would you stay for a moment?"

Everyone left the room except Joseph. He took his time gathering up papers, taking pleasure in the fury written over her face.

She waited until he'd closed the door before making her way towards G.

"I hope you can see Joseph's point. He's a damn good strategist and even though we know he has weaknesses when it comes to, well, certain things, his business acumen is certainly not one of them."

"I understand G. But I don't want to see this company lose

its share of the revenue pie when it comes to competitors like SKG. You know the niece of BP's former CEO, who's still on the board by the way, is married to SKG's president."

"I know."

"So what are Joseph's plans when it comes to handling that?"

"Don't underestimate Joseph."

She tried her best to conceal her annoyance.

"As always, I'm sure you're right, G. Will there be anything else?"

"Actually, there is. I'd like you to take Ary out to lunch for me today? I've been meaning to do that since she came to work for us but you know my schedule. I also think she'd benefit from your wealth of industry knowledge and from your success with ChemCo. I understand Joseph took her out for a business dinner when she first started, but no one has done anything since she brought in the Paris deal and I'm off to Texas for three days and Saudi Arabia for five or six."

"It's five days, G. And sure, I'll take her out for you."

"Thank you, honey."

"G, why aren't I going to the Middle East with you? We've gone together for the last two years. What's changed?" She wondered if it had anything to do with Ary or any other woman.

"Marguerite, you know this trip is different. With oil prices skyrocketing worldwide, and my Saudi contacts, I want to try and help negotiate the barrel prices down so that NPI can see some near-term profits. That's first and foremost on the agenda. And aren't you still meeting me in Texas?"

"Yes, and I'm looking forward to being there with you, alone. It's been weeks since we've spent time together and I miss you terribly."

He looked into her dark brown eyes. "And I miss you Marguerite Armstead—you're quite a woman, stunningly beautiful, artfully cunning and you have a keen eye for catching the attention of good looking men," he laughed. "And, most of all, you make me feel like I can climb any mountain, even when we're not making love!"

"G, I love you so much and I wish I could tell the world. But, I understand. It wouldn't be good for business. But how do you control your emotions?"

"Control is the operative word, sweetheart. You know most of my competitors have wives and children putting demands on their time, time away from business. Not me. With every waking minute, I'm thinking of ways to grow, expand and above all else, profit from this dogged industry. I've built this company from the ground up. I'm in control. And I've always told you that after my divorce, I married this company. That'll never change. NPI is my life. I love you Marguerite and I've always been fair and honest with you. The choice has always been yours, you know how I feel."

"I know, G." she said, holding back disappointment. She couldn't afford to show any signs of weakness in his presence.

"Did you have any place in particular you wanted me to take her?"

"How about the Four Seasons."

"I don't think I could get reservations on such short notice."

"Call Tony over there and reserve my private table. You should know that Marguerite."

"I guess it slipped my mind. I'm still thinking about the BP account." she pretended.

"Leave that up to Joseph and Dwayne. And after lunch,

why don't you go over to Victoria Secret, pick out something sexy, charge it to my account, and prepare a private showing for me at the ranch this weekend." G kissed her passionately. Marguerite longed for the day he would propose and she could at last be introduced as *Mrs. John G. Gicardi*. But with Ary in the picture, she suspected in-house competition. She knew there had been other women in G's life, even after they'd become lovers. But she felt as long as she gave him what he needed, when he desired it, and helped him grow the business, she would always be number one.

"The curtain rises at seven Saturday night," she said, walking towards the door.

"And so will I," he assured her.

Marguerite left the boardroom and headed for her office.

Her mind was in an uproar, worrying about what Ary might mean to her man and his company. She unequivocally regretted having to spend any time with her, especially dining with her at G's table—the table where they'd spent countless secluded lunches and romantic dinners.

If I have any influence on him at all, her career here will be very brief. She pushed the button on her speakerphone.

"Ann, would you please call or email Ary and *tell* her I'll be taking her out to lunch today. Meet me in the lobby at 2:00p.m. sharp."

"Yes Ms. Armstead. She's at the ChemCo meeting with Mr. Hargis until one o'clock but I'll let her know."

Marguerite curled her lip and tried to respond without sounding disgusted.

"Thank you."

CHAPTER 28

THE two women met in the building lobby. "I'm glad you could find the time to make it," Marguerite said, rushing in a frantic pace as she spoke.

Ary noticed the time on the grandfather clock centered in the atrium. It chimed at quarter past the hour.

She was the one who was fifteen minutes late, Ary thought as they sped through the glass doors.

"Normally, I'd have one of the guards hail a cab for me, but you look like the type who's accustomed to *catching* things."

"Taxi!" Ary shouted.

"Four Seasons, driver. Do you know where that is?" Marguerite sarcastically inquired.

The African driver turned to see who was asking such an asinine question of a New York City cabby.

"Who doesn't?" he asked, in a heavily accented defensive tone.

She turned to Ary. "Are *you* familiar with the landmark?"

"I waited tables there not too long ago," she lied. *This was going to be pure torture*. She prayed for time to fly.

"So, how was the meeting with ChemCo?"

"Smoother than I expected. They had a few objections about our aggressive project completion date, but we managed to get a second meeting with them, which I think is a very good sign."

"Uh huh, I see. A second meeting? And then what—a third, a fourth? When will it end, Annie?"

Before Ary could answer or correct her name, the taxi pulled up alongside the restaurant. Marguerite looked at the meter and slid $10 in the tray. The fare was $9.95. Ary followed Marguerite out, but stopped and reached into the open front window and gave the driver a $10 tip for having to put up with Marguerite's unwarranted insults.

The doorman greeted them. Marguerite entered first, walking up to the Captain's station and announcing her arrival.

"Ms. Armstead, welcome to the Four Seasons. Will Mr. Gicardi be joining you for lunch this afternoon?"

"No Tony," Marguerite said, rolling her eyes. "Mr. Gicardi will *not* be joining us and I hope his table is ready, now!"

"They're in the process of setting it up. We'll seat you in just a moment. In the meantime let me take your coats." Marguerite wore a ranch mahogany female mink. Ary sported a Shearling and wondered why the Captain asked if G would be joining them. *Would he usually accompany Marguerite to lunch or dinner there?*

"I'm going to the powder room," Marguerite announced as she walked down the hallway.

"Okay," Ary answered, taking in a deep breath, grateful for the few minutes alone. Every possible scenario of why she was really there ran through her mind—from having offended Dwayne to being reprimanded because of her intimate night with Joseph.

"He didn't come for us yet?" Marguerite said, disgustingly.

"Not yet. Hopefully it won't be *too much* longer."

Tony appeared from the vestibule, and not a minute too soon.

"Ladies, your table is ready. Please follow me."

He pulled out the chairs from the exquisitely set table, centered with a crystal vase that held three winter white lilies, then handed each woman a menu.

"Miguel will be your waiter this afternoon. If there is anything you need, please don't hesitate to ask," he offered, flashing a convincing smile from years of experience.

"Ladies, enjoy your time with us."

"We could have ordered our meals in the time it took him to finish that speech," Marguerite said, scathingly.

Ary laughed, although she was almost afraid to make the slightest move or noise in Marguerite's presence.

"So Marguerite, to what do I owe the pleasure of your company this afternoon?"

It's hardly a pleasure, she thought, but dared not reveal her true feelings lest they find their way to G.

"I wanted to let you know how much we all *appreciate* you working so diligently and how *proud* we all are of your recent accomplishments. You are truly an ass-set to our little firm."

"Thank you." *I think,* Ary mumbled. "I'm happy to have made a contribution in such a short time. G is a fascinating entrepreneur. I stand to learn a lot from him."

Marguerite felt her temperature rising.

"I remember in my last year of graduate school, discussing NPI as a business case study. It made everything about b-school come to life. He'd taken all of the knowledge he'd acquired at the larger firms and turned it completely upside down to win over their long time clients. Here was this start-up, with little more than the reputation of one man with the nerve and guts to take on the giant oil establishment. Using savvy, chutzpa and his life savings, he transformed a rough oyster into a multi-million dollar pearl."

Marguerite's disdain reached fever pitch at every sentence.

"Well, it certainly sounds as though you've done your homework. Now, did you have a job before coming to us or were you unemployed?"

Ary bit her bottom lip.

"And what exactly are your long range goals? I mean, how far do you want to go with us?"

"Before this, I worked for an energy company on Long Island where I gained invaluable experience. But I wanted to be mentored by the best and learn even more about the industry than I already know. And, of course, be rewarded for my successes. And at twenty-seven, I think I have more than enough time to accomplish my goals."

Marguerite arched her brow. "Oh really?"

"Well, I've already learned a considerable amount from Dwayne."

"Dwayne?"

"You seem surprised."

"Well, he's only been with us for a short time and I don't have that much contact with him, so I guess I wasn't all that familiar with his business savvy."

"Dwayne's been with the company for more than two years and in that time has brought in a total of $675 million dollars. And this year, with my contributions, I'm sure his numbers will exceed the billion dollar mark, easily," she said with confidence. "I know he worked tirelessly on the European Esso account for well over a year—but the fact that he won the business from a competitor, who by the way was larger and produced more revenue than NPI in the last three years, tells you something about his 'business savvy.'"

Marguerite frowned. Vertical lines appeared between her eyes.

"And you've only been with NPI for four years if my research proves accurate, and prior to joining, you had a remarkably successful career with a fierce competitor. However, for some reason you were tempted to jump ship and join G's team. I didn't get to complete my research to find out exactly why that was."

Marguerite was tempted to throw her glass of Perrier in Ary's face, but held back from fear of having to explain her behavior to G. Instead, she summoned an artificial smile. Although she almost admired Ary for her knowledge and dedication to the firm, she'd have to make sure the neophyte had very limited access to her lover. She couldn't afford the distraction.

The waiter appeared, saving Marguerite a response. "Have you decided on drinks ladies?"

CHAPTER 29

DWAYNE called Ary into his office late that evening after receiving a call from the ChemCo client saying their follow-up presentation would have to be postponed for a few weeks. He panicked. There was no additional explanation given. He wondered if Ary had said anything to offend the room full of curious men and women during her presentation. He hadn't noticed any resentment. Maybe he'd missed a subtle sign after having stepped out of the room for a brief minute. Could something have happened then?

Staving off the meeting would mean giving the competition a chance to come in before NPI could address any valid concerns. He was also aware of Marguerite's displeasure with G's decisions at the manager's meeting and smelled the skunk coming from her den. All this added to his frenzied state of mind.

She knocked before his thoughts ventured into uncontrollable fear.

"Come in. What'd you think of the meeting this morning with ChemCo?" he asked, before offering her a seat.

Ary was surprised. They'd already discussed this in detail.

"I think it's going to be tougher than we'd anticipated because of the demands of the client but I think we'll see it through," she said, slowly lowering her exhausted frame into the chair.

"What do you mean *'think we'll see it through.'* There's not one person on my team who talks about *'thinking'* they'll see anything through—they *'make'* things happen and that's all there is to it!" he shouted.

Ary looked at Dwayne as if he'd lost it. She didn't understand his hostility, and after spending an unbearable lunch with Marguerite, she couldn't stand it any longer.

She sat straight up in her chair and let it out. "What the hell is your problem, Dwayne? Ever since I've started working for this company you've been on my back. And to be quite honest, I'm sick and tired of it! For every word I say, you have a negative response. If I say 'good,' you say bad, if I say 'win' you say 'lose.' And in case you haven't noticed, Mr. Hargis, in my short tenure at NPI, I've brought in more revenue than you and most of your colleagues during your first year!" Ary leaned over and rested her forearms on the edge of his desk.

"So what is this really about? Is it about me being a woman that's making you uneasy or is it because you couldn't imagine in your wildest dreams a black woman accomplishing so much, so fast? Do you have a problem with my skin color? Or does it piss off your black male ego that I can hold my own with presidents and CEO's who just happen to be white? Maybe you resent me because I'm already smart enough to know how to play the game. Which one is it Dwayne? I need to know!" she screamed. "Because if I'm to continue reporting to you, brotha man, you'd better stop ridin' me." She leaned back in her seat. "Isn't that the way they talk deep in the black coal mines of West Virginny? You know Dwayne, every black person doesn't have to be born next to a railroad track to understand the struggle. But neither do you have to be white to ride the train of success. So whatever your problem is with me Dwayne Hargis, get over it. I'm here for the long haul. And by the way, there are only three people on your so-called team—you, me and that fresh off the sales track trainee. And the only thing he's talking about '*seeing through,*' is the way to your office in the next year or two. So if you want my advice, you need to take one of your prying eyes off me and keep it on him. And if you should happen to have a change in attitude and want to discuss either the ChemCo or Kendall Oil accounts, I'll be at my desk. Enjoy the rest of your evening, Mr. Hargis." Ary rose calmly to her feet and walked out of his office.

"I should pack my bags, cause I'm either in hot shit or out of a job," she thought.

CHAPTER 30

ARY went straight to Joseph's office to ask if she could accompany him to Colorado for an upcoming marketing seminar. She'd need him on her side if Dwayne had any plans of getting rid of her. What she hadn't realized was that Joseph had already planned to relive their Paris night. He wanted her as much as she needed him.

CHAPTER 31

DWAYNE sat in his office going over contract changes to share with Joseph for Friday's meeting. It was late. The floor was empty. He stretched his arms and groaned aloud, thinking about the conversation he'd had with Ary a few hours earlier. He felt bad… for a minute.

"How dare she. Who the fuck does she think she is? She's just a high strung, arrogant, expendable pretty face. I'll just wait until Joseph gets his hands on her, then grows tired of her. He'll be the one to convince G that she's not performing up to his expectations. I'll let him destroy her little game. Yeah, I wouldn't want it to look like I couldn't handle my professional responsibilities."

In reality, he knew how good she was at her job and tried to convince himself that she was probably going through some female, hormonal change. It was after nine o'clock, but he'd caught a second wind. *I'll stay for another hour.*

The phone rang.

"Hey G. I thought I was the only one here. Yes, Joseph and I are going over that contract Friday morning. Don't worry, we've got it under control. Alright, Good night G."

As soon as he hung up the phone, it rang again.

"Hargis here. Damn. I thought I'd made it extremely clear to you never to call me at my office. I send you money every month, enough to take care of you and your entire degenerate family clan. The only reason you should ever have to speak to me is when it concerns my son and that should only be in an emergency. Look, what I did was foolish and now I have to pay for it for the rest of my life. I've told you time and time again that I regret ever meeting you and I'm sorry for what came out of that so-called relationship. You were never good enough for me or my family. We were respectable, hardworking, church going people. My folks never asked anyone for anything. But you, that's how you made your living. I should have listened to my old man when he warned me about you years ago. He knew you were looking for black gold when you latched onto me. I didn't want to believe it and made a costly mistake. Now I know what we had wasn't built from love, it was rooted in lust and greed. So do us both a favor, if there's anything I need to know about my son, send a message through the mail. And like every summer, I'll send for him. And in the meantime, I'll continue to send child support payments, way more than what was stipulated by the courts. As for you, we weren't married, so I don't owe you a dime. And I don't care how much money you think I make and how often you threaten to sue me, those hillbilly lawyers down in Greenbrier County couldn't find the way to their asses without directions. Y'all could never scare me, or my attorney, so back off." He slammed the phone into the cradle.

Chapter 32

DWAYNE had always been a survivor. He came from a family that couldn't afford for him to go to high school, let alone get an undergraduate or graduate degree. But he'd always wanted more and knew what it took to get it. He was sure there were people that would criticize his methods of achievement, but to them he'd say: *Look at me and then take a good look at yourselves. My suits are tailor made, I live in a crazy expensive condo, I travel the world…things I thought only movie stars and rich white people could afford.*

He'd eaten at restaurants where his parents wouldn't have been able to afford the tip! He'd traveled to countries he didn't even know existed when he was a kid and whose names most of the people in his home town couldn't pronounce. *I make no apologies for my success.*

He vowed to never allow anyone at NPI to know anything about his personal background—it was no one's business. Dwayne stared thoughtfully out the window, gazing at the stars that formed the big dipper. His mother's Parkinson's disease was getting worse. She would need full time care when his brother Darrell moves out next month, and he still had a shit load of medical bills for his father's cancer treatments. On top of all that, it seemed like his brother Dion was calling twice a day for a 'little loan,' money he knew he'd never see again. But through it all, he wouldn't have changed a thing about his childhood. It made him *want* to do better, reach for more than what he had, and repay his folks in whatever way he could.

All anyone at NPI knew about him was that he was from Greenbrier County, and that he had two Masters degrees, Business and Political Science, which was more than they'll ever need to know, he thought. He knew his career at NPI wouldn't last forever, but while he was there, he would make the most of it. And no one was going to screw it up.

CHAPTER 33

"YOU know Joseph, you and I have so much more in common than just scoring in business," she whispered.

"Hmmm, you're right," he said, rolling across the satin sheets from his back onto his side. "But right now, my only concern is scoring with you."

She turned to meet him, smiling, impishly biting his nose and ear. Ary closed her eyes as his fingers traveled through her raspberry scented hair and down her velvety back, gently massaging her firm, round buttocks until she cried out his name.

He positioned her slightly above his heaving chest, but not before baptizing her tender breasts with kisses. She lowered her heated body onto his, sliding her moistened femininity up and down his bulging manhood. "Harder," he moaned. This time, she would lead the way to ecstasy. "Come to me, Joseph," her words, soft as silk. He shuddered, releasing a rapturous roar, pulling her down firmly onto his pectorals.

"You make me weak," he whispered.

Noticing the snow covered mountain summit against the evening sun outside their window, she felt her flesh peaking to an orgasmic high. "You make me strong," she answered, softly. The intimate aroma of sex and perfume filled the air as their hearts settled down to a smooth jazz rhythm.

As the sun rose, she kicked off the sheets, put on his flannel shirt and stepped out onto the balcony.

This is beautiful country, she remembered. At one time, Bruce loved vacationing here with his family. The children learned how to ski on some of the same mountains she now looked down upon. Tears welled up in her eyes as she turned away, shivering from the frigid air.

"Brrr, it's cold out there."

Joseph watched as she came inside—her face reddened, arms folded and long curvaceous legs standing in the light of the morning sun.

He walked over to her, dressed only in his bare skin and whispered softy in her ear, "let me warm you up."

They were lost in the warmth of arousing heat.

CHAPTER 34

MARCUS meandered up the Moroccan tiled walkway of his childhood home and unlocked the massive wooden door. He hung his coat unevenly on an African sculpted coat tree in the foyer and walked into the family room where he found his mother carefully dusting figurines in a curio cabinet.

Looking over her glasses, she called out, "Marcus you're home! Were classes cancelled tonight?"

"No mama. I just didn't go."

"Why honey? Is everything okay?"

"Actually, everything's not okay mama. There's something I need to discuss with you and I've put it off long enough."

"What is it Marcus?" she asked nervously.

"Sit down mama," he insisted, standing next to her.

Sonya slowly lowered herself down into a traditional chair from the Ivory Coast—her eyes looking up to her son.

Marcus had been dating Caroline for more than five months and their conversations were shifting toward marriage. He'd managed to keep her hidden from his mother, but now, the time had come—the time to discuss her connection to Bruce and Matthew.

Although he could never have imagined how this would affect the family, his intentions were pure. And while his sister had already shown some understanding, Sonya was still harboring deep resentment from the past.

151

He'd wondered if she'd risk losing a son or accept a woman who by no fault of her own, had fallen in love with a man whose father had deserted his family to be at peace with himself.

This would be more difficult than anything he'd faced since eavesdropping on his father's late night conversation, followed by that tragic Thanksgiving Day. He loved his mother dearly, and had played this scene in his head repeatedly.

He'd chosen not to rely on Ary's advice of keeping Caroline away until they were married, knowing that would surely kill his mother. He respected her for what he considered her quiet courage. He also still felt tremendous guilt for never having revealed what he'd found out about Bruce long before he'd left. But now he had to know whether or not she could put aside her years of suffering and anguish for his and Caroline's happiness.

"Mama, as you've probably guessed, I've been seeing someone for quite some time now. Her name is Caroline Grant, she's a law student at Columbia, and she's white."

Sonya sat still—without expression. She turned away from him, not sure of what to expect next.

"We're discussing marriage and I feel it's time the two of you met."

Her heart was racing. Her chest was heavy. A white man had already taken her husband and shattered her soul, now a white woman was stealing her son.

Slowly she turned to face him again. He kneeled down beside her.

"What do you expect me to say Marcus? *'Caroline, come on in, welcome to the family!'* You've been seeing this woman for almost half a year, going off on weekend junkets, not telling me at least the vicinity of where you were headed…in case of an emergency—and coming home on weekdays at one or two o'clock in the morning. I didn't know what to assume. You could have been lying on the side of a road, hurt or dead. I spent many nights worrying about you, Marcus, but chose not to invade a grown man's privacy by calling his cell phone. You never mentioned anything about her or brought her here, to *your* home—even when the two of you knew the relationship was getting serious. Why the secrecy? Did you think I would tell her about your father and his lover? I would never hurt you the way I've been hurt." Marcus took her hands into his.

"Mama, don't make this any harder than it already is."

"What?" she said, jerking them away, "It shouldn't matter to me that you couldn't find a *black* woman to get serious with? Maybe you wouldn't have had to keep *her* wrapped in a veil of secrecy. I should just ignore the fact that we've all been through emotional hell with the choices your father made with his *white* partner."

He grabbed her shoulders, stared deep into her sorrowful, chestnut eyes and yelled as loud as he could.

"Mama, would it have been easier if he'd chosen a *black* man to love? And if you're still hurting that badly mama, why did you choose to stay here? In this house—with all those memories? I could never understand it. Why didn't we ever move?"

She cast aside his questions, choosing instead to focus on a favorite painting hanging on the far wall and lament about her daughter.

"And now, Ary's involved with a man who I'm certain, when he's done with her, will ruin her life and career."

Turning back to face her son, she asked, "Are you telling me Marcus that all of these things shouldn't make a difference to me? Baby, you're only twenty-five years old. You haven't really experienced life and it's many challenges. There are prejudices out there that you and your sister have never really faced. Marcus, while he was here, your father provided us with an enviable lifestyle, the kind most people only dream about. And we exposed you to cultures most have only read about. Maybe the problem was that we sheltered you from the harsh realities of a cruel society. But we were only doing what we thought was best."

Shaking her head in disgust and sitting forward, near the edge of her seat, she continued to question his motives. "Is she pregnant, Marcus? Is that the reason for the mysterious hasty engagement? How can you prepare to bring someone into this family and the people closest to you know nothing about her?" Without giving him a chance to respond, she asked, "What about law school? How can you afford school, a wife and a child? Marcus, why are you doing this?" she shouted.

He moved in front of her, rose up on his knees, and placed both his hands on her cheeks.

"Because, I'm in love with her."

"Then why have you kept her away?"

"Because she's Matthew's niece, mama."

"Matthew?" she asked, puzzled.

"Matthew Conyers, daddy's lover."

Sonya drew a deep breath, sighed and fell back in her seat. Her arms drooped down along the sides of the chair as her head fell aimlessly onto her right shoulder. She could neither speak nor summon any tears.

Marcus' eyes widened in fear as he called out for his mother. "Mama! Mama!" Sonya's spirit however, had left the room.

CHAPTER 35

I T was her first day back in the office after her Colorado trip. She'd stayed late, going over client proposals when she received the frantic call from Marcus telling her that Sonya was in the hospital. Without mentioning a word to anyone she quietly gathered her files and left the building. Traffic was still heavy on the expressway, but she didn't notice—her mind was full of clouded thoughts. All she could think of was reaching her mother and brother and making everything right again.

She remembered Sonya bragging how she'd rarely gotten sick with a cold or the flu, because, as she'd say, *'all mothers made a pact with God to stay well, otherwise, who'd take care of their families?'* Tears streamed down her face.

The lighted sign for Long Island Medical Center came into view. Ary pulled into the driveway and parked her car as close as was allowed to the emergency room entrance. She ran inside, stopping briefly at the admitting window before racing down to the room, only to find Marcus pacing back and forth and Sonya, eyes wide open, lying motionless in bed.

"Marcus? What happened?" she screamed.

"I found her like this after coming home early from class tonight," he lied. I called her name when I came through the front door, like I usually do and when she didn't answer, I went upstairs to check on her and couldn't find her there either. So

I went back down and checked the family room. I saw here sitting in the chair and thought she was sleeping."

"With her eyes opened, Marcus!" she yelled.

"I hadn't noticed," he roared back. "I called her name again, went over and touched her arm. When she didn't respond, I called 9-1-1 and you."

"I can't believe this could happen. Mama has always been in perfect health."

"Ary, in case you haven't noticed, she's been depressed for more than a decade. You really think that depression can't lead to other illnesses?"

"I didn't say that—I'm not a doctor, I don't know. I don't even know if she was suffering from depression."

"What!"

"Marcus, there's a difference between sadness and depression. They're not the same."

"I'm willing to bet that after more than ten years of sadness, depression starts to kick in," he said, sarcastically.

She moved closer to him and whispered, sternly, "You didn't say anything to her about you and Caroline did you? You promised me you wouldn't."

"No I didn't. I told you that before. I didn't mention Caroline's name."

Marcus couldn't tell the truth now. He couldn't risk losing his sister. He kept praying that his mother would just wake up, regain consciousness. But if and when she did, would she remember his conversation with her? Would they ever speak to him again? He loved Caroline, but he also loved his family. Was she worth the sacrifice?

Ary began her rapid fire questioning. "Marcus, has anyone been here yet? What did they say? Has Dr. Murphy been contacted? He's been mama's doctor for as long as I can remember."

"I filled out the hospital forms as best as I could and I put Dr. Murphy's name down as her primary care physician, but I wasn't sure of his telephone number."

"I don't think that matters—they can find him, he's affiliated with this hospital."

"I can't stand to see her like this, Ary. I'm going to the waiting room down the hall."

"Wait, I'll go with you. You shouldn't be alone, you don't look well."

Ary held onto Marcus' arm and walked the short distance to the sterile waiting room. She sat. Marcus paced.

A young, charismatic African American doctor entered the room.

"Mr. Alexander?"

Ary jumped to her feet.

Marcus answered. "I'm Marcus Alexander, and this is my sister, Ary."

"I'm Dr. Ingram. I examined your mother earlier. She's in a state of mental trauma which caused her to lose consciousness."

Ary gasped. Marcus' knees buckled, but he held himself steady.

"However, all of her vital organs and brain activity are functioning normally. There must have been some horrific event that triggered this. Can either of you shed any light on what might have happened?"

"No," Marcus answered quickly and nervously. "Like I told my sister, I came home and found her that way."

"Well, right now she's doesn't seem to be in any danger, but I'd like to keep her here overnight for observation. If she remains stable, I don't see any reason why she wouldn't be aware and coherent by morning and hopefully she can tell us what happened. Oh, I also just closed her eyes. Do you have any questions?"

"I'd like to stay with her," Ary proposed. "I want to be here when she wakes up."

"That's fine. I'll notify the nurse's station."

"Thank you doctor. Also, do you know if Dr. Murphy has been notified?"

"He was. And a medical report was relayed to him. Either he or I will see you in the morning."

Dr. Ingram shook their hands and disappeared through the double doors. Ary looked forward to hearing a reasonable explanation from the soft-spoken physician, or Dr. Murphy, but for now she felt weak and sat down in the hard, plastic seat along the wall. Marcus walked towards the door.

"Aren't you staying?"

"I don't know. I have a client meeting in the morning and I need to get home and study for a law exam."

"Are *you* in shock? This is your mother we're talking about here. I think your *client* would understand rescheduling due to a family emergency! Don't you want to find out what triggered this so we can help prevent it from ever happening again?"

"Yeah, yeah I do. But I need to go home, pick up some information for my meeting tomorrow. I'll be back in a couple of hours."

"A couple of hours? You live fifteen minutes from here. Why would it take so long?"

"It won't. I don't know what I'm saying!"

"Have you eaten anything lately?" she asked, concerned about his mental stability.

"No, but I think I should probably stop and get something before I come back. Do you want something to eat, or drink?"

"I think both of us should eat something. I imagine it's gonna be a long night."

She thought for a few seconds and recommended that he stop at the diner on Route 10, the main strip in the quiet town of Bedford, an equal distance between her mother's home and the hospital.

"Ok. What do you want?"

"A Caesar salad and a large black coffee. Here, take this." She offered him a fifty dollar bill. "This is all I have in cash. Get yourself something too, and take your time driving. I don't want you rushing behind the wheel. We've been through enough tonight already."

Marcus didn't hear her. He was panicking. He couldn't face Sonya once she woke up and he didn't feel the need to explain any of his actions or behavior to his sister. While driving home, he called Caroline from his cell phone.

"Hey baby, it's me. I just had a huge argument with my mama and I think the time has come for me to move out. What? I can stay with you? Alright, thanks babe. We'll talk when I see you tonight. Love you too. Bye."

CHAPTER 36

ARY left the waiting area and walked towards her mother's room, pausing before going in. She prayed at the door. *Oh God, please let her wake up.* Stepping carefully over the threshold, she looked over at her sleeping mother.

"Mama, how can I help you? If you can hear me, please give me a sign." Ary placed her own unsteady hands atop her mother's and bent down to kiss them. Amidst her own fallen tears, she whispered in Sonya's deafened ear. "What happened mama? What caused this? I should have done a better job of protecting you." She turned to leave, then hesitated, asking, "What would you want me to do right now, mama? I feel so helpless. Please just give me a sign." She lowered her head and walked back towards the waiting area.

Sonya, the accomplished artist, talented sculptress and youngest of two daughters had certainly experienced her share of pain. Her father, Charles Dodd, an up and coming musician, died unexpectedly of a massive heart attack shortly after her 5th birthday, robbing her of any chance of ever knowing the man who cherished *'the girls'* as he'd affectionately called his small family. Her mother, Mary Anne, struggled for years afterwards as a nightclub singer, taking jobs as a maid and waitress when they were available. She was often forced to bring her daughters to smoky clubs and speakeasies between singing gigs when she couldn't find a neighbor to watch them.

But by the time she was eight, her mother had found steady employment as a voice coach, finally able to provide a stable life for her girls—exposing them at every opportunity to music, art, dance and singing, believing that a love and appreciation of the arts would open their limited world to unlimited opportunities. Although Mary Anne's desire to achieve widespread stardom faded as time went on, she continued to perform locally, insisting that dreams were a continuous work in progress. Each night before they closed their eyes, she reminded the girls of how life's roadmap to personal success and happiness would be full of detours. *You may be forced off the main road before you reach your final destination,* she'd say, *but if it means bringing you and your family love and peace, it'll only feel like a minor irritation."*

Ary lowered her drained body into an available chair and closed her eyes. Out of the blue, childhood images of she and her father tossing the football in their backyard entered her thoughts. She reached for her phone in her purse and tried dialing his number. Her mind, cluttered with worry and confusion, wouldn't allow it. She paged through her contacts until she came to his name, *'Bruce. A'.* The phone rang twice before he answered.

"Daddy, it's me."

He took a quick look at his watch. "Hi Ary, is everything ok? It's pretty late there."

"I'm at the hospital, with mama."

"What happened? What's wrong with Sonya?"

"We don't have a clear understanding yet, but Marcus came home from class and found her sitting motionless in a chair in the family room…staring at the walls. I don't expect you to come, I just…I just thought *maybe* you'd want to know."

"Of course, I'd want to know. Ary listen, as I told you before, I'll always care about your mother and this is no time to rehash ancient wounds."

Unprovoked mental wounds stormed her mind. Her brow tightened and her tone change. "Well daddy, I guess you just have a different way of showing it."

"Ary, you obviously called because you knew I'd be concerned, and I am. I'm trying to get information from you so I can determine if I should come out there. Now what did the doctor say?"

"I don't know what might have possessed me to call you, but really, the last thing on earth I think mama would need is to wake up and find her ex-husband and his lover at her bedside! I apologize for bothering you with these *family* matters. In normal circumstances families support each other by being there for one another."

"You're not making any sense Ary!" he yelled. "I don't really want to hear about what families do or don't do. Tell me what hospital she's in?"

"You know what, go to hell. I must have been out of my mind to call you," she shouted back. "Stay with your partner there in San Diego. The partner you left behind to wither away in sorrow is lying here unconscious and for all I know, it could have been memories of you that caused this!" she screamed.

A woman sitting nearby gave Ary a contemptuous look and walked out of the room. She realized she was yelling, but didn't care.

"You listen to me young lady, I was married to your mother for eighteen years, and no matter what happened between us, I still care. So you either tell me how she ended up in that hospital or I'm on the next plane to New York."

"No, you listen to me daddy, I never felt like I could tell you what you took away from me, but now seems like the appropriate time. You took away my belief and trust in *any* man. I loved you more than life itself and I never wanted to disappoint you so I busted my ass in school, in sports and every extracurricular activity you ever enrolled me in—including learning two foreign languages! I wanted you to always be proud of me. I wanted to be perfect daddy, like you. And then you turned out to be a man's man, a person none of us knew—not me, not Marcus and certainly not the woman you slept with all of those years. So *you* turned out to be imperfect daddy. You turned out to be a liar, you ripped our *perfect little family* apart," she cried. "And then, I ended up taking your place! Yes, a fifteen-year-old, head-of-household 'cause mama just couldn't deal with you walking out on us. I wasn't prepared for that!" she screamed. "But I didn't have a choice. It was up to me to keep everything together. Do you know how difficult that was for me?" she yelled. "Mama couldn't do it. She never had the chance to come to terms with her own grief, so she pushed it aside to try and take care of Marcus—there was nothing left in her for me. And now you're *so* concerned that you want to take the first thing smokin' to New York. For what? To fix things? To try and make up for what you did to her, to us? To right the wrongs of the past? Well, I'm here to tell you that you can't. I don't expect you to come here and wait by her bedside. As a matter of fact, I'm begging you not to come. I'm old enough and mature enough to handle the situation now daddy, and I intend on doing just that." Ary pressed the *end call* button without giving him the chance to respond.

"Ary, Ary!" he yelled. But it was too late. He slammed the receiver against the wall.

"What the hell was that about? What am I supposed to do now?" he screamed.

He'd been the bad guy for all these years, and if he didn't do something now, he would be blamed for Sonya's deteriorating health or possibly death, for the rest of his life. *Ary and Marcus were adults. They should be able to handle the situation. Why did she really call?* Ary had never called to tell him about her mother's health in all the years they'd been apart. So why now?"

For eighteen years I provided them with life's luxuries and waited until I thought the kids were old enough to handle a change. Is it so wrong to want to finally live your life free of guilt and deception?

He thought about the happiness, contentment and peace his family had—all of which had eluded him for far too long. He'd found his happiness with Matthew and over the years had tried to remain a part of his children's lives. At times, it had proved difficult. They were still to this day, he thought, unable to accept him in totality. He'd tried explaining everything to Ary when she was in college. He'd tried to make peace—to reunite with his daughter. She'd refused to hear him out, just like now. What more could he do?

Bruce had grown up the eldest of four children born to Alma and Ray Alexander of Elgin, Illinois, thirty-eight miles northwest of Chicago. His father, a successful entrepreneur in the steel business, ruled his house as he did his company, with an iron fist. His word was gospel. No one was allowed to challenge him. And no one dared. But as Bruce grew up, he questioned his father at every turn and opportunity. His mother, a shy elementary school teacher who instilled a love of reading, learning and debating in all of her children, cautioned her fiery son not to cross the line as often as he did. But in reality, she secretly enjoyed the spirited confrontations he instigated with the patriarch. Bruce, she felt, acted as the voice of reason in a house where rationalism went out the door once Ray entered his self-imposed kingdom.

Alma took special pride in her eldest—reminding him how the birth order of each child had a unique meaning, with a distinct purpose being placed on the first born. *You're destined for greatness,* she'd remind him. *But sometimes it could mean sacrificing a part of who you really are.*

He sat down with his head bowed at the kitchen table. The dangling phone beeped as a reminder to hang it up. He pulled the tangled cord up from the floor and placed the receiver on the wall base. A sudden uneasiness waved over his body.

Would they accept me if I'd left for a woman? Should I go to New York anyway, stay at a hotel and speak to the doctors from there? Or call from here?

He wondered if Marcus had been at the hospital with Ary. *I'll call the house. Maybe he'd be willing to talk.*

Using his iPhone this time, he dialed the number of his former residence, but paused before pressing the last digit.

I don't think I can handle another dramatic scene. He hung up.

He thought about calling Dr. Murphy in the morning. They'd remained friends over the years. He'd ask his opinion of whether his being there would cause more harm than good.

Matthew came out of the shower wrapped in a towel from the waist down. He'd heard bits of Bruce's phone conversation and the phone banging against the wall. He noticed his partner staring out the window into the sweeping ebony skies.

Matthew placed his hand on Bruce's shoulder and asked, "What's wrong?"

Bruce turned around, unaware of his presence.

Drawing a deep breath, he recounted the story. "I don't know what to do Matthew—whether to go, stay, call, what?" His facial muscles tightened. "Why do I still feel the need to explain my actions from years ago? Matthew, I really am concerned about Sonya." Matthew's touch reached even deeper.

"Then go. Go and find out how she is, even if you don't go to the hospital. I don't think calling will be enough and staying home will only cause you to worry. Stay at the beach house. I'll call and see if I can get you on the red eye tonight."

"I have depositions tomorrow afternoon," he worried.

"This is family Bruce. Should I call your assistant to reschedule?"

"No, I'll call and tell her to postpone everything until next week. I may be gone for more than a day or two. I need to talk to my daughter, Matthew, and try once and for all to put some closure to this. No matter what, I'm still her father and I deserve respect. Am I supposed to subject myself to her emotional tirades whenever there's a crisis? No," he said, answering his own inquiry. "I won't have it," he declared finally, pounding his large, copper fist on the table.

"Sonya and I have been divorced for a long time. What do they expect from me?"

"They expect that you should care Bruce, about their mother. Our relationship is obviously still hard to accept— even with adult children."

Matthew wondered if he should mention meeting Marcus at the surprise birthday party. But quickly decided against it.

"I'll call the airline, pack a bag and schedule a car service to pick you up. Just call and let me know you're okay once you arrive at the house."

Bruce leaned his head against Matthew's steady hand and whispered. "I love you."

Matthew stood there silently, knowing that Bruce, who was more often than not the anchor in their relationship, needed him this time. He'd never probed Bruce about Sonya or the kids, leaving any conversations about his past life up to him to discuss—which wasn't often. The same held true for Matthew. His memories of Rockport were just those, memories. The two men chose to keep their former lives separate and apart— preferring to build a new life together. And up until now, they'd been successful. All he'd really been told of Ary was how strong-willed and determined she was, like her father. He knew Marcus didn't care for him—his discomfort and speedy departure at the party was proof of that. And the times he'd answered the phone when either Marcus or Ary called rendered only a brusque *'is my father available?'* He needed Bruce. And although he'd sanctioned this trip to New York, in the back of his mind, he was worried about the Alexander reunion, especially at such a vulnerable time as this.

He answered softly, "I love you too."

CHAPTER 37

ARY looked around the corners of the waiting room as if Marcus had snuck in without her noticing. She was starving and filled with regret for placing the call to Bruce without her brother being there for support, unwilling and still unable to deal with what she'd labeled, *'daddy's issues.'* With an aching head, racing heart, empty stomach and trembling hands, she felt like a time bomb waiting to explode. She clenched her teeth together and shifted positions in a chair that seemed to grow more firm as time passed.

She needed someone there, someone to talk to. She closed her eyes for a brief second and thought of Joseph and dialed his number without thinking it through, unaware that it was one o'clock in the morning.

"Hel-loooo," he dragged, drained from a night of drinking and promiscuity.

"Joseph it's me, Ary. I apologize for calling so late but I'm at the hospital with my mother. My brother found my mother just sitting in a chair at home, in a state of shock."

"I'm sorry to hear that."

At that moment, his bathroom door opened slightly and a topless woman sporting a red-laced, thong peeked around it. Joseph didn't notice.

"Hey baby," she whispered. "I'm ready."

Joseph immediately turned and pointed to the phone.

Ary was certain she'd heard a female voice.

"I'm sorry, I didn't realize how late it was. I didn't mean to interrupt….."

"No, it's ok. Is anyone there with you? I can come if you need me."

"No, no. Look, I apologize for calling. I guess I needed someone to talk to and I thought of you."

"Ary, what are you talking about? There's no need for an apology. What hospital is she in?"

"Long Island Medical Center, in Bay Shore. Look, really, that would be asking too much. I can handle this alone."

"Hey, I know you think you can, I get that. But right now isn't the time to be *superwoman*. You need someone there with you. I can be there in less than an hour."

"Do you need directions."

"No, I'll use GPS. See you soon." Joseph wondered about Ary's brother or friends and relatives. Where were they? But he'd offered assistance to a friend at a difficult moment and he intended on keeping his word.

His evening guest lay seductively in wait in the middle of his massive bed.

"I'm really sorry love but we'll have to pick up where we left off at another time.

I promise to call you soon," he fibbed.

CHAPTER 38

TAKING a deep breath, she got up and walked down the winding hallway to room 212. The first thing she noticed was the peaceful aura surrounding her mother. The fine wrinkles on her forehead seemed to have disappeared and she seemed to be smiling. But it turned out to be the way the dim room lighting poured over her face. The green jagged lines of the heart-monitoring device served as visible reassurance that life had not yet cheated her. She walked over to Sonya's bed and affectionately spread her soft graying locks across the pillow.

How beautiful she was, even in this fragile condition, Ary thought. She wondered how they could ever go on without her if she remained unconscious. Marcus still relied on her for shelter and home cooked meals, even as he desperately tried to assert his independence. They couldn't bear to lose her.

"If you can hear me mama," Ary pleaded, "squeeze my hand, I'm here." Tears streamed down her face. Every thought and complaint she'd had before coming into Sonya's room was now a faded memory. Her only concern was for her mother's recovery.

"Mama, when you wake up please tell me what was *so* wrong that you had to shut everything and everyone out of your life. Was it me? Was it something I did or didn't do? Whatever it is or was, you're going to have to talk about it sooner or later so that it doesn't happen again. I'll get help for you, mama, for us," she offered. "I've been meaning to do something nice for your birthday next month. Let me take you away if it's okay with the doctor. How about a trip to Africa? Just you and me. And not to the Southern or Western countries of the continent, no, this time we're going North, to Morocco! We'll stay at ancient hotels, feast on exotic dishes, dance until the break of dawn, practice Arabic or have conversations in French with handsome Moroccan men, and…who knows, maybe we won't want to come back!" she laughed. "That's what we'll do. And we'll talk all night, like we did when I was a little girl. We'll talk about anything that comes to mind. Just wake up mama, please." Ary laid her head gently on top of Sonya's chest, rising and falling to its own beat.

CHAPTER 39

JOSEPH drove along deserted city streets. The only noticeable activities were vagrants searching for warmth and safe
havens in building vestibules and alleys. Typing his destination
into the GPS, he settled comfortably into his prized, classic
Mercedes sports car. The computerized voice suggested the
Queens Midtown Tunnel as the best route to the Long Island
Expressway to reach the hospital.

His car traveled smoothly over the causeway. The system
prompted him to veer right onto the approaching expressway.

"What am I doing? I'm her boss, not her boyfriend. What
am I supposed to say once I arrive? *'Honey I got here as quickly as
I could. How's mom?'*"

He had to find a way off the expressway. An exit sign
announcing a *U-turn* before crossing the Queens border into
Long Island shone from his headlights in the distance. Joseph
exited and headed back towards Manhattan.

"Ary, I'm sorry. I'm not ready for a serious relationship. I
shouldn't have told you I'd come. I'm very attracted to you, but
being at your mother's bedside takes what we have to a place
I'm not willing to step up to right now. Forgive me, baby." A red
traffic light halted his thoughts and finalized his decision. He
turned on the radio and tapped a finger on the steering wheel
to the soft music.

CHAPTER 40

"**PLEASE** return to your seats. The Captain has put on the fasten seat belt sign. If you have any cups or trash that needs to be removed, please pass it to the center aisle."

The flight attendant wakened Bruce from a much needed sleep. He was grateful to Matthew for being able to book a flight out tonight. But unsure of what to expect upon seeing Marcus and Ary, he'd drank two vodka martinis to unwind. Bruce debated whether to go straight to the beach house and call the nurse's station or venture to the hospital, facing his son and daughter first hand.

"Ladies and gentlemen this is Captain Neilson. We'll be touching down at JFK airport in about eleven minutes. If you look out of your window on the left side you can see New York City's beautiful skyline and a few of her radiant bridges. I'd like to take this opportunity to thank you for flying American Airlines and hope to see you again on the return."

Bruce's heart raced. Adrenaline rushed through his body like his recent experience riding the waves on the Island of St. John in the Caribbean.

"Please remain seated until the Captain has turned off the seat belt sign and we are parked safely at the gate." The flight attendant's rhythmic voice slowed the pace of his pounding heart. "Thank you for flying with us and enjoy your stay in New York or wherever your final destination may take you."

Bruce unbuckled his seatbelt and placed the tiny pillow over his lap. The nose of the plane seemed to kiss the windows of the terminal before the jetway locked firmly to the door. He rose up and instinctively opened the overhead bin to retrieve his briefcase as he'd done hundreds of times before. It wasn't there. This time he wouldn't need it. What he would need was strength, resiliency and level-headedness, the qualities his family had once depended on.

Downstairs in baggage claim, Bruce searched the white cardboard signs of the limousine drivers. His was held by a tall lanky man wearing a chauffeur's cap and a cheap black suit. This was not his usual driver, the one he relied on whenever a business trip brought him to New York. He needed to make a decision. What had Matthew told the car service? Where did he think he should go? Bruce looked the driver in the eyes and said, "I'm Mr. Alexander. Please take me to Long Island Medical Center in Bay Shore."

CHAPTER 41

ARY had fallen asleep hours ago in a chair next to her mother's bed. Her neck was stiffened and her stomach growled from hunger. *Oh my God, what time is it?* She pushed up her sweater sleeve. It was nine o'clock in the morning. She surveyed the room. *Where's Marcus? What happened to Joseph?* She sat up and looked at Sonya. "Mama, Mama?" Sonya lay idle—in the same position as when Ary last kept watch over her. The expression on her face had not changed, neither had the green line on the monitor. There had been no movement. She placed her hand over her mother's blanketed chest to see for herself if she were still breathing. The door swung open. Ary spun around sharply, startled, but reassured at seeing a familiar face.

"Dr. Ingram! Hello. Do we know anything yet? I must have fallen asleep."

"Good morning, Ms. Alexander. We were here earlier to check on your mother and there've been no developmental changes yet. We were hoping to see some improvement by now."

"We who?" she asked, rising hastily to her feet. "Was Dr. Murphy here? He's been caring for my mother for years. He knows her medical history and..."

"Ms. Alexander..."

"Please stop calling me that!" she said with obvious frustration. "Just call me Ary, please!"

"Ary, Dr. Murphy was here with me this morning and we discussed your mother's condition. We decided to wait a few more hours to see if she woke up on her own before speaking with you."

"What on earth are you talking about? Do you mean to tell me that the two of you came in this room and made a decision about *my* mother while I was asleep and didn't bother to wake me?"

"Ms. Alexander, we made a clinical decision to wait for any unassisted movements from your mother. We didn't feel it necessary to wake you and notify you of that. I'd intended on returning in a couple of hours to speak with you."

"Really? Well maybe you can answer a few questions right now, Dr. Ingram. Is my mother actually suffering from mental trauma or is it something else? How long will she remain like this? And do we have any ideas what caused it?"

"There really are no changes from last evening. Dr. Murphy consulted a psychotherapist and has subsequently requested a meeting with your family this afternoon."

"A psychotherapist? I don't understand," she said, her voice rising to a sharp crescendo. "Why should *we* speak to a psychotherapist when the one person who can tell us what happened is unable to speak? Shouldn't we wait until my mother can communicate?"

"We're not sure when that might be. So in the meantime, we need to take preventative measures."

Ary was stunned. *Preventative measures.* What did that mean? What needed to be said to the family in the presence of a psychotherapist this afternoon? And what family would they be talking to? She was the only one there. She could neither speak nor respond to his statements.

"We'll meet at two o'clock in a private room. Check in at the nurse's station and someone will escort you there. If you have any additional questions prior to that time, I can be reached by beeper and Dr. Murphy will be here around 1:30p.m."

Dr. Ingram's attention went from Ary to Sonya. Silence filled the room except for the occasional beep of the heart monitor. His bowed head spoke of his frustration. He didn't know whether to comfort Ary in some way or escape her incredulous gaze as quickly as he could. He turned and walked out the door.

Ary slumped into a nearby chair falling across Sonya's lap with outstretched arms and cried. She wept for her mother—a woman who'd given up on living long ago, whose agony laid buried deep within her subconscious. She cried for herself, feeling more alone and abandoned. Her sorrow could be heard from the hospital corridors. No one was there who cared enough to ease her suffering.

"Ary, I came as soon as I'd heard." She never heard him come in, her wailing had blocked out all intrusions.

She raised her head slowly from her mother's lap and wiped her face with the back of her hand, hesitating before turning around—afraid to acknowledge if the voice she recognized in her mind was in fact the person who stood behind her. *Was it really him?* Her heart pounded like a snare drum against her diminutive chest. Her mouth went dry as she swallowed hard. Carefully rising from her seat, she turned towards his voice.

"I didn't know…" But before she could continue, he walked over to her and searched his pockets for a handkerchief. Unsuccessful, he resorted to wiping her tears with his long fingers, smoothing her hair behind her ears, which he'd never seen before. They were shaped perfectly, with lobes generous enough to hold the brilliant diamond studs found resting against them. Her grief stricken eyes exposed the vulnerability she'd fought so hard to suppress.

He removed his suede jacket, wrapped it around her shivering body and directed her head into the hollow of a neck that had thickened from years of football drills. His arms found their way around her narrow shoulders, pulling her closer. Feeling helpless, she placed her hands over his heart taking refuge in its soothing rhythms as he embraced her in protective custody. He held her tighter, trying hard to hold back the impulsive instincts that were natural between a man and a woman.

Dwayne shut his eyes and imagined kissing her salted, wet lips. Without the shield of his coat to prevent bodily contact he could feel her round full breast pressing against the walls of his chest. She released a prolonged sigh as he slid his strong hands along the curve of her back. Feeling his manhood rising, he wished hard at that moment for different circumstances.

Ary's concern for her mother was momentarily relieved as she willingly consented to her boss' embrace. With her eyes closed, she questioned how this could be. They'd gone through professional pandemonium and now, this tender scene. *Did he actually care? Could that have been why he was so tough on her?* Right now, it didn't matter, all she wanted was to linger in what was once an unthinkable moment. She leaned back, just far enough to see the impassioned expression on his face. He could've held her for eternity. Instead, a sudden interruption robbed them of any ensuing course of action.

"How is she?"

Bruce had come in while his daughter was locked in the

arms of a stranger. He walked around the surprised couple and gazed at the woman who'd held him responsible for her misery.

Ary didn't know what to say at first. She was unsure of how to react.

She backed away from Dwayne's embrace.

"Daddy!" she said, surprised to see him. "Dwayne, this is my father, Bruce Alexander. Daddy this is my boss Dwayne Hargis."

"Mr. Alexander, I'm sorry we had to meet on such a somber occasion."

Dwayne extended a hand to Bruce, who waited, what seemed to be minutes instead of seconds before reciprocating. Feeling uneasy, he determined it best to leave the family alone.

"Ary, I'm gonna step out into the hallway."

"Thank you for coming," she whispered, softly.

She wanted him to stay, but the time had come to take care of family matters.

Bruce was exhausted from the flight and apprehensive about the inevitable discussions he'd have to have with his kids. He watched Dwayne as he left the room, not turning away until the door closed after him. He then turned to his daughter, whose flushed complexion was the answer to a question he didn't need to ask.

"So what do we know from the doctor?" Bruce asked, speaking more like an attorney than a father.

"Dr. Ingram, the resident who I met last night has set up a two o'clock meeting this afternoon with us, and of course Dr. Murphy to inform us as to what they're recommending as next steps. Mama's condition is called, 'mental trauma.'" Ary answered her father with just the facts, as she'd done so many years ago. "There'll also be a psychotherapist at the meeting."

"A psychotherapist?"

"Dr. Murphy consulted with the specialist."

"By the way, where's Marcus?" he inquired, looking puzzled, "I haven't seen him since last night and I've been too preoccupied to call the house."

I'll bet, he thought.

"Well, let's make sure he's ok," he suggested. "And I'll track down Dr. Murphy."

"I was told he wouldn't be here until one-thirty."

"I'll get to him before that. I'd like for us to talk to him before meeting with the others. Now please, check on your brother."

His position as head of the family felt all too familiar. He was suddenly comfortable in the role he'd left a world away. He stroked Sonya's cheek, standing watch over her as treasured memories of she and the kids flooded his mind. But the moment was short lived. Flashbacks of a beleaguered denial of who he really was painted a very different recollection.

Ary felt relief now that he was there—relieved that he'd left Matthew to be with his *real* family. She felt a sudden surge of triumph. Maybe he'd realize the lasting impact of his actions and try and make amends. Seeing her mother and father together brought temporary logic to a world filled with confusion. Thoughts of Sonya's failing health being the catalyst for bringing them back together only made it more meaningful.

"Ok, I'll find Marcus."

"I'll meet you back here in an hour." He reached in his pocket and pulled out a business card holder. "Here's my pager number if you need me before that."

"Thank you, daddy."

CHAPTER 42

"**MARCUS**, I called your office and they said you'd called in sick. I would've stayed home with you if I'd known you weren't feeling well."

"Caroline, you worry too much. I only told my boss I didn't feel well because I didn't want to deal with anyone today. I told you last night why I was upset and I thought I could put it out of my head by now, but I can't."

"Sweetheart, maybe you shouldn't be alone right now. You were extremely agitated last night. I can come back and work from home."

The fact of the matter was—she was a large part of the problem.

Marcus held the phone away from his ear and shook his head. How did he let this happen? What kind of man would run away from his family when they needed him most?

Dad, he thought. *I'm no different from him.*

One irrefutable distinction was that Bruce was certain of his sexuality, while Marcus still questioned his.

It began in his freshman year of high school. A classmate approached him in the gym locker room as he dressed, and without warning, kissed him on the lips. No one else noticed. But the fact that he did nothing about it, not even a justifiable punch, made him wonder if homosexuality was inherited.

This incident haunted him for years, causing him to question his masculinity.

"No, I don't want you to come home and I don't want you to worry. I'll be fine—I'll work this thing out somehow. I'll make it right again…somehow." Marcus hung up the phone, not wanting to hear another word from Caroline. He sat on the side of the bed resting his lean elbows across his knees. His cupped hands held a face wrought with anger and despair.

Ary had never depended on him for much, he thought, she'd always been the anchor. Now, when it was his turn, he jumped ship.

He thought about calling the hospital. But what excuse would he give Ary for not coming back. What if Sonya hadn't pulled through? What then?

"I can't believe this shit!" he screamed.

"My mother is fucking lying up in a hospital bed because of me! All because of what I said. What the hell was I thinking when I told her about Caroline. I'm a fucking idiot," he yelled, raising both hands toward the ceiling. "Those two people are my family, my life, and I ran away, like a coward. I'm supposed to be the man—the person they can turn to in times like these. Instead, I'm the culprit. I'm responsible for my mother's illness," he shouted.

"How could I ever look them in the face again? God help me."

Marcus cried so hard his slender body trembled, sliding helplessly onto the floor, striking it repeatedly with his clenched fist. He needed to feel brute pain. He felt crazed, like a rabid animal hunting for prey. He found a framed picture of Caroline and her family, including Matthew, hanging over the fireplace mantle in the living room. He hastily put his fist through it, splattering glass everywhere. Undaunted by his bleeding knuckles, he reared back with all of his might and punched a gaping hole in the wall. Blood splattered over the sofa and onto the beige carpet. He looked at his butchered arm and hand. Moaning, he fell to the ground.

CHAPTER 43

DWAYNE went back to the room to find Ary and her father gone. He searched the corridors and located her in the waiting room on her cell phone. She motioned for him to come near.

"I'm trying to find my brother. There's no answer at the house or his cell. I called his office and they said he'd called in sick. I don't know what to think."

"What about friends. Have you tried any friends?"

"No. But maybe I should try his girlfriend, Caroline, but I don't have her number."

"Do you know where she works?"

"She's in law school with Marcus at Columbia and he told me she clerks for a new firm up in Harlem."

"What's the name of the firm?"

"I don't know. All I know is that it's new and it's uptown."

"I'll call a few of my lawyer friends to see if I can find her. What's her last name?"

"Uh, Caroline, Caroline, Grant! Do you think you can find her? The doctors want to meet with the family in a couple of hours."

"I promise you I'll find her. Let's just hope she can tell us where your brother is."

"I hope he's okay," she whispered.

"Don't worry, I'm sure he is. Why don't you go down to the

cafeteria and get something to eat. I could hear your stomach growling as I walked down the hallway," he teased.

She managed a half-hearted grin.

"I haven't eaten in a while. I'll grab something and bring it back up to mama's room, just in case she wakes up."

"Good idea." He stared at her leaving the room, not able to blink an eye. He hadn't noticed this soft side before, or maybe he'd chosen not to. He'd convinced himself that he couldn't afford to get seriously involved with anyone—his career was too important and there wasn't much time left over for a personal life. But right now, all he wanted was to be near her.

She looked back at him and smiled before disappearing through the door.

His cell phone rang just as he was about to make a call. "This is Dwayne."

"Dwayne, it's Joseph. How's Ary and her family?"

"She's holding up as best as she can under the circumstances. I found her crying on her mother's bed when I got here."

"Really?"

"Yeah. But once I held her, she calmed down." He waited for any reaction.

"I see. Well, looks like you have everything under control. Please give her my best and tell her I'll speak with her later on today."

"I will." Dwayne stared at the phone before pushing the end call button. This time maybe he'd won the girl.

Chapter 44

"**J**ONAS, it's Bruce Alexander—how are you?"

"Bruce, I'm good thanks, but I was sorry to find Sonya in the hospital. How are you, man?"

"Best I can be under the circumstances."

"I know, I know. Listen, I'm glad you caught up with me. I left word with Dr. Ingram that I wanted to meet with the family this afternoon at two o'clock. Did you get the message?"

"Yes, I did. What do you know thus far? I'd like to have some idea before we meet with the kids."

Dr. Jonas Murphy explained in detail what he'd found in his diagnosis of Sonya. Bruce listened carefully, hearing each recommendation as if he were in a fog: *assisted living; speech therapy; home health care; rehab; medications; What would this mean for his life now? What decisions would they expect him to make?*

"I see."

"If it comes down to assisted living, I can suggest some very reputable facilities in the area. I'm sure the family would want her nearby."

He answered a quick, "Yes," as if *he* were in shock.

"I appreciate your help, Jonas." His temples throbbed at the pace of a rapid heartbeat.

"Okay, Bruce, I'll see you all in a few hours."

"Yes. Thanks Jonas." Bruce had walked down to the

cafeteria to take the call and fell back in his seat, tucked away in a corner, away from the hospital staff and patient family lunch crowd. He stared into a cup of steaming, hot black coffee, preoccupied with how to tell his son and daughter.

"Shit, I forgot to call Matthew! He pushed number 6 on his cell's contact list. It rang once before his daughter suddenly appeared at his table.

"Daddy. I didn't know you were coming down here."

Matthew answered on the second ring. "Hello."

Bruce hung up before replying.

"Bruce, hello?"

Bruce placed the phone back in his blazer pocket. "Any luck in locating your brother?"

"Dwayne is helping me..."

Before she could finish explaining, Bruce's phone rang.

He checked the display and decided to let it ring rather than have Ary listen to his conversation with Matthew. He also decided that he should be the one to deliver the news about her mother, not Drs. Murphy or Ingram.

"Let it ring, they'll call back. What were you saying about Dwayne?"

Matthew was persistent.

"Why don't you get that? Sounds like they really need to reach you. It could be Matthew," she said sarcastically.

"If it is, he'll leave a message. I'll call him back later. What were you saying about Marcus?" he insisted.

"I checked his office. They said he'd taken a sick day. Dwayne's trying to get in touch with his girlfriend, Caroline Grant to see if she's seen or heard from him." Ary surveyed her father for any reaction upon hearing Caroline's last name. His poker face proved formidable.

"You do know who Caroline Grant is, don't you?"

"Yes Ary, I do. And I know she and Marcus were dating."

"It's not that they *were* dating, they *are* dating and....oh my God!" Ary's face suddenly went pale. She grabbed onto the side of the unsteady table causing the hot cup of coffee to spill over Bruce's shoes. Her eyes widened. "Jesus help us!"

"Ary, what are talking about? What is it?"

"Marcus! He probably told mama they were dating or talking about getting married. That's why he disappeared. He probably told her who Caroline was and she went into shock. Oh my God! Oh my God!" she screamed, raising her hands up to her mouth. Bruce grabbed her shaking body and held her. She wrestled herself away—intentionally scratching the sides of his face with her fingernails.

"You bastards, you and Marcus." Bruce pushed her away as the blood trickled down his face and onto the floor. She lunged at him again. Two hospital orderlies on lunch break rushed to his aid. She screamed louder, fighting them off.

"Get away from me, all of you! Let me go, let me go! Dwayne," she yelled. "Help me, please."

"Ary stop it, Stop it! You don't know what you're talking about. Calm down."

She tried to free herself from the grip of the orderlies, fighting harder, unleashing her fists, striking one on the side of his head. They could barely suppress her violent blows.

Dr. Ingram was notified and rushed to the cafeteria. He grabbed Ary's arm and stuck her with a needle. She turned and looked at him before collapsing in her father's arms.

"Take her to an empty room," he ordered.

"I gave her a sedative. She'll be out for a couple of hours. What brought that on?"

Feeling the blood rolling down his face in the spot near his throbbing temples, Bruce took the last dry napkin from the table, blotted his face then responded to the doctor's question. "My daughter thinks she knows what caused her mother's condition."

"You're Mr. Alexander?"

"Yes."

"Why don't you have the nurses take care of those scratches."

"Who are you?"

"I'm Dr. Ingram. I've been collaborating with Dr. Murphy in caring for your wife."

"What the hell is going on here?" he demanded without correction to his former role. "First, I find out that she needs possible long-term rehabilitation and now my daughter is drugged because she tried to assault me."

"Mr. Alexander, could we continue this conversation privately? I'll see if I can reach Dr. Murphy right away."

Bruce's lips tightened when he noticed the blood soaked napkin in his hand. He looked down at his coffee-stained shoes and his eyes grew cold.

"Yes, let's do that."

Dr. Ingram stared into Bruce's enraged eyes knowing that any decisions made now would probably not be rational.

"Dr. Ingram. There's no further need for your services. I'll be in the family waiting room. Have Jonas page me when he's available."

Dr. Ingram shook his head, then walked out of the cafeteria, which by now had attracted curious onlookers.

Dwayne peeked into Sonya's room looking for Ary.

Hmmm. I guess she decided to eat downstairs. I'll catch up to her there and give her the news.

Walking briskly through the corridors, he could see inside patient rooms—some empty, some with family or friends by their bedside. He was glad he'd made the hasty decision to drive out and comfort her. Initially, it was just the right thing to do. Now, it was much more. He approached the last of the rooms instinctively turning to look inside. There in bed lay Ary. Her eyes were closed and her arms lay stretched by her side.

"What the hell," he screamed. Dwayne rushed in the room, frantically looking around as if someone were there to give him answers.

"Ary! Ary wake up. What's wrong?" He shook her shoulders.

"Ary," he shouted.

"Doctor, nurse, anyone!" he yelled outside in the corridor. "What happened? What is this?" he said, spreading his arms wide as he ran down to the nurse's station.

"Why is she in there? What happened? Tell me what's wrong," he demanded."

"Sir, please lower your voice and control yourself. Are you a relative?"

"I'm her fiancé," he lied, pounding an opened hand on the desk. "And I need to know what happened."

"Sir, I'll get the Charge Nurse, but please hold your voice down." She looked around to see if any aides were in the area in case he became violent.

"If you'll wait here, I'll call for her to come immediately and explain everything to you." Dwayne paced back and forth, wringing his hands, biting his bottom lip and taking deep, heaving breaths. He was seething.

Bruce walked down the corridor with tunnel vision to Jonas Murphy's office, never noticing Dwayne, or his daughter, who lay sleeping in the room across the hall.

"Where-Is-The-Nurse?" Dwayne demanded, pausing after each word.

"Sir, I'm the Charge Nurse." A redheaded, large woman rounded the corner. "Are you the fiancé of the patient in room 247?"

"Yes. Can *you* tell me why she's now a patient instead of a visitor?" The nurse recounted the cafeteria incident in detail and informed him about the medication she was given by Dr. Ingram. His demeanor went from concern to absolute anger.

"I'd like to speak with this Dr. Ingram, now!" he shouted.

"Sir, may I remind you that you are in a hospital and…"

He held back a tumultuous eruption. "I know damn well where I am. And I sure as hell don't need *you* to remind me of that. My fiancée is lying in a hospital bed and all I'm getting is some cockamamie excuse that she went wild for no reason. Get the good doctor so we can straighten this out and I can take her home."

CHAPTER 45

"SO Jonas, when can she be released and taken to Hilltop?"

"I can call and have her placed there this evening Bruce. It doesn't make sense to prolong her stay here and I know you want what's best for Sonya. I was sorry to hear about Ary. It is overwhelming, but, you're right, someone has to remain focused to make the right decisions."

"Yeah, well, I'm heading over there right now to complete the paperwork. Call me if there is anything else I should know." Nothing mattered now except admitting Sonya to the Hilltop Rehabilitation Complex at the eastern tip of the Island, near the ocean. At that moment, he wasn't thinking about Ary or Marcus, only what he felt was best for Sonya.

CHAPTER 46

"SO you see Mr. Hargis, I felt it best to sedate her before she became a threat to herself or anyone else. She should be awake in a couple of hours and I'll release her in your care."

"Ary mentioned something about a family meeting with the doctors. I hope that can be postponed until she wakes up and her brother can get here.

"Unfortunately, not."

"What are you saying?"

"A decision was made to send Mrs. Alexander to the Hilltop Rehabilitation Complex."

"What! When? How could a decision be made without the consent of her family?"

"My understanding was that her husband made the decision."

"Her ex-husband. They're divorced. Where is Mr. Alexander?"

"He may be on his way to the facility to complete the paperwork. I know he wanted to place her there by evening."

Dwayne scratched his head and sighed, "Jesus, Mary and Joseph, this is straight out of the movies."

He knew he'd have to get to Marcus. Caroline told him earlier that he was at her place, distraught.

"Thanks, doc, I'd like to go and see Ary now."

"Sure. I'll check on her later."

He'd already had enough personal problems to fill a calendar year. Now he was involved with the one person he'd vowed to keep a safe distance. Shrugging his shoulders, he put his hands in his pockets and walked down the hall to room 247.

CHAPTER 47

WHAT *have I done?* Marcus maneuvered himself off the floor and onto the blood soaked sofa. He felt dizzy, hopeless, shameful, and filled with remorse. But how would he apologize? He couldn't, not now. He'd hurt Caroline too. She didn't deserve the wrath of his rage.

Where can I go? I need time to think this through. He stood up and rubbed his hands up and down his thighs with thoughts of his mother chipping away at him.

He realized suddenly, that his world had been turned upside down, and again, Bruce was partly to blame.

Ok dad, when are you gonna just disappear from my fucking life. Why do you keep haunting me? You won't even let me meet a woman without her having some kind of connection to you. What is it that you want from me? Am I being punished 'cause I didn't turn out to be the son you really wanted? 'Cause your daughter was more of a jock than I was? 'Cause I wasn't brilliant like you and Ary? he shouted, into the mirror. *Would it have made a difference if I'd told you I might be gay—like you? Would you have loved me then? Would you have stayed? But dad, I want to be straight. I want to love Caroline like a man.* Marcus wanted to cry, but his tears were spent. He lowered himself onto the arm of the sofa, defeated, overcome with agony. *Just go away dad, please.*

Dwayne pulled the vinyl chair up to the bed railing

protecting Ary. He typed on his laptop computer. Every so often, he'd glance at her and lose his thought, wondering what would happen once this was over and they returned to work. He'd heard the office rumors about Joseph's salacious activities with Ary on business trips, but he'd chosen to ignore them. But he also knew that Joseph would stop at nothing, as he'd done before, to see to it that Dwayne presented no challenges to his female conquests. Jeopardizing his career wasn't worth it. But how could he walk away now—especially after holding her in his arms. He'd felt the magic, the desire and tenderness felt between lovers. He wanted her, but not like this. He wanted Ary to be free of any personal anguish, wanting him for the man he was, with all of his flaws and imperfections. He needed her to realize that she could break through the glass ceiling without compromising herself. He would compromise himself instead.

Dwayne put aside the rest of his work and fell asleep. His computer dangled dangerously off the edge of his lap and his cell phone lay on the floor underneath the chair.

Ary awoke, her eyes were heavy from sedation. She sat up slowly.

"Mama? Where am I?" She heard a man snoring.

"Dwayne. Dwayne wake up." She climbed down off the bed, knelt beside him and placed his laptop on the floor. She shook his arm.

"Dwayne."

He opened his eyes, awkwardly turning to look down at her.

"Ary, you're awake." He positioned himself upright in the chair. "What are you doing out of bed? How do you feel?"

"Dwayne, what happened? Why am I in here? Did something happen to my mother?"

"No, Ary. But I really think you need to speak with your father."

"Where is he? Did you find Marcus?"

Dwayne swallowed hard, before standing up.

"Sit here. I need you to stay calm. I kept my promise of finding your brother. But before I tell you where he is, I need you to promise me that you'll *listen* and not just *react* to what I have to say."

All she could manage was a pensive stare. "I promise."

"Marcus is at Caroline's house and your father is on his way to a place called Hilltop to check your mother in."

"The rehab facility? What's happened to my mother?" she cried.

He stooped down in front of her. His arms reaching around to hold her as she wept.

"Ary I'm sure it's for the best. They waited for you. They wanted your input," he lied. "But you were sedated and they didn't want to wait any longer."

"Is she gone? Did they take her already?"

"I'm not sure. I'll get the doctor so he can explain everything to you. I'll be right back, I promise." He rolled up his sleeve to check the time. It was six forty-five in the evening. He knew Sonya would more than likely be on her way to Hilltop. He reached the nurse's station, this time, he hoped, there would be no need to raise his voice. "Nurse, I'd like to speak to Dr. Ingram or whichever doctor is responsible for Mrs. Alexander's care."

"That would be Dr. Murphy," a nurse from behind the counter answered.

"Ok, then, Dr. Murphy."

"I'm afraid he's not in the building."

"When will he return?"

"Not tonight."

"I need someone to talk to my fiancée about her mother, right now." Now it seemed natural describing her as his fiancé.

"I can get Dr. Ingram for you and send him down to her room."

"Thank you," he said as calmly as he could muster at that moment.

Dr. Ingram spoke to Ary through her tears. Dwayne watched as she hunched over in her chair, arms folded, holding her stomach. It was tough watching her grieve. How could he keep a safe distance, yet reassure her that he cared. Doctor Ingram provided the solution.

"Ms. Alexander, it would help for you to be with your family tonight, someone to make sure you're okay. The medication will take a while to work its way completely out of your system. I can assure you that your mother will be fine. She'll be admitted and prepped tonight. I suggest that you wait until morning before going out to see her. Your father is there completing the necessary paperwork this evening."

CHAPTER 48

DWAYNE opened the door to his bachelor quarters, cautiously peeking inside before giving her the all clear. "Just wanted to make sure I wasn't gonna embarrass myself. I couldn't recall if I'd cleaned up, in the last month or two."

She smiled.

"I'm kidding. I have a cleaning service." Ary was too distraught to notice the dark décor or the impressive artwork in the dimly lit room. She reached down to remove her shoes.

"Here, please sit down and let me do that for you." Dwayne directed her to an overstuffed love seat and held one foot at a time, slipping off her size eights.

"May I take your coat?"

She leaned forward and handed it to him. Dwayne offered her a drink, forgetting that she been heavily sedated just a few hours earlier. She declined.

"Well, I hate to drink alone, but after what I've seen you go through today, I think it might be unavoidable."

He walked over to his mini bar and poured a glass of scotch. He turned to look at her. She stared into the distance. Her thoughts drifted back to the hospital.

"Dwayne, did my father talk to you at all?"

"No. It all seemed to happen at lightning speed. And once I found out what had happened to you, well, my whole focus changed."

He took a slow sip of his drink.

"Were you able to speak to Marcus?"

"No, I didn't get to speak to him. Ary, do you remember what you told your father about Marcus?"

"I think I'd figured out why he ran away. His behavior the night it happened. It all makes perfect sense. I'm sure he told mama about Caroline. I remember saying something to daddy about it." She stood up, unsteady, but determined to leave. "Dwayne, I need to see her."

"Whoa!" he said, placing his drink on the nearby coffee table. "Where are you off to young lady? It's after 10 p.m. I hardly think you're in any shape to drive out to the Island from Manhattan right now. But if you want, I'll drive you there first thing in the morning. Tonight though, I strongly recommend you get some rest."

Ary noticed a complete turnaround in his demeanor. Just a few weeks ago he didn't seem to care whether she worked for him *or* the company. Although she was grateful for him being by her side at the hospital, this was family business and they'd look to her for strength.

She rose up and headed toward the closet.

"Look Dwayne, I'm sure you have my best interest at heart, and I appreciate everything you've done, but I have to go, I need to get some answers. She slipped on her shoes. "If you'd give me Caroline's number, I'd like to try and call my brother."

Dwayne needed to stop her.

"Ary," he said, walking over to her. "The doctor suggested that you not be alone tonight. He said something about the medication not completely working its way through your system for a while. I honestly don't think driving is safe, and any decisions you'd make tonight, might not be what's best." His sinewy hands held on to her weakened arms.

"There's really nothing you can do tonight, and you've been through so much. Hey, you're welcomed to stay here. I'll even relinquish my very comfortable bed," he said, putting on his saddest, puppy face, the kind women find totally irresistible.

"Seriously, use my phone to call your father and your brother. And in my opinion, I don't think you should be alone when you talk to Marcus. Ary, outside of business, I don't ask you for anything, but now I am. I'm pleading with you not to leave. I wouldn't be able to forgive myself if something happened to you and I could have prevented it."

She stood with her back to the closet, perplexed. Ultimately, she succumbed to his offer. They bore into each other's eyes— his, dancing wildly across her troubled face, hers, focused on his parting lips. He planted a light kiss on her forehead, and brushed each soft eyelid with his lips. She instinctively rose up on her toes. Dwayne unleashed her golden locks, causing them to fall like wisteria around her face as he inhaled a long breath, savoring her natural scent. Suddenly, a maddening force below urged him to take her to the bedroom. He moaned, managing to hold back, willing the moment to linger.

"Ary," he whispered in her ear, "I just want to hold and protect you."

She leaned into him, relishing his strong embrace. He opened and closed his mouth, gently pulling and sucking her lips—careful not to let them slip away.

"I need you, Dwayne." She looked upward into his eyes. His thoughts became unintelligible, leaving his emotions to assume the lead.

The recessed lights silhouetted her shapely body underneath

her peach colored blouse. They stood face to face. Slowly, he unbuttoned her blouse. Her satin bra could no longer contain the swell of her creamy breasts. He fondled her hardened nipples between his fingers, playfully biting each one, alternating between the gentle grasp of his teeth and the heat of his tongue. Ary's legs weakened as she held onto the corners of his solid shoulders for support. As he pushed back, inches from her embrace, she placed her hands over his belt, her eyes meeting his amplified stare.

"Oh, Ary," he groaned, reaching around to rub the smooth moist skin in the curve of her back. She slithered out of her pants and scant bikini panties, unmasking the contours of her hips and the cusp of her sumptuous sexuality.

Removing his belt and watching it as it fell silently onto the thick Persian rug, she knew this would be a memorable moment. He stepped back to witness her unequaled beauty, and without taking his eyes from her, unzipped his pants and tore off his shirt, revealing a chocolate colored chest and the full extension of his manhood. She marveled at his muscular legs, athletic thighs, and fully erect manhood. For Ary, at that instant, he embodied all that any man should be. She caressed his firm buttocks as his heart rumbled like thunder. His chest tightened, propelling his senses into a higher orbit. His thoughts exploded with a euphoric moan.

"Arryyy…"

He swept her up into his arms and led her to his room and onto his king sized bed, supporting her head with down filled pillows. Gently, he spread apart her long, shapely legs and let the tip of his tongue explore every magnificent curve of her lithe frame. Her body tingled, gyrating smoothly as he pulled her further into his mouth.

"Dwayne," she cried, "I want you. I need to feel you inside of me."

Willfully obliging, he reached around and anchored her legs securely across his back, delving deep inside of her, in and out, simultaneously discharging cries of ecstasy.

"Oh…Dwayne…!" He was relentless.

"Ary, let yourself go."

She freed herself from his loving grip, leading him on an exploration of her exquisite body that would be impossible to forget. Her hips pivoted in unison with his, absorbing the sensuous sweat of seduction. Climactic tremors surged through their heaving bodies. His eyes watched fiercely as she worked her magic. "Ahhhh!" he screamed, as the hot liquid flowed like satin inside her. "Ary!" he yelled, jerking as if struck by simultaneous bolts of lightning. Her trembling fingers dug deeply into his back. They rolled dangerously close to the corners of the bed, holding tightly on to each other. With his heart relentlessly pounding, he thought, *this was meant to be.*

CHAPTER 49

JOSEPH was on his way to the office even before the sun rose. It wasn't unusual on a Saturday morning for him to hammer out last minute details of a proposal before presenting it to a client for a Monday meeting.

Passing Ary's cubicle reminded him that he hadn't spoken to her since the call from the hospital.

He tried her home number first. There was no answer. He called her BlackBerry.

"Oh my God, is that my phone?" Ary jumped out of Dwayne's arms, nearly falling out of bed. She raced to the living room and heard a ringing coming from her purse.

"Don't stop, don't stop," she begged.

"Hello."

"Ary, it's Joseph."

"What happened to you yesterday?"

"I'm sorry I didn't make it there but G called with a client emergency right after you'd called and by the time I quelled that fire, it was two or three in the morning," he lied.

"How are you? How's your mother?"

"I'm ok. I'm going out to Hilltop to see her this morning. And because it's all the way at the end of the Island, I want to get an early start."

"Hilltop? I thought she was at…" he fumbled for a name.

"Long Island Medical Center," she interjected. "Not any longer."

"Well, I tried calling your house but…" Ary interrupted him before he could offer any further explanation.

"I spent the night at Dwayne's apartment. Long story. But he's been wonderful and he also offered to take me out to the facility to see her."

Joseph seethed with anger. "Are you still at his place."

"Yes."

"Well, I'm glad I was able get him to stand in for me on Friday."

"What do you mean? I didn't know you'd *told* him to come." Her thoughts flashed from Dwayne's appearance in her mother's hospital room to last night's tenderness. She never imagined that he'd been ordered to stand by her side. She looked towards his bedroom, lowering her head in disappointment.

"Listen, I can swing over there in a matter of minutes and take you to see your mother while I visit with an old friend who lives near Hilltop. I'm sure Dwayne needs to finish preparing for the ChemCo presentation which is still on for Monday."

"ChemCo! I forgot all about it! Joseph, I can still do it. I've been ready for more than a week…I"

"Hey, I have every confidence that you can. But this time I have to insist you take a few days off and tend to family matters. You'll need a clear head when it comes to this account 'cause we'll only get one more shot at it. Ary, I truly am sorry I wasn't there for you. So let me make it up by taking you to your mother today."

"Thank you, Joseph, I know you are, and your concern and confidence in me means more than you'll ever know. I'll see you soon."

"Let me speak to Dwayne."

"Sure. I'll see if he's awake."

Dwayne stood in the hallway between the bedroom and living room listening to the entire exchange. His heart was filled with disillusion and disappointment. How could she do this? Say that? Especially after what they'd just experienced. How could he allow himself to get so involved with her? After hearing about her family's misfortune, he'd taken it upon himself to go and offer support. There was never any prodding from Joseph. And there certainly was never any preconceived intention on his part of comforting her in his arms at the hospital or sleeping with her, especially at such a vulnerable time.

He stared at her blanket wrapped body. The memory of last night was still fresh in his mind and as he inhaled, he could still smell her fragrant scent clinging to the air. He hesitated before exhaling, prolonging the moment. Ary was in *his* house talking to a man he despised. How should he confront her? Dwayne quickly jumped back into bed and pulled the covers over his head.

Ary tiptoed in, gently poking him under the comforter.

"Dwayne, are you awake? It's Joseph."

He'd managed not to move a muscle. Ary went back to the living room to finish her call. "I'm sorry, Joseph, but he's sound asleep. Where can he reach you once he's up?

"On my BlackBerry."

"I'll have him call you. Goodbye now." She walked into the bedroom and eased the silk blue comforter off Dwayne's head, kissing him on the neck. His muscles tensed. She brushed his smooth cut hair with her hand, then crawled into bed beside him.

"Dwayne, wake up. It's almost eight o'clock. Joseph called. He wants to talk to you about the ChemCo account. Dwayne?"

Dwayne turned slowly towards her— an icy stare fixed on his face. He sat up and leaned against the cherry wood head-board with only his chest exposed and his actions of the prior night quickly fading into a chapter of obscurity. Ary stared back at him, sensing something had gone terribly wrong. She moved closer, placing her hand on his shoulder. He grabbed it and slung it away.

"What's the matter? What did I do?"

"Ary, cut the shit. I overheard your conversation with Joseph. What the hell was that about? You're up in my fucking house fucking my brains out last night, and when the morning comes you're sweet-talking that rich, white, male whore. What happened last night? Didn't that mean anything to you? Or was I just a substitute for him 'cause he was tied up with someone else? Tell me!" he shouted. "Tell me what the *fuck* is going on here, 'cause woman, I don't play stand-in for no man."

He got out of bed, grabbing his robe from a nearby chaise. "I don't know how many black men you've had in your life. But girl, we don't play by the same rules as the white boys. They don't seem to mind if they share the flavor of the month, but once a brother has chosen a sister, he plays for keeps. No man comes between them, unless she fucks around and messes things up. And it's plain to see that your lack of understanding has cost you dearly. I didn't see your boy Joseph coming to your aid when you needed him. Did you ask him why? Well baby, if you haven't, you'll get that chance sooner rather than later. Get the fuck out of my bed and get your clothes on. Call yourself a car service and charge it to the firm. And do me a favor. Forget about what took place last night, 'cause as soon as you walk out my door, as Michael Jackson once said, 'You're His-Story.'"

Ary sat frozen in confusion. In her mind, what she'd experienced with Dwayne was memorable, but that was all. There was never any relationship established and no commitments made. What was his problem? They hadn't set any rules and there was never the type of unspoken sexual understanding she had with Joseph. How could he have gotten the impression that she was somehow his? She *belonged* to no one! And how dare he try and define her in his world.

"You're absolutely right Dwayne Hargis," she said, staring into his enraged eyes. "Black men don't play by the same rules as their white counterparts. But fortunately for me, I've found their way of playing to be much more entertaining."

Ary picked up her cell phone and dialed the office.

"Joseph, it's Ary. I'll be waiting out front."

Dwayne sent his fist against the headboard. Ary flinched, getting up slowly to retrieve her clothes and walking cautiously into the bathroom. Dwayne's hand and head were throbbing. He watched as the bathroom door closed, wondering whether or not he'd sufficiently communicated his pain. She was no different than what he'd left behind in Greenbrier. He needed to get her out of his thoughts. A business trip out west— anywhere to avoid contact for the next several days. But right now, what he really wanted was to slap some sense into her. Maybe it was stress over her mother's condition that caused this irrational behavior. Maybe it was the drugs still in her system. Ary came out of the bathroom fully dressed, hair pulled back and tied with the same clip he'd untied in a moment of passion. Even in his state of fury and despair it was difficult for him to deny her beauty. She stopped at the foot of the bed and placidly addressed him.

"Dwayne, I appreciate all you've done for me. And I know you're angry right now because you feel I misled you. But please understand, that was not my intention. I think we were both caught up in a vulnerable moment. Look, we have a decent working relationship and I'd like for it to continue."

He held onto the same stack of pillows he'd placed under her head—only this time, it was to keep his hands from choking her.

"Joseph said to tell you that the ChemCo meeting is still on for Monday morning, and to be prepared. I'll also be there so please don't start without me."

She was just outside the room when she heard him tearing the pillows to shreds. She turned to look, then picked up her pace. He got out of bed walking quickly into the living room just as she'd closed the front door. With his head fallen, he stood in the center of the room trying desperately to decide his next move.

Moments later he looked out of his tenth floor window, wondering if he should go after her. He spotted her looking in both directions. His heart pounded erratically—his mind was in turmoil. Maybe he was too hard on her. Maybe he didn't have all the facts. Maybe he'd let his emotions get the best of him. He'd obviously let Joseph get the best of him, again. Dwayne knew in his heart that he was the better man and Ary would soon come to realize it. Besides, everyone in the industry knew about Joseph's reputation with the ladies.

He went into the bedroom, grabbed his pants and shirt off the floor and raced back to the living room window. What he saw was Joseph holding the car door open and Ary giving

him a hug before getting in. That was it. Every emotion he'd
experienced last night was flushed from his body. He'd vowed
years ago that no other woman would use and trap him like the
mother of his son. From now on, he'd only be out to fulfill
his bodily needs. He recalled his dad saying: *Son, don't make any
lasting commitments to women unless you know in your heart it's right.
And you'll recognize the right one when she walks into your life.*

And she's not worth the time it takes to blink, he thought. At
least, that's what he wanted to believe. Dwayne fell into the
comfort of his recliner, grabbed the TV remote and stared at
the empty screen.

Ary and Joseph arrived at Hilltop in less than two hours.
Ary spoke briefly to a nurse who led her to her mother's room.

She found her lying in bed, her hair neatly laying across
a firm pillow. The expression on Sonya's face hadn't changed
from the one she'd seen at the hospital. Ary folded her arms
tight to her chest and bit hard on her lower lip. Joseph pulled
her close, burying her head in the safety of his chest. The
moment ended when the attending doctor came in to explain
Sonya's condition. She was told that Sonya had moved her toes
when being given a bath that morning—a definite sign of progress. Ary's face beamed at the news.

"How long do you think she'll need to remain here,
doctor?"

"If she continues to make improvements on a daily basis,
I don't think we're talking very long at all. However, she'll need
in-home care for a while, as I'm sure you've been told, and
we still need to get to the root of the problem. I recommend
therapy when the time comes. But that's something we'll discuss
as she gets better."

Ary stayed at her mother's bedside for the next few hours, while Joseph met up with an old flame. Upon returning, he roamed the grounds of Hilltop, taking in the breathtaking scenery. As he walked back towards the building, he noticed Ary coming through the revolving doors. Taking her by the hand, he led her to the end of the complex to witness the inspiring views along the Long Island Sound. He took her into his arms and held her until the pain of seeing her mother eased, little by little.

CHAPTER 50

"**M**ATTHEW, hello."

"Bruce, I've been worrying and trying to reach you. Are you ok?" Matthew stood near the window of his den. He'd spent most of the sunny, cool, San Diego morning at his desk working on briefs, but his concentration was in New York. He'd longed to hear Bruce's voice, but didn't want to appear as though he was unsympathetic to the Alexander family crisis. "How is everyone holding up?"

"They're fine," he answered curtly. "Listen, I'm at the beach house right now but my flight leaves at two fifty-six this afternoon."

"What happened with Sonya?"

Bruce shared very few details, choosing not to replay the past few day's gripping events. "I'll explain more when I get home."

Home, he thought, sounded wonderful. And hearing Matthew's voice provided a moment of comfort.

Matthew, however, detected chaos in Bruce's tone but

didn't push the issue. He wanted him home and began to feel uneasy about the trip he'd insisted Bruce take.

"Don't worry about picking me up at the airport, I'll catch a cab."

Matthew answered a quick, "Ok."

CHAPTER 51

DESPITE the mess she'd found in her apartment, Caroline was concerned about Marcus. She had no idea where he could have gone and tried calling some of his friends. They had neither seen, nor spoken to him in days. *It was time to contact his family,* she thought. The only phone numbers she had were Sonya's and Matthew's. She called her uncle first. Matthew gave her as much information as he'd known—which was very little. She'd asked for Bruce's cell number, determined to find Marcus.

Marcus had found a dingy hotel room downtown. He'd driven back home to get clothes and work files, managing to avoid any inquiries from the neighbors. He struggled with the untenable decisions he'd made and the damage he'd caused his family and Caroline, and knew she'd try and find him, although he felt relatively safe that it might take a couple of days, giving him time to begin sorting through this impasse.

CHAPTER 52

JOSEPH parked in front of her condo and didn't press the issue of coming upstairs. During most of the drive home, Ary slept. He looked at her when he could afford to take his eyes off the road and daydreamed of what it would be like to settle down with one woman.

His mother would often ask, when they spoke on the phone, if at thirty-nine years old, he'd considered whether or not the time had come to start a family. But the thought of being a responsible husband and role model to a son or daughter had always sent chills down his spine, until now. Now he was intrigued by *this* woman, a woman who was not only intelligent and beautiful, but also courageous, even while she was sleeping. Joseph's plans for Ary weren't fully flushed out in his head, but he was sure she'd be the one to help him fulfill his dreams.

"Ary, wake up, you're home."

"I'm exhausted," she admitted as she stretched and yawned. "Sorry I wasn't much company for the ride home."

As she turned to push open the door, he tugged on her shoulder and kissed her tender lips. She smiled, but couldn't find the strength to respond. She thanked him for the day and tried again to assure him that she'd be prepared for Monday's meeting.

CHAPTER 53

ARY put the key in the lock and opened the door to her sanctuary. She drew her body down to the sofa and promised her Chinese evergreen that after ten minutes of rest, she'd water it. But her eyes were heavy and her brain was mush. Preparation for Monday's meeting would have to wait. The sun was beginning to fade, and the glow of a distant sunset peeked through her window. She appreciated the familiar beauty of home more than ever and within minutes, was sound asleep.

Several hours passed before the ringing telephone forced her awake. She considered letting voicemail answer but reconsidered after thinking it could be Marcus or Bruce.

"Hello."

"Ary, this is Caroline Grant, Marcus' girlfriend," she announced cautiously. "I'm sorry, did I wake you?"

Ary sat up, brushing back fallen strands of hair from her face.

"Yes, but that's okay. Is Marcus with you?"

"Well, he was here on Thursday and rather upset about the argument with his mother. But when I came home after work on Friday, he was gone. But not before trashing my apartment."

"What are you saying?"

"I don't care about the house," she cried, "I'm concerned about Marcus." Tears streamed down her face as she tried to convey her anxiety to a woman she'd up until now, only heard

Marcus speak of. "I don't know where he is, and I'm terrified that he might do something irrational. I really need to find him," she wept. "He shouldn't be alone."

Ary wiped the sleep from her eyes, realizing she'd need to focus and remain calm in order to get any useful information from her.

"Caroline, please tell me exactly what happened."

She drew in a deep breath and tried to remember everything she and Marcus talked about on Thursday night. Ary surmised from her discussion with Caroline that Marcus had in fact told Sonya about his marriage plans and it was most likely the cause of her condition. She was angry all over again, but careful not to reveal her feelings. Ary recounted for Caroline how her mother never fully accepted Bruce's homosexuality and hasty departure.

"The problem is deeper than you can imagine, and unfortunately, because of your connection to Matthew, you're a part of it now."

Caroline sobbed silently into the phone.

"Listen, I'm sure Marcus is okay. He's dealing with a lot right now, but if I know my brother at all, he's feeling a tremendous amount of guilt. Marcus loves mama and I know he's struggling. He was never really able to express his emotions, but I guess at some point, they had to come out and unfortunately, your house bore the brunt of his pain. I don't think he'd do anything stupid. So, let's give him until Monday to get in touch with either of us. I'm sure he just needs some time to clear his head. Try not to worry."

Given the circumstances however, she could do little else.

"I just can't sit around and do nothing until Monday Ary, I

need to go and at least *try* to find him. Are you willing to help me?"

Ary shook her head and silently asked for God's strength, realizing Caroline's persistence.

"Meet me at my place, so we can strategize."

"Thank you. I'd appreciate that very much."

"Let me give you directions." But before she could begin to spell out her address,, there was a call waiting. "Can you hold on for a second, that's my call waiting."

"Sure."

"Hello."

"Ary."

"Marcus! Where *are* you? We need to talk. You fucked up big-time Marcus. But that doesn't mean you had to run away and hide."

"Is mama ok?"

"She's in rehab and she might be there for awhile. She's still not able to talk. Marcus, I know you told her about Caroline. In fact she's on the other line right now getting ready to come over so that we can search for your ass together."

"Ary, I need to be alone for a while. I feel confused. I feel like a coward and right now I just wanna end it. Look at what I've done to everybody….."

"Marcus B. Alexander, you are *not* a coward," she shouted. "You're an *Alexander* and we stand up for what we believe in, no matter what. If you want to kill yourself, go ahead, just know that you'll also kill her. Is that what you want Marcus? Be a man, go talk to her—even if she can't respond. Explain your love for Caroline. Tell her it was pure coincidence that Caroline's his niece. I know she'll understand because she loves us. And afterwards, if you feel like you still want to commit suicide, the only one who can convince you that it's wrong, is you. I'm not going to pretend that what you did wasn't detestable, but I'm also not going to put all the blame on you. We need to rectify this situation and we have to start by talking."

Marcus listened to his sister's words. She'd always known what to say in desperate times, just as she'd done all throughout their childhood. But this time he wasn't sure she could help. He wanted to make amends with Sonya, but he also wanted to know if she could forgive him.

"I hear what you're saying and I agree with you, but I'm gonna need some time. I'll be in touch. Tell Caroline I love her and I'll pay for the damage. Goodbye Ary."

CHAPTER 54

"THE damage to her home or to her heart, Marcus?" she shouted.

But he didn't respond—he'd already hung up. She clicked back over to Caroline.

"I'm sorry I kept you waiting. That was Marcus."

CHAPTER 55

DWAYNE was in his office before seven a.m. on Monday. He'd hiked around the corridors to see if G or Joseph were in theirs. They weren't. Thoughts of Ary were still fresh in his mind as he reared back in his chair. He'd tried everything to forget her over the weekend. On Saturday afternoon, after making several calls, he was able to connect with a couple of friends who were on their way to the gym. He needed to get rid of the negative energy flowing through his veins and a good workout was the perfect solution. He was hurting inside, and the tight grip of his ego prevented him from coming to terms with his true feelings. *Could his friends have been right all along about NPI? Was is time to start looking for a job with more of a diverse environment?* His thoughts raced for a few moments. He knew Joseph would always be an issue and his very presence repulsed him. Would he be able to look at the man who'd once again stolen his night of passion and memories.

But with sudden renewed determination, he decided that no one would push him out. *She'll have to find out the hard way, that it's only money that ensures your longevity at NPI.* Dwayne poured over the presentation that was scheduled for nine o'clock. He was so involved in his work that when she walked past his office and peeked in, he never even noticed.

Ary set her briefcase down on her desk. But before she

could open it and gather the file she'd need for the meeting, the telephone rang.

"Ary Alexander."

"Ary, it's G. I was sorry to hear about your mother. Is there anything I can do to help? Name it and it's done."

"G, thank you, but everything is okay for now."

"Are you sure? Why are you even here today? Shouldn't you be with your family?"

Ary swallowed hard. Her eyes filled with tears, but she quickly composed herself.

"They're fine and I'm here because of the ChemCo presentation."

"Joseph or Dwayne would've postponed the meeting. Up until six o'clock this morning, I wasn't sure whether or not I'd even make it, just having returned from Saudi last night. Listen, you know I understand the importance of winning that account, but I'm also human, and I care deeply about my staff. Remember when I told you that I consider all of you family, these are the times when it matters most."

"I know G, and believe me I sincerely appreciate your concern. But really, everyone's fine and I'm more than ready to win this contract for NPI. So please give me the opportunity to present the proposal this morning."

"Well, I won't argue with your perseverance. I'll see you in the boardroom in fifteen minutes."

Ary waited to make sure he hung up first before placing the phone in its cradle.

She was mentally and physically drained and didn't know if she could keep her cool exterior for the entire day. She wished everyone would just leave her alone. Relationships and non-relationships were putting pressure on her. Even though she blamed Marcus for what happened to Sonya, she couldn't help but think that her recent actions played a major role. But she also felt strongly that men shouldn't always have the upper hand when it came to determining how women lived their lives. *Females should have more control when it comes to business and personal relationships,* she thought.

Facing Dwayne and Joseph in the same room would be tough, but she was determined not to let them upset her. She'd seen enough weakness in the last few days to last two or three lifetimes. She picked up the meeting materials left on her desk by the marketing assistant and walked down the hallway to the boardroom.

As the doors opened, everyone fell silent. The banter taking place between Joseph, Dwayne, G, the client and a couple of NPI marketing managers hung in the air like a cumulus cloud. No one could speak. "Please excuse me, I had to wait for a few more printouts of the presentation." She walked slowly around the table handing each attendee a packet.

Ary's hair was pulled straight back and twisted into a conservative bun. A pearl comb held the coif in place, and like every day in the office, her makeup was flawless. She'd chosen burnt orange lipstick to compliment the stylish orange Versace suit hugging her perfectly proportioned figure. Dwayne dropped his pen on the floor, Joseph cleared his throat and G brought them all back to reality.

"Ah-hem," G coughed. "If we're all composed and ready, I say we proceed."

Ary knew at that moment she was in full control. She'd made an extraordinary entrance, and this time, she'd gotten more than what she'd expected. She'd gotten G's attention.

Now, he too was fair game. But she'd have to tread lightly.

His reputed lover was protective and watchful and any wrong move could cost her her job.

"Dwayne, should I begin?"

He gulped, barely able to answer. "Yeah, I mean yes, please, begin."

Joseph glared at him from across the table, covertly rolling his eyes.

G's self-restraint was much more refined. He settled on flipping futilely through the document.

Ary's presentation was tight and faultless. She hit each major point with precision. Even if Dwayne had intended on getting revenge for her weekend performance, at this moment, he didn't stand a chance.

Ary's quick successes had already impressed her CEO, but this time, under the tremendous strain and stress of personal problems, G felt her performance was beyond what he expected from a rookie.

After the presentation, the client stood up with his entourage and motioned to G, with a nod that he'd like to talk one-on-one. As G stood up to leave, Joseph, Ary and the others rose from their chairs. Dwayne was already standing at the far end of the room after having wrapped up his segment with a PowerPoint presentation. G paused at the door and turned to face the group, "Ary, in light of what you've just gone through, I'd like to commend you for a superb job. Thank you." He smiled, winked and walked with the client through the board-room doors.

The accolades from her colleagues reverberated throughout the room.

Ary, great job, congratulations.

Flawless performance, Ary.

You hit that one straight out of the ballpark!

Welcome to the multi-million dollar NPI club, Ary.

"Thank you all. Thank you Joseph, Dwayne, I couldn't have done it without your help and guidance."

Dwayne was shocked at her gratitude. *Was this the same seditious woman he'd argued with over the weekend?* Without warning, the memory of Friday night began playing in his mind like a familiar love song. An impulsive gaze and grin swept over him.

Joseph was enraged. "Dwayne, meet me in my office in 10 minutes. There's something I need to discuss with you."

"Sure." Dwayne brushed his hand slowly over his hair. He summoned a deep breath not knowing what to expect as Joseph left the room without any further discussion or explanation.

He lowered his head, not wanting to make eye contact with her. "Ary, that was...a great presentation." He quickly unplugged his laptop, packed up his gear and disappeared into the corridor.

Ary loved every minute of it. The winning deck was in her hands. The only question now, was how she'd play out the rest of her cards.

The emotional high from the meeting still loitered in her mind as she made her way back to her cubicle, and she wanted to relish it a while longer, when the ringing phone demanded her attention. She chose to let voicemail respond.

Bruce's message was short and explicit. He'd apologized for having to leave without getting the chance to talk things over with her, but he'd done what he thought was in Sonya's best interest. *Bastard,* she whispered.

CHAPTER 56

"COME in." Joseph's voice was stern and condemnatory. "What just took place in the boardroom? This, from an NPI Manager? I have to tell you Dwayne, I've seen better from you...much better. Is something on your mind? Is something going on between you and Ary? You know how I frown on inter-office relationships—they tend to get in the way of rational thinking. Do you know how hard I fought for your promotion, Dwayne?" he lied. "I wouldn't want to see you throw that away for a piece of ...you get my meaning."

Dwayne was shocked and appalled. He wanted to jump across the desk and strangle the life from Joseph's despicable body. It took everything he had in his nature to summon restraint. Looking Joseph squarely in the eyes, he said, "I understand. And *nothing* is going on between me and Ary Alexander. There is no inter-office relationship. Maybe I was a little off because of her family crises over the weekend." Dwayne cringed at the words he was about to express to his manager. "I appreciate that you fought for my promotion Joseph and it's a privilege to work for someone who is both admired and feared as a force to be reckoned with in the oil industry. I continue to learn so much from your worldly experiences, every day. So from now on, it's strictly business, and if something misfortunate does happen to someone under my watch, well, I'll have my secretary send a card."

His blood was boiling. Thoughts ran from extreme disgust to profound hatred. He'd listened to his own words and felt the need to wash out his mouth with soap.

"Well, I'm glad we've cleared the air. I think we needed it. And by the way, I'd like to see your BP presentation tomorrow morning. That's all for now."

Dwayne's head throbbed. He'd taken just about all he could from Joseph, a man who'd already stolen one woman, now he was being instructed, ordered, threatened to stay away from another. This time he'd gone too far.

Dwayne went back to his office and slammed the door shut—he was steaming.

"How dare that callous, ostentatious, loathsome excuse of a man chastise me and criticize my work!" He threw a glass paperweight across the room, causing it to shatter against the wall. "Joseph Larsen, this time you've crossed the line."

CHAPTER 57

A week after the meeting with NPI, Robert Moss, CEO of ChemCo Inc., invited the NPI team to his office.

"We look forward to a profitable, long-term, professional relationship with NPI," he toasted. "Our attorneys should have the final contracts to you early next week. And to you Ms. Alexander, well, I told John Gicardi earlier on the phone that I would have been hard pressed to agree to all the terms he'd snuck into the final proposal except for the fact that you were so convincing and knowledgeable."

"Thank you, sir. I look forward to working with ChemCo."

"I'd also like to extend an invitation to all of you to join us tonight at the Polo Club for drinks and hors D'oeuvres."

Moss had been presented with an offer that he literally could not refuse. NPI did what was necessary to save the client money up front—knowing that it was just a matter of time before those dollars flowed back into the company's coffers. The firm had used this strategy successfully time after time with its smaller customers. The projects were always completed ahead of schedule, saving the client millions of dollars, which eventually were later won by NPI in subsequent bids for future projects.

"We'd love to join you tonight," Dwayne said, sporting an air of self-confidence and speaking on behalf of the NPI staff.

"Then it's set. We'll see you all tonight at seven. And Ms.

Alexander, when you're done working for that handsome Italian, making him richer, maybe you'll consider joining our team."

"Well, that's certainly an offer I'll keep in mind, sir," she smiled.

CHAPTER 58

AFTER the meeting, Dwayne suggested to Ary and the others that they take a taxi back to the office, explaining that he needed to walk the more than ten blocks to savor the ChemCo victory. In truth, he needed to clear his head and wanted to be nowhere near his understudy. He called G from his BlackBerry to update him on the meeting and extend the Polo Club invitation. Pleased, G called Marguerite to invite her to tonight's celebration. Although she'd made other plans, she thought it best to rearrange her evening. Ary, she felt, would require close monitoring.

"I'd love to be your date tonight, and it'll be great to see the ChemCo folks again."

"Wonderful! Let's mingle with old acquaintances and afterwards, come home with me. Be my special guest."

Marguerite closed her eyes, pressing the phone closer to her ear. G was the only man who could diffuse her fears.

CHAPTER 59

THE Polo Club was busy on this Wednesday night. There seemed to be meetings and receptions taking place in every room. Parlors were filled with CEOs, Vice Presidents and Managers, all prospects for Ary's ambitions.

Thin, vertical strips of red and purple velvet adorned the ornate walls of the private chamber for the ChemCo affair. Crown molding carved by nineteenth century artisans bordered the twelve-foot high ceilings, which was further complimented by gold leaf tucked carefully in each of its four corners. Oversized framed portraits of famous Polo horsemen, including Prince Charles of England rode along the outer walls. Pictures of white men on black horses hung separately from black men on white horses, divided by the expanse of the room. *Even the pictures require a safe distance,* Ary thought. Black wait staff wearing white tuxedos moved skillfully about, offering colorful delicacies on shining platters. This was an atmosphere in which time had long since passed, and old attitudes weren't likely to object.

Ary and Joseph enjoyed a glass of imported Chardonnay as they surveyed the room full of people. "I don't see anyone here from NPI, do you?" Ary said, after scanning the space.

"No, not yet," he answered, "So far, only *old*, ChemCo farts."

They both laughed. But the jollity was interrupted by the intrusion of an old acquaintance.

"Joseph Larsen. It's been too long since we've bumped into one another."

"Leslie Daniels how *are* you? It's been quite a while." Joseph greeted her with a kiss on each cheek. "Leslie, I'd like for you to meet Ary Alexander, our not-so-new- anymore marketing representative, who, by the way, is mostly responsible for this celebration tonight." Ary offered her hand but was greeted instead by an ineffectual tilt of Daniels' perfectly coifed, blond head. Joseph stepped in at just the right moment. "Ary, Leslie is Vice President of Research at ChemCo's West Coast branch."

Sensing feminine hostility but wanting to remain professional, Ary managed a swift, "It's a pleasure."

Leslie turned her attention back to Joseph.

"Could I steal him away for a few minutes," she asked, finally acknowledging Ary's presence. "We really should catch up," she suggested seductively.

"Please Ms. Daniels, take as long as you want," Ary smiled, sarcastically.

"Well then," Joseph said, thwarting what could have turned into a cat fight, "shall we go and reminisce?"

Ary ventured through the crowded room, nearly colliding with a waiter carrying a tray of vintage white wine when she spotted Dwayne walking in with a tall, young, beauty. "I'm so sorry," she apologized. "May I take one of those off your hands?"

G and Marguerite crisscrossed through the room, heading over to Robert Moss and his entourage. Ary wanted to leave, but decided to take refuge in her glass of wine near a corner entrance. *This is beginning to get very boring*, she mumbled.

"I'd have to say I agree with you." Startled, Ary turned to find a man wearing round, bronze-rimmed glasses standing behind her.

"I'm sooo...sorry. I didn't know anyone could hear me...I"

"No need to apologize, Ms?"

"Alexander, Ary Alexander," she answered, still embarrassed.

"Ms. Ary Alexander," he repeated, moving closer beside her. "I've attended at least four of these things in the last month, and after about the second one, even a billion dollar deal becomes routine."

Ary hadn't recognized him from any previous meetings at ChemCo. *Who was he?*

"I'm with the BP Corporation," he said, almost whispering. "I'm Darias Woolfolk and we're having a small affair a couple of doors down and I decided after being in there for over an hour, it was time to crash someone else's party." She extended her hand. Instead of shaking it, he raised it up to his lips and softly kissed her slender fingers. Ary could only stare into his chivalrous blue eyes. "Your hand is shaking. Are you cold? Would you like my jacket?"

"No, I'm fine, thank you," she said, still feeling somewhat embarrassed.

Darias unbuttoned his sport coat, draped it around her shoulders, placed both hands in his pockets, drew in a deep breath and scanned the room.

"By the way, it's very nice to finally meet you, Ary."

"I beg your pardon."

"Isn't this party partially in your honor?"

"Well, I wouldn't exactly put it..."

"What is it, a three or four hundred million-dollar collaboration between NPI and ChemCo?"

"Wow. Very good, Mr. Woolfolk," she laughed. "Now if only I knew as much about you."

"In time you will," he told her. "There's a technique to staying on top of important things. And if you're willing to learn, I'd be eager to teach you." Ary was struck by his candor.

"Now, if you're still wondering how I knew about the deal, no, I'm not clairvoyant, just very intuitive."

He had her full attention.

"I'm sure you, like everyone in the industry knows the rags to riches story of John G. Gicardi, poor little kid, son of Italian immigrants from the close knit community of Little Italy in New York and his meteoric rise to fame. How he started out in the belly of the mailroom for a small oil firm, in time working his way up to marketing assistant. He worked even harder and smarter to become a marketing rep in six months, making quota ten times over in his first year. Gicardi figured out pretty quickly that if he could make this kind of money for someone else, he'd be insane not to do that for himself. So after just six years of savvy selling, Gicardi founded his empire, NPI. The man's a damn near business genius and he makes sure that he only hires the best and the brightest. If anyone ever does voluntarily leave the company, and I couldn't imagine why they would, they wouldn't be jobless for more than a minute. And you, young lady, are one of those best and brightest. Corporate eyes are upon you."

"Wow. What are you saying? I just started at NPI."

"Ahh…but you must be the only one who hasn't checked the score board lately."

"I didn't realize I was in the game."

"Oh, you're definitely in the game. And let me compliment you on how well you play."

"Okay, now you're scaring me."

His gaze grew intense.

"Ary," he said, now standing in front of her and taking her hands into his.

"Remember what I said to you a few minutes ago about a technique for keeping on top of important things in this business?"

"Yes."

"Well, there are certain rules you'll have to be aware of when you choose to play, and I'm sure by now Joseph has instructed you on some of them."

Ary's heart skipped a beat.

"That's where I come in. I've been around for as long as Gicardi, and I've learned by watching him that you never divulge your true self to the players. They'll most definitely use your *weaknesses* against you and your *strengths* to frame you."

Her mind raced. *Who was this guy, really, and why disclose this information to her, a total stranger he'd only recently come to know.*

"Your wine glass is empty. Can I refill it for you?"

"I already feel as though I'm hallucinating. So, no. I think I've had all the wine I should drink for one night."

"Nonsense young lady, this is a time for celebration. Waiter!" he summoned. "If you're worried about driving home, don't be. I'm volunteering to be your designated driver. Besides, there's something I believe you'd be very interested in knowing. I'll meet you in front of the building when the party's over."

Darias left Ary standing in the doorway. She watched him casually stroll down the corridor, back to his firm's reception and felt maybe, he'd be her inside tract into BP. But it all seemed too easy. *What would he want from her in exchange for information? And the bigger question, would she be willing to give it up.* Her mind sprinted wildly.

"Hey, I've been looking for you," Joseph said, catching her off guard. "Sorry I left you alone like that, but when a business opportunity seeks you out you'd be a fool not to chase it, right?" She didn't respond.

"I hope you haven't had to endure *too* many boring conversations."

"Actually, I've met some very interesting people just standing here," she said, smiling mischievously.

"Hmm," he reflected, curiously. "Well, right now you're needed center stage. Moss and G are ready to uncork the champagne and make the formal announcement. And by the way, your dress is much sexier without the jacket."

Darias' suit coat still hung from her shoulders. Giving it a snug pull and folding it across her arm, she caught hold of Joseph's hand and followed him through the crowd.

Praise and toasting replaced idle, business chitchat. Dwayne, Ary and the ChemCo team were thrust together to accept the accolades. She managed to keep a tolerable distance from Dwayne. But while he delighted in the attention of his colleagues, he found the time with her disquieting. For her part, Darias Woolfolk was the only one consuming her mind.

CHAPTER 60

EXHAUSTED and anxious, Ary walked outside the Polo Club into the brisk night air along with NPI's newest clients. People clamored for taxis or stepped into waiting Lincoln Town cars. Joseph stopped to ask whether she'd be interested in sharing a ride. She politely declined and wished him a goodnight. Ary watched as he caught up with Leslie, curving his arm around her waist, and eventually disappearing into a limousine. Dwayne exited the building with the woman he'd arrived with, stopped for a few good-byes and handshakes then walked down the avenue. There was an unexpected twinge in her heart to which she summarily ignored, and continued the lookout for Darias.

A man wearing a black cap approached from a black stretch limo directly across the street and inquired *Are you Ms. Ary Alexander?* Managing a cautious reply, she affirmed her identity. Ary followed Darius' driver to the polished car and looked around to see if anyone was left to notice. The sweet smell of flowers greeted her once he opened the door. Small bouquets of red, pink, and yellow roses were arranged securely around the floor of the passenger area. As she settled in her seat, the driver handed her a card which read: *Please join me for a late night brandy. Should you accept my invitation, the driver will be waiting for a nod of yes or no.*

Darias

Ps:

I trust that my coat provided you with enough warmth for the duration of your celebration.

She sat back for a moment, inspecting the beauty surrounding her, then nodded her head a simple yes.

The driver returned a quick, "Very good."

After whisking through the still busy streets of the City, the limo came to rest at the side entrance of a building with the number, *770* inlaid within a marble block. 770 Fifth Avenue was a forty-two story, luxury high-rise that housed those whose names were not easily recognized: Foreign financiers, successful U.S. stockbrokers, and people with money passed down from generations of wealth all called it home. The driver hurried out of the car to open the door for Ary, exchanging swift pleasantries with the building's doorman, who tipped his hat as she stepped out onto the carpeted entryway. He directed her to the private elevator inside and wished her a good evening. She wondered what would happen to the flowers. But as she turned to look for the car, all that was left were the trail of taillights in the dark distance. *What am I doing? I just met this guy a few hours ago.* She questioned her impetuous judgment, but decided to put the blame on alcohol and curiosity. The high speed elevator delivered her to Darius' rooftop suite. The doors opened quickly to a small entryway whose walls were lined with impressive works of art.

"I'm delighted that you didn't have a change of heart," he said, greeting her from behind a huge wooden door. "Come in, I promise not to bite you." Clad in relaxed silk pants, a complimentary short sleeve silk shirt that seemed to hug his muscular physique, and the absence of his eyeglasses all combined to make him look noticeably younger than his forty-seven years.

It was far easier now for her to distinguish the rugged details of his handsome face. "Hey, thanks for returning my jacket, it's one of my favorites." Sliding the jacket off her shoulders, she handed it to him who promptly tossed it over a nearby chair. He walked over to a fully stocked bar. "Make yourself comfortable," he urged, looking over his shoulder. "Can I get you that Brandy?"

She noticed the fireplace, crackling with flints of burnt logs. She pulled her dress further up her thighs and settled down on the warm wooden floor. "I'll have Dom Perignon instead," she requested, testing his savior faire.

"What year?"

"1996," she challenged.

"Great year."

"Now don't tell me you keep every year in your wine cellar?"

"Of course not. I'm not that self-indulgent, I just get *damned lucky* every once in a while," he laughed.

After filling two flutes with champagne, Darias walked over to the fireplace to join her and proposed a toast. "Here's to the beginning of what I hope will be a mutually rewarding friendship."

They spent the next few hours drinking, talking and subtlty flirting. He revealed his past relationship with Marguerite, whom he'd dated for two years prior to joining BP. He recalled how she'd constantly push him to new heights, encouraging him to network with the largest oil companies—introducing him to people she'd met along the way in her rising career. But after five years of vigorously seeking VP status, he left the firm, realizing his goals would not be met during his self-imposed timeframe. He subsequently landed a position with

BP and within three years of joining the oil giant, he'd not only accomplished his goals, he'd surpassed them. However, his relationship with Marguerite fizzled because of their hectic schedules and never being able to see one another. Ary inquired about Marguerite's ethnicity. "She's so attractive, and it's hard to pin down what she is. But truthfully Darius, I'm too *afraid* to ask," she laughed. He claimed that she was always evasive, but admitted to having British, South African and French lineage, which, she said, accounted for the olive complexion, dark brown hair and eyes. He admitted that he too felt there was more to Marguerite's identity than she'd let on, but he never pressed her. That wasn't the focus of his attraction. However, he did recall one incident where he'd spent the weekend at her apartment in Greenwich Village. While Marguerite was in the shower, he relaxed in bed with the Sunday New York Times until the ringing phone upset his concentration. Reluctantly, he answered after the fifth ring and a baritone-voiced male was on the calling end, asking to speak with his sister. Darias relayed that she was unavailable, but would pass on the message. He questioned her after she came out of the shower because she'd never mentioned having any brothers or sisters, she'd always talked of being an only child born in South Africa to a British father and an American mother who moved them to the States when she was five years old. Marguerite often mentioned how nice it would have been to have had a sibling, and assured him the caller had the wrong number. To change the subject she allowed her plush, full-length towel to drop slowly at his feet and suddenly, he said, his prior curiosities faded .

He went on to describe Dwayne's pursuit of Marguerite after their breakup, before she joined NPI. "She made it quite clear that she wasn't interested. I believe her exact words were, *'I don't date men of color.'*"

"Wow! Sounds like she has some definite issues, which might explain the friction between those two."

"I don't know about that, but what I do know is that he has some 'issues' of his own."

"What do you mean?"

"Marguerite and I remained friends after our split, and she told me Dwayne was romantically pursuing her. So, naturally as her friend, I had him checked out by a buddy of mine who ran a detective agency in Washington, D.C. He found out that Dwayne fathered a child with a woman in West Virginia, a child he preferred to keep secret."

"You're kidding! Why would he want to keep it a secret?"

"Oh, I'm guessing it was because the mother of his child turned out to be a former prostitute from Richmond who'd moved to Greenbrier to try and start a new life."

"Oh-my-God!" she let out, with eyes wide open.

"They met, dated and fell in love. She became pregnant and they planned to marry without him knowing much about her background until his father, a retired Navy cook who'd worked in Richmond, and had probably been solicited more than a few times in his career, asked around and discovered the nature of her former profession. Dwayne was young, stubborn and didn't want to believe it at first. So he took a trip to Richmond to find out for himself. Well, when he found out it was all true, he went ballistic and moved as far away from his roots as he could—ending up here, in New York. And as far as I know, he's never mentioned having a son to anyone. And although he pays child support, his son's mother is always hounding him for more money."

"Darias, does Marguerite know about this?"

"No. There was no reason for her to know. Had she still been interested in him, I would have told her so that she could decide for herself whether or not to get involved. Otherwise, I didn't see the need."

"Does *anyone* at NPI know?" she asked, with heightened curiosity.

"I doubt it. Dwayne is an extremely private man. He never mentions his family, relationships or any problems or concerns outside of work to anyone. But I do know that he takes care of his ailing parents, financially."

"I'm shocked, I mean, about the whole thing. I don't know what to say right now." She rose up on her knees, positioning herself in front of him.

"So if you know all this, what do you know about me?"

He sat up slowly, studying her face, the gleam in her hazel eyes, the flutter of her lashes, the slant of her perfectly shaped nose and the natural fullness of her lips. Lifting up her chin with his finger, he lowered his mouth in slow anticipation of discovering hers. Her body felt weak from the smooth intoxication of champagne and desire.

"Only that you remind me of a younger, even more beautiful Marguerite," he whispered, gently biting her lower lip, "before she became corrupted by the industry," he finished.

"Why are you telling me all this?" she managed, backing away slightly.

"Stay with me tonight, Ary," he appealed, softly in her ear. "Please stay with me and learn the truth." She looked into his eyes and decided to give in to intuition.

CHAPTER 61

JOSEPH pushed the button on the speakerphone, paging his assistant. "Michelle, make reservations to L.A. for me. I need to pay a visit to the West Coast office."

"Yes, Mr. Larsen. Will you be traveling alone?"

"How long have you worked for me, Michelle? You, of all people know the answer to that." She forced a grin. "Hey now, I can picture that sarcastic smile on your face, young lady," he teased. "But this time, my dear, invaluable assistant, you're wrong. I will be traveling alone."

"For how long, sir?"

Joseph rolled through his BlackBerry calendar. "Let's see. Tuesday's meeting with G and the B."

"Pardon me, sir?"

"Nothing, nothing. I was just thinking about Marguerite." Michelle laughed silently. "Let's see. Marguerite, Marguerite who will you defeat this week," he sang. "Uh, three days, beginning Wednesday."

Michelle quickly checked the airline itinerary from her desktop connection to the air carrier's website. She located Joseph's *preferred traveler's* status and booked the flight.

"Okay, Mr. Larsen, I emailed you the information, but just to recap, you're traveling Wednesday, to L.A. out of Kennedy at 6:49 a.m. American Airlines, returning Friday, leaving 5:30 p.m.

out of LAX. Hotel reservations are confirmed at the Bel-Air Hilton. Will there be anything else?"

"Yes, remind me to give you a raise when I return."

"I always do," she laughed before disconnecting the call.

Joseph swung around in his leather chair and stared out the window. His thoughts centered on snagging the BP account. The stakes were higher this time. Although ChemCo was a significant win, BP was known in the industry as the *'Academy Award'* for any firm. At one time, Joseph would have been confident using Morgan Reynolds as bait, but now that her uncle was retired, and his own interest in her fading, he'd have to re-examine his strategy.

Although initially, he'd tossed Dwayne's hat in the ring to secure the information he'd need to help structure a winning bid, after seeing Darias cozying up to Ary at the Polo Club, and knowing his power, influence and position at BP, Ary seemed like the better candidate to help him realize his dream. Joseph stood up, spread his hands along each side of the window and peered down at the bustling City streets. *Soon they'll all recognize me as the genius,* he thought.

Dwayne arrived at 9:15 a.m. Ann checked the time on her computer screen. *He was always the second one to arrive after G,* she thought, usually around 7:00 or 8:00am at the latest. Her eyes followed him down the corridor until he abruptly turned around trapping her stare. "Ann, Good morning. I'm sorry, I was lost in thought. Got a lot on my mind."

"No worries, Mr. Hargis."

"Would you please have Ary stop in to see me?"

"Of course," she called back, leaning over the receptionist desk."

Dwayne unlocked the door to his office and immediately reached for the ChemCo folder laying in the center of his desk. He sat down, opened the file and energetically spun around in his chair toward the gentle warmth of the morning sun. He removed a pair of rarely worn, designer eyewear from his suit coat breast pocket, propped his feet on the windowsill and began reading.

Ary's head was throbbing from the night before. All she'd planned on doing this morning was to quietly read over the ChemCo contract and review the project's team members before her scheduled afternoon meeting with Dwayne. After settling into a comfortable groove, she was startled suddenly by a phone call from Ann conveying Dwayne's message. Reluctantly, she grabbed her files and made her way to his office.

"Knock, knock," she said, poking her head in first. "You wanted to see me?"

Dwayne turned to face the doorway. "Yes, come in. You could've taken off your coat before you came down."

"I'm fine," she said, unaware that she was still wearing it. "I must be more eager to meet with the ChemCo project team members than I even realized. I've already thought about who would take the technical lead and...

"Hey, hey! Not so fast. Take a breath, have a seat, relax for a minute before you fire off *your* choice for team leads. Last time I checked the company organization chart my name was still listed as 'Marketing *Manager*,' unless of course, things changed overnight," he finished, cynically.

She frowned. "I apologize. I guess I *can* be a little aggressive at times."

"A little?"

"Should I continue?"

"Yeah, but shut the door."

"What I was trying to say was I'd like to take the technical lead on the account, freeing you to do managerial oversight."

Dwayne was shocked. Who was she to tell him *anything*?

"I know by now you're aware of my project management skills, as well as the fact that I've accomplished all of my assigned tasks, independently, and on time. And nothing personally, but the fact that I was the first rep in the history of NPI to have closed enough deals to satisfy her first year's quota in just under six months only confirms my business aptitude and acumen."

He could only stare in disbelief.

"And also," she continued, "I know that to be successful, you *always* separate your personal and professional lives. So what I'm asking is your permission to be Principle Marketing lead on ChemCo." She sat back in her chair, pleased that she was able to communicate her wishes in spite of last night's hangover.

Dwayne considered reaching across his desk and slapping her with all his strength. *This woman is impossible*, he thought. *How can I continue to work with her?* She was definitely the female version of Joseph. The only meaningful difference was that he'd slept with this adaptation, even cared for her, and pretended to be engaged. Maybe it was time to take a few weeks off, test the waters at another firm—leave these ruthless, conniving people to themselves, let Ary self-destruct in the dangerous world she was creating for herself. He drew in a hard breath and pulled his thoughts together.

"You don't need to remind me of your accomplishments, I'm *very* aware of your capabilities. And as far as taking *anything* personally, believe me, I learned a long time ago that sometimes, it's better to just let things slide off your back. But for you and I Ary, I think we've reached that plateau where we can no longer have an effective *business* relationship. So I think I'll suggest to Joseph that you work for another manager, possibly on the fifteenth floor. And truly, I hope you continue to enjoy many more successes with the company. So, I'm sure I'll see you around, maybe when you've scored *another* major account." Dwayne adjusted his glasses around his face and turned his attention to the ChemCo file. Without looking up at her, he said, "Close the door when you leave."

He'd hoped she'd leave quickly. She didn't. She was infuriated. And as she rose, so did the fine hairs on the back of her neck. She opened then slammed the door shut and shouted, "Are you kidding me? Are you doing this because of what happened in your apartment? I'm not here to *begin* a relationship or *recover* from one. I'm here to make money and a name for myself in this industry, just like you, G and Joseph. I thought the name of the game was *'Get as much as you can, by any means necessary, as long as it's perceived to be legal.'* Isn't that right, Dwayne? And here's a newsflash, because of me, you stand to double your commissions this year." She placed both hands on his desk and leaned forward. "Look, we work well together, and what we shared intimately was wonderful and I'll never forget it. But I don't *want* or *need* a relationship right now—I don't want the burden of caring too much for someone who'd eventually leave me anyway. Right now, my only interests at NPI, is climbing to the top of the corporate ladder. But if you feel uncomfortable having me report to you because of what happened between us, then I'll move up to the fifteenth floor, and wish you the best of luck."

He looked up from his file.

"Well, I'm glad we agree on something. I'll talk to Joseph today to make the arrangements. And by the way, you should hold off on any further talks with the ChemCo folks. Joseph and I will announce the change at our next meeting with them."

"Wait a minute," she said, shifting her petite frame in her three and one half-inch heels. "Do you mean I'd lose control of the accounts I've already won?"

"Well, yeah, but you'd still be compensated and credited for the initial wins. But any future commissions would go to the acquiring rep."

Her eyes were ablaze. "You've obviously lost all sense of reality if you think I've busted my ass and come this far to let *anyone* rob me of future commissions just because I won't sleep with them anymore!" she screamed. "You may not want me working for you, Dwayne Hargis, but it'll take more than a scorned lover to make me give up my accounts!"

She walked towards the door, then slowly turned to face him.

"You're not so naïve as to believe that most people don't have something in their lives they wished would stay hidden forever are you? Even within the hallowed halls of NPI," she scoffed. "I know about your illegitimate son and his whore mother in Greenbrier, and maybe that's the reason for your anger. But Dwayne, I won't just stand here and foolishly be the scapegoat for all your frustrations. I'd have surely given you more credit than that," she whispered through a slight grin. "Oh, and one last thing. In case you're wondering, Joseph wasn't the one to tell me about your little secret, and so far, no one at NPI knows. But that could change at any moment. So I think it'd be in your best interest to cooperate with me 'cause I'd hate to be the one to snitch."

His head pounded. His temples throbbed. His heart raced.

"So, now that we've cleared up that little misunderstanding, I'll resume my work on ChemCo, and assume that I'm still reporting to you, Mr. Dwayne Hargis."

"Get out!" he demanded. "Get the fuck out of here, now!"

She looked back at him, winked and slowly closed the door.

CHAPTER 62

MARCUS' room mimicked his new neighborhood, dark and drab, filled with dejected men and women hanging out in front of the building. He worried about his safety and the few valuables he'd brought with him to his temporary home. But for now, this was all he could afford while he contemplated his future of leaving the law program, and saving his money for a nice apartment on Long Island, closer to his job. But the very thought of being on the Island, near his mother, was overwhelming.

His irrepressible thoughts of Ary, Sonya and Caroline caused him to work overtime, just to keep his mind free. Caroline called the office at least once a day, despite the promise she'd made to Ary. She'd left messages, reminding him that she loved him no matter what had happened. She wanted him back. She needed him in her life. Neither Ary, nor Bruce made any further attempts to contact him. He reasoned they no longer wanted him in their lives. His own recent attempts at deciphering right from wrong had failed. His friends counseled him, assuring him that families had forgiven far greater transgressions than what he'd committed. They suggested he start by making amends with his sister and perhaps she could help heal the deep wounds he'd inflicted on his mother. Marcus knew he couldn't live the rest of his life without his family or Caroline. Somehow, he had to rectify it all.

Before heading home one evening, he decided to get the rest of his things from the house he was now a stranger in. As he pulled into the driveway, he noticed the lights on in the living room and his mother's car sitting in its usual spot. He sat in his metallic silver BMW, under the glow of a full moon, wondering what he would say, or do first. He turned off the engine and the headlights, then looked around at the neighboring houses. Carefully positioned spotlights shone on precise areas of manicured landscapes. Luxury cars waited to be tucked away behind garage doors and soft shadows moved about through large, undressed windows.

Marcus checked his key ring, making sure he'd brought the right ones. He breathed heavily, letting his head fall back as he exhaled. Taking one last look around the car's interior, he opened the door and stepped out onto the cobblestone driveway. It felt familiar and safe as he crossed over to the winding esplanade leading to the wooden double front doors. He paused, throwing his shoulders back and turning the key in the lock. He opened the door slowly and was greeted by the sound of a beeping alarm. After nervously fumbling a few times, the combination of numbers he and Sonya had decided upon together, came back into memory.

He tiptoed through the foyer, peeking cautiously into the living room where the dimly lit table lamps, timed to turn on at dusk, greeted him. He crossed over to the dining room where the same crystal chandelier hung over the table where his father made his stunning announcement years before. Marcus closed his eyes and tried to forget, but when his mind wouldn't cooperate, he walked quickly to the kitchen. He hesitated before going into the family room—his heart beating as though it was making a desperate attempt to escape his chest. The muscles in his arms, legs and neck tightened, he couldn't move. He could see the chair where his mother fell into unconsciousness.

Standing there, on the steps dividing the kitchen from the family room, he allowed his entire body to weep. His emotions were no longer in control, only the sounds of sorrow. *"Forgive me mama,"* he cried. *"I need you. I need to tell you how sorry I am for everything. I should have told you about daddy's conversation with Matthew that night,"* he confessed. *"Maybe you could have talked him out of leaving. Maybe you would have been better prepared for how to go on after he left. Please mama, I'll do anything now, I love you. I didn't mean for this to happen, not to you. Please mama, come back home."*

His words were heard only by the emptiness of a deserted home. Marcus stared at her empty chair. *Tell me what to do, what you want. Tell me I'm still your son.* He sat on the cold, marble tiled kitchen floor and wept for hours until his eyes were dry and swollen, and he felt empty of life.

Later on that evening, rising up from his pain, he noticed a small tan envelope on the family room coffee table. Approaching it slowly, he saw his name centered on the face of it, and his sister's in the top left corner. His fear of opening it was followed by an urgent desire to know if he could return to his family. He began to read.

Dear Marcus,

I knew you'd return home and hopefully have the courage to open and read this note. We've all been through a lot, but we also need to move forward, it's what they taught us to do, even if one of them wasn't strong enough to follow that sage advice. I never stopped believing in your love for us, Marcus. I've always been there for you in the past…but it's time you be responsible and stand on your own. Talk to me when you're ready.

Love,
Ary

Marcus picked up the telephone sitting on the round table near the sofa and dialed Ary's number. Her recording assured callers that she'd get back to them as soon as possible. He spoke swiftly and with desperation. "Ary, it's me, Marcus. I'm at home. I'm ready to talk. I want you to hear the truth from me about what really happened that night. I need you and mama. Please call me back."

CHAPTER 63

ARY had taken Tylenol throughout the day trying desperately to get rid of her nagging headache. Nothing helped. She'd managed to stay clear of everyone, working from the safety of her cubicle. She contemplated how much longer she should stay tonight. It was already after ten o'clock. Her stomach felt queasy and unsettled, but her morning conversation with Dwayne and his next move prevented her from leaving.

She wondered if Dwayne would confront Joseph—mistakenly accuse him of disclosing his pint-sized, Greenbrier secret. Her thoughts ran wild. She laid her head on top of the desk as a last attempt at stopping the pain, but her mind refused to let her rest. She speculated whether or not Joseph was still in the office and decided to dial his extension. "This is Larsen," he answered, from the speakerphone.

"Joseph, it's Ary. I didn't mean to disturb you. I thought you'd left already. I was going to leave a voicemail."

"Don't be silly. What's on your mind? And why are you still hanging around at this ungodly hour," he joked.

With her voice vacillating, she asked, "Have you spoken to Dwayne today, about, well, one of the accounts?"

Never taking his eyes or fingers from the keyboard, he questioned, "Which account in particular, Ary?"

"You know what, never mind, it's not important. I just

thought maybe he'd mentioned something about the ChemCo team, you know, who might lead the project."

"Nope, he hasn't mentioned anything to me yet. He should really be communicating with you on that. Just like the Paris deal, this is your baby. We trust you now, young lady," he finished, still concentrating on his computer screen. "I would have thought the two of you were already on top of that, especially in light of him going away for a couple of days. Oh and listen. I need you to stop by my office before you head out. I want to discuss the BP account."

"Okay. Thanks Joseph." She hung up the phone, curious as to why he'd need to speak with her about any account at that hour. *Wasn't Dwayne the account lead? What was this late night meeting really about? What did he know?* This day was ending as grimly as it had begun. She wondered if in fact she was digging a hole too deep to climb out of. Ary pulled herself and her thoughts together, gathered her coat and briefcase and walked down to Joseph's office. The door was wide open.

"Hey love, come on in. By the way, how's my old friend Darias Woolfolk?" Ary swallowed hard before answering. "I didn't know the two of you were friends. And if that's the case, I guess Dwayne won't have to work too hard to win that business," she laughed.

"Darias made it his business to meet me last night, said he'd heard all the publicity I'd been receiving." She folded her slim arms together, feeling confident in her explanation.

"I don't think there's a worthy soul who hasn't been affected by your recent success. You know Ary, rich oil men, unlike ordinary rich businessmen are extremely egotistical when it comes to who has possession of what."

"I'm afraid I'm not following you."

"I've been told that old man Moss has plans of recruiting you in the middle of the project. Then maybe you could spill NPI's well-planned strategies on future contracts and possible acquisitions."

"What are you saying?"

"What I'm saying, is that some of these old fogies are envious of G for having had the courage and foresight to hire you."

"Courage, foresight?"

"Yes," he continued, leaning back in the chair. "Certainly by now you've encountered enough of these geriatric fools, most of whom haven't had much contact with African Americans, except maybe as housekeepers, or chauffeurs. And until you came along, I can assure you, they weren't willing to accept them in any other capacity."

Ary was shocked at his frankness.

"What? Housekeepers and chauffeurs? You mean to tell me that they hadn't noticed Dwayne was black, and might I add, brilliant, *and* successful? What about him?"

Joseph winced at her description. "I don't know. Maybe they think he's an exception to the norm."

Ary's face flushed. Her eyes widened.

"What are you saying?" she asked, pacing across the room. "Do you consider him and me anomalies? That somehow, when it came time to hand out brains to whites we picked up a set without being noticed?" She kicked the door completely shut with the back of her heel, conjuring up the energy that had escaped her all day. She moved closer, meeting his stare across the desk.

"Is this racist attitude coming from them or from you, Joseph? You, of all people, a man I held in the highest regard.

I didn't want to believe that I was just a good time for you, a diversion from the lily white norm you're accustomed to conquering." Ary slammed her hands down on his desk, ignoring the pain throbbing in her fingers. "This entire conversation is putrid!"

"Stop it!" he shouted. "How dare you come into *my* office screaming and yelling, accusing me of racism. You work for me! I'm in control here. I'm the one making sure you get those premium accounts and I can just as easily make them disappear. You never question my motives or intentions!" he commanded, standing to meet her revolting stare.

"I didn't say that I was the one with narrow minded assumptions. All I'm saying to you is that I've been in this business longer than you probably ever will be, and I understand how the game is played. You may be smart, beautiful and one shade darker than me, but the fact remains—men rule this industry. And in the good old U.S. of A, that boils down to men who look like me."

Ary was appalled. Her eyes held onto his infuriated gaze.

"And by the way, keep up the good work with Darias Woolfolk," he finished, smiling, "We may need his help on this one."

Ary grabbed her briefcase and ran from his office.

CHAPTER 64

"**G**OOD morning, NPI. How may I direct your call?" Ann answered cheerfully.

"Ary Alexander, please."

"May I ask who's calling?"

"Dr. Jonas Murphy, and it's personal."

"I'll connect you now, doctor." With her curiosity raised, Ann wondered if something was wrong with NPI's newest prodigy.

She answered as though the call were an unwarranted interruption. "Ms. Alexander speaking.".

"Ms. Alexander, this is Dr. Murphy."

Ary's heart raced. A knot formed in her throat, preventing an immediate response. She closed her eyes and waited. "Yes, Doctor?"

"I tried reaching your father several times yesterday, but I was unsuccessful. Anyway, I caught up with Dr. Ingram this morning and he gave me your work number. I wanted to tell you that Sonya is awake and coherent. She asked for you late last night.

She desperately wants to go home, and I see no reason why she can't. She's alert and I think it would be beneficial if she returned to a familiar setting, getting a head start on the road to a full recovery. Is it possible that you could come out to

Hilltop today or tomorrow?" Ary cried silently on the phone, tears streaming down onto the papers spread across her desk.

"Hello? Are you there?"

"Yes," she answered, sniffling, wiping away the tears and hoping no one passing by had noticed. "I'll leave right away. Thank you doctor. I owe you a debt of gratitude."

"You owe me nothing except to make sure that your family gets to the bottom of what happened, and that Sonya receives the proper counseling she'll need to ensure this won't happen again. She'll need someone full-time to care for her and drive her to therapy during the first couple of weeks. After that, maybe 2 or 3 days a week. I'll leave detailed clinical instructions and a recommendation for a psychologist with the nurse. It may be tough going for a short while, but I know that with love and understanding, everything should turn out fine. I wish you the best of luck. Good bye."

Ary looked around her small office space as if she would find answers to all the questions speeding through her head. She would need to find someone right away to take care of Sonya while she was at work. Would her mother even be open to therapy? Where was Marcus? Now *she* needed *him*. She logged onto the computer to check her daily calendar and saw that Dwayne had scheduled a 10:00 a.m. meeting. She stretched out her arm sleeve to look at the time. It was 9:20a.m. *I have to go,* she whispered.

Ary slung her coat over her arm, picked up her briefcase and headed towards the reception area. Colleagues passing in the hallway greeted her. She walked right past them, without any acknowledgement. As she reached the glass doors in the reception area, leading to the elevators, Ann called out her name.

"Ary, sweetheart, is everything okay?"

She turned abruptly.

"I'm sorry, but I have to go. If anyone is looking for me they can reach me by BlackBerry, I won't be returning today." She pushed opened the doors.

"Ary," Ann called, "Wait a minute." Leaving her station, Ann walked over to her and spoke softly. "I don't mean to pry honey, or be intrusive, but you look as though you could use someone right now. Let me call Dwayne. He's your manager."

"No!" she said sternly, "Not Dwayne. Listen, I'm fine. I'll call him from the road." After noticing the frightened look on the receptionist's face she altered her harsh tone. "I'm fine, Ann, really," she said, placing her hand on Ann's shoulder. "Don't worry about me. I just have something I have to take care of. But I appreciate your concern." She disappeared into the elevator.

Puzzled, Ann went back to her post trying to determine if and when she should alert the managers. As the elevator reached its destination, Ary realized that she'd pressed 'L' for lobby instead of 'G' for the parking garage. She banged the close door button on the panel trying desperately to prevent the doors from opening in the lobby. It was too late. People piled in, pushing a myriad of buttons to reach their office floors. She shoved her way out and ran through the lobby towards the door emblazoned with the large 'G.'

"What's the hurry Miss Ary? Are you alright?" She stopped in her tracks.

"Bob! I'm in a bit of a rush. I'll have to talk to you later."

"Hey, if you're 'bout to drive looking like that, I'd strongly suggest you get somebody to go with you."

"You don't understand...I...I'm fine," she replied, wiping sudden tears from her eyes. She quickly tried to compose herself, avoiding any further inquiries. "It's just that I need to get somewhere fast and it's going to take me a while to get there."

"Hey, I've seen and heard a lot from where I stand here in this lobby. And after twenty-three years of eight hour days, five days a week in the security business, you start to develop a knack for identifying when something doesn't look or sound quite right." Ary stared into the faded whites of his eyes. This was the first time she could exhale after having gotten the news from Dr. Murphy. "Come with me," he suggested, ushering her to a room filled with the building's security monitors. They sat in a corner, near a percolating glass coffeepot. "I'm gonna have a cup. Can I pour one for you," he offered.

"No thank you. I'll be alright."

"Miss Ary, ever since that day you stopped to talk to me out in the cold, I felt that you were, well, different, caring. Maybe it's cause people don't usually take the time to stop and have conversations with security guards and I don't see too many of *us* coming and going in the building either," he smirked. "And maybe for that reason, I started to feel, well, protective of you, like a father almost. So, that's why I thought it'd be best if I stopped you just now. I don't want to see you hurt."

"I don't understand. Why would you feel 'protective' of me? And what do you mean about not wanting to see me hurt?" He paused before answering and checked on the boiling brew.

"I know you need to get somewhere, so I don't want to take up your time, but it looked to me like there was somethin' wrong. I could tell from your eyes, from your quick pace. And I'm usually right when it comes to these things. Now ordinarily, I'd never interfere in anybody's personal or business affairs, but that company you work for upstairs seems to run their people real hard, even take away their spirit, their friendliness. All except for the big fella G, they call him. He's always got a nice word to say. I guess it's 'cause he's the owner. But I hear he demands a lot from his people. Now I don't know what kind of money there is to be made in the oil business, but I'm assuming by the looks, clothes and cars of the employees, it's pretty damn good," he said, with a tired laugh. "You see Miss Ary, I do know something 'bout the oil business. I have a sister, a half sister really, who works in it." Ary's concentration was now squarely focused on his every word. "She'd lost her soul before she started working in the business, but that just seemed to make it worse. She got caught up in the game of rich men, money, and fancy living. She forgot her roots," he confessed, the hurt still visible in his eyes.

"Family's important, no matter who they are or what they become. Outsiders can promise you the world, make it all seem too good to pass up, make you do and say things that one day, you might regret. I still love my sister dearly and pray that one day, she'll understand that the bond of family blood is more powerful than the promise of false riches."

Ary placed her soft hand on top of his rough, cracked knuckles resting on the gray metal desk. He shook his head and reached in his back pocket, pulling out a wrinkled handkerchief.

Ary squeezed his hand tighter to reassure him that he wasn't alone. His shoulders hunched up and down as he let out what seemed like years of sadness.

"Bob," she asked softly. "Who is your sister?"

He looked at her, slowly returning the dampened cloth to his back pocket.

"Marguerite Armstead," he said, through redden eyes.

Ary's mouth dropped open. She covered it with both hands to keep from uttering a sound.

CHAPTER 65

"**O**H yeah, she's perfect. No one would ever suspect her. And now that she has an in at BP, we're closer than I ever expected to be at this point. So don't worry, I have everything under control on my end. You just make sure everything is in place on yours. I'll see you on the Coast next week." Joseph clicked the 'end call' button on his cell and tucked it into his pocket. The pieces were coming together for what he referred to as the '*final plan.*' His excitement will be difficult to contain, but for the past year, he'd managed to keep it in tact.

Dwayne, who'd needed to speak to his boss about an account, waited outside Joseph's slightly opened door and listened to the conversation. Michelle had taken an overdue bathroom break.

He rushed back to his office and shut the door.

"What the hell? She's perfect? This sounds like something I don't want any part of," he thought. He sat in his chair for the next twenty minutes trying to figure out what Joseph was up to now. In the past, he'd been annoyed with Joseph's weakness for women, and his methods for cutting deals, which narrowly escaped industry ethics, but intentionally sabotaging the career of an NPI colleague, even that seemed out of character for Joseph. Was the '*she*' he referred to Ary or Marguerite? He knew Ary was involved with Joseph, and now, possibly Darias. Dwayne knew how important a BP victory would be for NPI

and that's partially why he'd put up with so much crap from Joseph in return for landing the lead on the account strategy. But was he planning on using Ary to score the deal?

Maybe I need to find out what's going on here before that asshole destroys all of us," he thought.

Michelle returned to her desk to multiple phone lines ringing.

"Joseph Larsen's office."

"Hey Michelle, is he available?"

"I'll check, Mr. Hargis." After a few seconds, she patched him through.

"Dwayne, I'm glad you called, you're just the person I need to talk to."

"O-k, why is that?" Dwayne asked, with raised skepticism.

"Listen, maybe we should talk over lunch. What's your schedule like at say, 1:30pm?"

Dwayne scrolled through his BlackBerry calendar.

"Actually I have a client meeting at 1:00 and it's gonna take more than half an hour. Can we push it to back to 2 o'clock, maybe?"

Dwayne's calendar showed no 1pm meeting, just the 10:30 with Ary. He also knew that Joseph's afternoon would be filled with management consults.

"Let's see, I have a 3pm with G and the others, hmmm. By the way, that one o'clock you have wouldn't be with the BP folks, would it?"

"No it's not. Why do you ask?"

"Because that's what I want to talk to you about. I've come up with a brilliant…"

"Joseph, hold that thought, the red light on my phone is flashing, it's G on the other line, hold on for just a minute."

Dwayne pushed the hold button and switched over to G. After a mere minute he switched back to Joseph.

"I'm back. I apologize for keeping you waiting. Actually, G wants to get together at one-thirty today, before his meeting with you and the others to discuss BP. So I guess I'll have to cancel my client meeting after all. How about dinner this evening? You name the time and place and I'll be there."

"Marucci's at seven," he said, annoyingly. "What exactly did G say about BP?"

"He just wants to alert me to a few client pitfalls to avoid before you and I get together for the preliminary strategy. I told him I really hadn't put anything down on paper yet, so his comments would be very helpful."

"Okay, perfect. I'll see you tonight."

"See you there." Dwayne felt both relieved to put Joseph off until the evening and disgust for his unscrupulous behavior. He needed time to come up with his own strategy for retaining control of BP. He was certain that if Joseph wanted to discuss the account, it could only mean he wanted to pass it off to someone else, possibly himself or his protégé, Ary. But why? Especially after promising it to him and convincing G that he was the man for the job.

He wouldn't stand for it. Not only would a BP win be extremely important to NPI, it would surely mean more autonomy for himself over future high profile accounts, and the boost he needed to propel his career to VP. Dwayne decided to use the morning hours away from the office to plot his course of action. He picked up the telephone and dialed the receptionist.

"Ann, I'll be out in the field today until one o'clock. Please forward any voice messages to my email." He'd forgotten all about the meeting with Ary.

"Yes, of course Mr. Hargis. Uh, sir, I'm a little worried..." Ann stifled her thought in mid-sentence.

"What's that Ann?"

"Nothing, I'll forward your messages." Split between betrayal and duty, she weighed her responsibility to inform him about Ary. She decided against it and returned to the phones— only this time her usually light-hearted greeting was teeming with indifference.

"This is NPI, who do you wish to speak with?"

CHAPTER 66

ARY sat in the parking lot of Hilltop for more than half an hour, not knowing what she'd say first. *What would Sonya want to know? What would she remember about that night? Would she be upset?*

There were patients everywhere, in wheel chairs; holding onto walkers; strolling with men and women in flowered coats; and walking around the grounds with loved ones. Before stepping out of the car, she stared at the pathway she'd walked down with Joseph where he'd held her in his arms. A sudden chill washed over her.

She entered the facility, carefully approaching the reception desk. "Hello, I'm Ary Alexander. I'm here to pick up my mother, Mrs. Sonya Alexander," she said, managing a weary smile.

"Please have a seat Ms. Alexander, we'll be right with you." Ary sat nervously as overworked nurses, and chart-carrying doctors discussed the private health concerns of the convalescing over a counter across from the receptionist station. Upon hearing her mother's name, she perked up and sat forward, but it was virtually impossible to eavesdrop with the bustling activity of people moving around.

"Excuse me," she interrupted, rising slowly from her seat, "Is everything all right with my mother? When can I go in and see her? The last time I was here, I didn't have to wait, I was told to go right in. Is everything alright?" The staff turned to face her. A doctor approached and relayed something she wasn't prepared to hear.

"Ms. Alexander, your brother was here after Dr. Murphy gave the discharge orders and took your mother home. I'm sorry you weren't notified before coming."

"What do you mean, my brother took her home. How is that possible? He couldn't have gotten here before me." Suddenly, she recalled how much time she'd spent with Bob at the office.

"As I was about to say, he was visiting early this morning and Dr. Murphy thought he was here to take her home. Nothing seemed out of the ordinary," the young doctor said, his tone coated with trepidation. Ary breathed deeply, trying to calm down.

"Where are the discharge forms? Do you still have copies of those?"

"Yes. I'll have the nurse make a copy for you."

"And what about the instructions, the medical information…"

"Those were given to Mr. Alexander before leaving."

"Is Dr. Murphy still in the building or somewhere on the grounds?"

"Uh, no. He left a few hours ago. Would you like to speak to the resident physician?"

"Uh, no, I wouldn't," she answered cynically. "Is there anything I need to do or take or…"

Sensing her growing hostility, the young doctor wanted to quell the conversation as quickly as possible and interrupted her before she could complete her question. "There's nothing else for her here, Ms. Alexander, she's been given a full release."

"Meaning?"

"Meaning, we've sent her home with all the medical discharge instructions." He turned his back to her, walked over to the counter, picked up a chart and walked down the glistening corridor. Ary stood facing the nurse's station, trying to determine if there was any reason to lash out at anyone else. She repositioned her purse hanging from her shoulder and rushed out to her car. It was time to confront the inevitable.

CHAPTER 67

DWAYNE relived the scene with Ary at the Polo Club, over and over again in his head after he'd arrived home. He poured himself another scotch and declared, *"That woman is gonna drive me to pure alcoholism. She's caused me nothing but heartache since the first day I laid eyes on her...even threatening me with my own son!"*

He wondered why, out of all the other managers at the firm, most of whom were more experienced in managing personnel, she had to report to him. He began questioning whether G had put the two of them together because of their shared ethnicity, although, in his heart, he truly didn't believe it. But his thoughts were raging.

What am I supposed to do now? Just sit around and wait to be manipulated by him and her whenever they feel the need to be amused? He was tired of being a doormat for Joseph, caving in to his outrageous demands.

He wanted to concentrate on business for now. What would his next move be to counter Joseph's dinner proposal tonight? He picked up his laptop, sat down in his familiar recliner and began typing. He suddenly remembered his morning meeting with Ary.

"Damn!"

Reaching for the cordless phone, he called her at the office but was told by Ann that she was out due to a family emergency.

He pressed for more details, insisting that Ary would have at least left a destination. She was adamant, but did relate that she'd suggested Ary talk to him before leaving. She said Ary assured her she'd check in from the road. He decided on calling her cell.

CHAPTER 68

SHE circled the block twice before pulling into the driveway, not sure if she was ready to face what lie behind the doors. She said a quick prayer, got out of the car and used her spare key to get in. "Mama," she called, walking through the foyer towards the family room.

"We're upstairs Ary," Marcus answered, routinely. "In mama's room."

Her heart skipped a beat. Now, she'd have to face them together—even though she'd forgiven him on paper, would her forgiveness translate in person. She took one cautious step after another up the winding staircase. Disturbing flashbacks stepped with her. She held tightly onto the banister that was badly in need of a dusting and made it to the second floor where memories of racing Marcus from room to room, and playing hide and seek brought a delicate smile. She peeked into her old bedroom where she and two girlfriends had stayed up all night whispering about the cutest boys in school, then continued slowly down the hallway whose walls were decorated with her academic achievements, her mother's artwork and pictures of Marcus in school plays. There were also family photos with Bruce. She recalled the cozy corner near her parent's exquisite bedroom master suite, where she'd heard them making love one night—prompting her to run and get Marcus so he could listen to the funny grunts and groans of a fulfilling marriage. Ary closed her eyes tight, squeezing out reluctant tears and paused at Sonya's bedroom door. There, she found Marcus, casually dressed, sitting at the foot of the bed facing Sonya, who appeared tired and worn.

"Ary darling," Sonya said, smiling weakly and placing a cup filled with brewing green tea on the nightstand. "I'm so happy to see you."

Ary walked straight past Marcus. "Mama," she sighed, "I've missed you terribly. I prayed you'd come back to us. I love you so much." She hugged her mother gently around her shoulders and kissed her lightly on her moist forehead. "I went out to Hilltop this morning to get you, but I guess my timing was a little off," she said, turning to face her brother for the first time. Marcus lowered his head.

"Baby, you can't imagine how happy I am to be home, to be with my family."

"How do you feel, mama?"

Sonya's dilemma revealed itself in her gaunt face, through her hollowed eyes and the lean arms that were visible through the sheer sleeves of her salmon-colored nightgown.

"I've had a slight headache, as I told your brother, since last night and I'm hungry for some *real food*," she laughed. "They gave me applesauce and a slice of wheat bread this morning, hardly enough to make up for all the meals I guess I've missed."

"Mama, what can I get for you?"

"I was getting ready to go downstairs to get something for her when you came in," Marcus explained guardedly, not knowing what to expect from his sister. "I didn't know if I'd find anything still edible in the fridge, so I thought about going out to pick up some things."

"You mean you'd have left her here alone?" Ary didn't

expect that her hostility would slip from her lips so suddenly. Although she'd forgiven him in her heart, her brain was yet unwilling.

"Well I, I wasn't sure…"

"Weren't sure? Didn't the doctor give you instructions? Where are they?"

"Honey, it's okay," Sonya mediated. "I'm fine. There's no need to scold your brother. I'm not an invalid. I think I'm capable of being alone in my own home for just a little while."

"I'm sorry, I didn't mean to upset you, mama," she apologized. She smoothed down her mother's hair, which seemed to have grayed over the course of her illness. "Can I get you something for your headache?"

"I'll get it," Marcus interrupted before Sonya could answer. "They gave me all of her medications before I left, and wrote prescriptions for refills. I'll also get the papers the doctor gave me."

Marcus left the room in a hurry, racing downstairs to the kitchen where he'd put the plastic bag of medicine on the counter top. He grabbed a bottle of water from the refrigerator and returned upstairs as quickly as his feet could propel him, but stopped short before returning inside because of what he was hearing in the distance.

"Mama, I…I know you need time to rest and recuperate, and I understand that you're going to need someone to help out with everyday things before you're on your feet again, but I need to ask you one question."

"What is it Ary?"

Marcus stood discreetly to one side of the doorway, hands trembling, struggling to hold onto the bottle of pills and water.

"Do you remember what happened that night?"

"I don't remember a thing. After I woke up last night, it felt as if I'd been asleep for only an hour or two. My neck was sore, like I'd slept the wrong way on my pillows. When Jonas came to my room later on, he told me that I'd suffered mental trauma." Sonya heaved her chest and released a drawn-out breath, then turned slightly, to face her daughter. "But Ary, right now I'd really rather not discuss it. I only want to spend time with the ones I love. Jonas told me not to rush any recollection—to let it come naturally. So please, no more questions right now. I only want to listen to you and Marcus tell me what's been going on in your lives." Sonya pushed herself upright and leaned back against a stack of down filled pillows supported by a custom-made upholstered headboard. "So, what have I missed?"

Marcus nervously bumped into a wall as he walked back into the bedroom. Ary turned to look over her shoulder. "Here's your medicine mama."

Before she could continue, her BlackBerry's ring tone of Robin Thicke's, *Lost Without You* interrupted any further questioning, or conversation she might have had for Sonya or Marcus.

"Hello."

"Ary, it's Dwayne. Is everything ok with you?" he asked, half caring, half angry.

"Yes, everything's fine, thank you. Listen, I apologize for running out of the office and not speaking to you beforehand, but I'd planned on calling later on in the day and going in early tomorrow to catch up."

"Well, it's already kind of late in the day and tomorrow's Saturday you know."

"I know that."

"Do you also know that I'm still your manager, and as

such, if you have to leave the office for any reason, emergency
or not, I should be alerted through voicemail, email or phone?"

"Yes."

She tried to keep her cool in her mother's presence but her
annoyance was discernible in her tone, and painted across her
face.

"Dwayne, can you hold on for just a second please?" Not
waiting for his reply, She pushed the 'hold' button.

"Mama, I'm gonna take this downstairs. It's a business call.
It shouldn't take long."

"Ary? Is something wrong?"

"Oh no! I'll be right back."

Sonya watched as Ary gathered up her purse and left the
room. She closed her eyes and breathed softly. Marcus desperately wanted to ask her forgiveness with Ary out of sight, but
noticed how peaceful his mother appeared and decided against
tempting fate.

"Dwayne, I'm back."

"You do know I'd scheduled a ten-thirty meeting with you,
don't you?"

"Yes, but I didn't have time to respond. I…"

"How do I get through to you?" he interrupted. "You work
for me! I'm responsible for *what* you do at NPI, *how* you do it,
when you do it and *where* you do it. Tell me what it's gonna take
for you to understand that?"

"Dwayne, I…"

"If G, Joseph or Marguerite approaches me with a question about an account that you've been assigned to, and I don't
have the answers to their interrogations, then my ass looks
bad—and let me be quite clear to you, I consider my ass one

of my best assets. And oh, for the record, the conversation we had a few days ago, along with your little threat, is still fresh in my mind."

"Did you call to remind me of something I feel needs no further discussion, or to assert your position as my well-endowed manager?"

"Neither. I'd planned on meeting with you this morning to discuss ChemCo in light of the fact that you're remaining on the account. But after I'd found out that you'd left the office with no explanation to anyone, I called to find out for myself what the hell was going on."

"Is there something about ChemCo I need to know right this moment that I'm not aware of?" she quizzed.

"I don't know. Why don't *you* tell me," he answered, guardedly.

"Tell you what? You're sounding a little strange. What is this really about?"

"I don't know Ary. Maybe you can shed light on why Joseph wants to meet with me this evening to discuss the BP account. Who or what am I up against?"

"I *really* don't have any idea what you're talking about," she confessed.

"Well, the only reason I can see him asking me out to dinner these days is to let me know who'll be taking over the account. And if memory serves me correctly, you *are* the newly christened golden child."

"Were you the old one? Is that what's bothering you? Are you afraid I've replaced you?"

"I've worked long and hard to even warrant us being considered as a player in the competition for the BP account. NPI is small potatoes compared to the other companies vying for that gold mine, and Joseph has been well aware of my efforts throughout the process. And now that we have our foot in the door, it seems his plans have changed regarding who'll get credit for scoring that deal. So my question to you is, are you replacing me as lead on that account? Listen, I've already conceded defeat to the two of you once. When is it gonna stop?"

"What are you saying? I don't know anything about your dinner with Joseph tonight or what he plans to discuss with you. The only thing I do know is that Joseph called me into his office yesterday and told me he wanted to discuss the BP account. It surprised me because I knew you were assigned to it. But then we started talking about other things and he never mentioned it again. So as far as *my* involvement with the customer goes, it just doesn't exist."

"Then, if what you're telling me is really true, you should be aware of something going down."

Ary's heart pumped faster than she could think as she paced around the kitchen center island.

"What are you saying, Dwayne?"

"I think Joseph is up to something explosive, and you're part of the flame."

"That's nonsense. This time you've gone over the top."

"You still don't get it do you? Ary, these oilmen are ambitious to a fault and Joseph is no different. In fact, he may very well lead the pack when it comes to scoring the greatest business deal at any cost. His main problem is that he's too headstrong, he doesn't think everything through and that's why he's been so accommodating with me for the past couple of years. He knows how detailed I am when it comes to strategy. We've essentially fed off each other's talents for mutual gain.

But with a major victory like BP, Joseph sees more than just a pat on the back from G or a hefty raise."

"Ok…." she said, cautiously.

"I know Joseph has lofty goals, and he needs a stooge to help him reach them. The problem I have is, I'm not sure what those goals are."

"Dwayne, do you know what you're accusing him of?"

"No, I don't. But I'm gonna find out and I need your help."

"My help?"

"Will you join us for dinner tonight?"

"Tonight? I don't know. What purpose would I serve? I can barely digest what you've just told me."

"Ary listen, maybe between the two of us we can figure out what he intends to do and be able to save our jobs in the process."

"Oh, now my job is in jeopardy? This all seems too far-fetched Dwayne. And weren't you the one who just said I was the golden child? Listen, I've done everything right since I've joined NPI, exceeding my own expectations! How could *my* job be at risk?"

"Ary, I heard Joseph talking to someone on his phone about BP, telling them he had everything under control and that he had the perfect person to help carry out the plan."

"Yeah, so?"

"I'm sure that person is you."

"You're crazy."

"Oh am I? Do you know Morgan Reynolds? The wife of SKG's president, Brian Reynolds?"

"No, I don't."

"Well, she and your boy Joseph had a thing going on for years. I know for a fact she was passing him secrets from her husband's company. That's one reason how we won so many clients away from SKG. We knew their strategy before their proposals were ever written. Her uncle, Franklin Lowell, the former CEO of BP, sat on their board until recently. He had to step down because of health problems. So, Joseph feels that Morgan has outlived her usefulness."

"Why are you telling me about her?"

"Because Ary, you're the new Morgan Reynolds in Joseph's life. But instead of getting cast aside when he's done with you, you can turn it all around to your advantage if you're smart."

There must have been some truth to what he was saying, she thought. The conversation she'd had with Joseph and his interest in her relationship with Darias. But she'd rather be the one to discover these so-called plans for herself.

"Why are you suddenly so interested in helping me, Dwayne?"

"To be honest Ary, I'm not sure. Maybe I'm a fool, or maybe I'm just trying to save the company, and my job."

"This all sounds so implausible. Right now, I'm just trying to get my mother settled, she'll need me to help with…"

"You don't have to explain. I have parents that need help too. It's a huge responsibility. But I guess you probably already knew about that just like you knew about my son," he said, sarcastically. "I apologize, I shouldn't have said that."

"So what time is this dinner?"

"Seven o'clock at Marucci's, in midtown."

"I'll be there."

Ary stood in silence, lightly tapping the phone against her chin. She found herself gazing through the kitchen windows into the backyard. Without warning, she recalled the fun times she and her father spent together, sharpening her field hockey skills or swimming laps in the kidney shaped pool. Sonya and Marcus would cheer them on while sitting on the enclosed patio, surrounded by imported trees, colorful flowers and exotic plants. She forced her thoughts back to the present and looked towards the stairs that lead to her mother's bedroom. She remembered telling her mother not to worry about the phone call. Now, she had to convince herself.

She cleared her throat outside Sonya's room to get her brother's attention. Marcus sat on the edge of the bed reading over the medical release forms. He turned to find her motioning for him to join her.

"I need to go out tonight," she told him as he came near. "If it wasn't important, believe me, I wouldn't leave mama's side. So, can I count on you not to disappear or say anything else about your relationship with Caroline when she wakes up?"

"That's not fair Ary. You don't have to push the blade in any further than it already is. You know how terrible I feel about what happened—why would you say something like that?"

"Listen Marcus, you're lucky I'm even this calm. Look at her," she demanded, in a stern whisper.

He lowered his head.

"That's what you did by making your little announcement after I told you not too."

"I'm not twelve anymore Ary. I don't need you to tell me what to do. And you certainly can't blame me for everything that's happened to her. What about you and dad? Are the two of you completely innocent of all charges? Do me a favor Ary, get off my back. Stop treating me like I'm some kind of criminal," he yelled.

Sonya flinched, opening and closing her eyelids, before returning to sleep.

"I'm not finished with this conversation Marcus Alexander, but I'm not going to continue it here where she might hear us. We'll need to discuss the care she'll require immediately, and also choose a good psychologist to help her get through this. And I'm not going to be responsible for it all by myself—not this time—do you understand me?"

"Oh, I hear you loud and clear, big sister," he saluted.

Ary walked over to Sonya and kissed her soft cheek. "See you tonight mama."

Marcus' eyes followed her as she left the room. His initial thoughts were to grab her before she reached the stairs and explain everything he'd been through—from the secret he'd kept of Bruce's divulgence, to bearing the pain of not knowing whether he too, was gay. Marcus wanted to cleanse his soul and walk away from the nightmares he'd been living with for so long. His laughter had ceased more than a month ago and the despair was taking its toll. Marcus loved Caroline, but recently began struggling with the possibility of leading a deceptive life, like the one his father had suffered. He heard the front door slam shut. Everything would have to wait.

CHAPTER 69

TRAFFIC was heavy going into the city. Ary wondered if she'd make it to the restaurant by seven o'clock. Her thoughts were too preoccupied with the shocking news she'd heard from Dwayne to notice her favorite tune playing softly on the radio. As she neared the posh eatery, goose bumps formed on her arms. She felt tiny drops of sweat rolling between her breasts. Two cars ahead of her pulled into the busy driveway, met by precision paced attendants with an offer of valet services. Ary waited her turn. She could see inside the well-lit establishment and spotted Joseph and Dwayne sitting at a table for four, engrossed in conversation. She wondered if they were they discussing her role. *Was Joseph actually willing to ruin several NPI careers in order to spearhead his own? What could this mean for Dwayne and his position on the BP account? Would Joseph have to destroy the company in order to attain more power?* She hadn't noticed the man waving her car in or the time on her watch—it was seven-fifteen.

"Ma'am," he said, thumping lightly on the window. "Are you getting out?"

"Oh my God! I can't do this!" she shook her head furiously through the glass pane. "No, no, I've got to go." Ary backed up nearly hitting the car behind her and sped off without looking for the oncoming traffic whose horns blasted unmistakable annoyance. "I'm sorry," she cried through blinding tears. But the drivers were unforgiving, yelling and gesturing obscenities.

Making an illegal left turn onto Park Avenue South, she headed over to Madison Avenue, swerving to miss startled pedestrians crossing the street. *I'm not ready for this,* she thought, continuing uptown for twenty blocks. *This cannot be happening.* She parked jaggedly at the side entrance of 770 Fifth Avenue and rushed out of her idling car. The same doorman who'd graciously wished her a pleasant evening not so long ago approached her and said, "Miss, you can't leave your car parked there."

"Please. I'm here to see Darias Woolfolk, he's expecting me," she lied.

"Wait here."

Walking over to a red phone near the outside door while keeping an eye on the visibly distraught woman, he punched in three familiar numbers. Ary stood anxiously on the red carpet, praying for Darias to be home. She never even considered whether or not he was entertaining a guest.

"Your name?" he asked, lacking the customary smile.

"Ary Alexander," she answered, eyeing the perimeter of the lobby, hoping not to miss Darias should he pass through.

He turned his full attention back to the now trembling young woman.

"Please use the private elevator to the penthouse," he said, forcing a half grin.

Ary raced into the elevator, pounded the letter 'P' along with the close door symbol on the panel and supported herself against the back wall of the small paneled cage. The ride was quick, whisking her up to where Darias curiously waited in the doorway to his apartment. Her watery eyes found the way into the comfort of his embrace. His previous curiosity turned into genuine concern.

"Hey, I'm here," he said, reassuringly. "It'll be alright."

CHAPTER 70

"SO you see Dwayne, Ary has the '*in*' if you will, to BP. Her relationship with Darias is worth more to NPI than all the work you and I have done together my friend," he beamed.

Dwayne looked desperately towards the entrance, hoping to wave her over once she walked through the door. He covertly glanced at his watch as Joseph discussed his brilliant plans to make all of them richer than they'd ever imagined. Finally, at eight thirty, Dwayne succumbed to the realization that she'd betrayed him once more.

"Joseph, what can I do to change your mind? I hear what you're saying and I agree with you that Ary might be able to help set the stage for retrieving information from Darias, but only up to a certain point. I mean, he's not stupid and you know better than I do that illicit business relationships collapse at the most crucial times and we can't afford for that to happen—not with this account. G wouldn't stand for it."

"G won't know about it, Dwayne," he interrupted. "Listen to me, this is one time we won't ask for G's opinion. Need I remind you of how many accounts we've taken from that asshole, Brian Reynolds at SKG because he doesn't have what it takes to hold onto his bride? G didn't know about those, and neither did he care." A wicked smile complimented the brazen look on his face. "You know G only cares about winning, and we've done that—over and over again—and every time, so far, it's been *'perceived'* as legal. I keep telling you Dwayne, I'm not throwing you off the strategy team, I'm just switching the bait and G will be none the wiser. And after we've won, I'll be the bird that sings *Dwayne Hargis for VP* in G's golden ear. Do I make myself clear?"

Dwayne tried to conceal his disbelief.

"Very. But why would you do that for me if ultimately, Ary is going to be the one to clinch the deal?"

"Hey, you've covered my ass more than a few times," he laughed. "And I never forget a friend, Dwayne. Listen to me, everyone knows your contributions to the firm have been invaluable. And believe me, your real payday is coming."

Dwayne was speechless.

"Now that we have a *'true understanding'* of how this will go down with BP, I'm afraid I'll have to run. I have someone more *attractive* than you waiting for me at home," he smirked. "Take care of the bill won't you."

Dwayne could only nod, yes. When Joseph was out of sight, Dwayne took one last look at his watch, pounded his fist on the table, then summoned the waiter for the check.

CHAPTER 71

IT was after midnight. Marcus concluded that his sister wouldn't be returning to the house. He stood next to Sonya's bed contemplating whether he should wake her to confess, but just as quickly abandoned the thought. He wasn't certain that his mother was ready to hear what he'd have to say.

Inside her bedroom, spread across the dresser were playful childhood photos of himself and Ary. An exquisite work of Sonya's own sculpture sat on a 4-foot pedestal near a striking self-portrait, leaning slightly against a weathered, antique artist's easel. On a far corner wall, separated from the other photos and artwork, hung a small photo of the family vacationing on Martha's Vineyard. Marcus wasn't convinced that she'd let go of the past, and her present condition was proof of how difficult it still was.

He leaned over his mother's head and whispered, "Mama," I'm not sure if the timing is right, and to be honest, I'm not really sure I'll have all the answers to all the questions you might have one day—questions about why I did what I did. I'm not even sure you'll ever remember what took place that night. I'm still searching for answers mama, looking inside my heart and my soul. I need to find out who *I* really am, once and for all. And this time, I won't be hiding—I'll just be stepping back to gain a better view. I hope you'll understand and accept *my* truth, mama. He kissed her exposed hand which lay on top of the soft cotton blanket, and took a step back away from the bed.

Marcus felt the energy siphoning from his body as he walked down the stairs into the family room where he picked up his leather jacket from the sofa, tossing it across his shoulder before making his way out the front door. Once outside, he looked up to his mother's faintly lit bedroom window and deeply inhaled. Climbing into his car and settling his body against the smooth, black Bavarian leather, he exhaled. As the engine roared to life, a soulful melody from a preselected jazz station helped put his mind at ease as he backed out the driveway.

"I love you more than life mama, and I'll be in touch soon, I promise." With that he sped away as fast and far as his sports car could take him.

Chapter 72

THAT night, Darias held her in his oversized Peruvian armchair before taking the sleeping beauty to rest in his bed.

The following morning, after hearing her mutter a few indecipherable words, he asked, "Are you awake? Do you want to talk about what happened?"

Turning to face him, confused, sleepy and staring in his eyes, she asked, "What time did I get here? How long have I been asleep?"

"Last night around eight. And you fell asleep shortly afterwards, never getting the chance to explain what brought you here or why you were so upset."

Suddenly recalling the troubling phone call with her boss, she screamed, "Oh my God, Darias, I think Dwayne is being set up to lose his job! I might even lose mine!"

"What are you talking about?"

"Darias, there's a plan involving Joseph, me and BP," she paused, studying his expression of raised eyebrows.

Recounting the conversation she'd had with Dwayne the previous night, she questioned him about the consequences of passing information to a bidding firm. Could the New York State Oil and Gas Regulatory Agency or even the Securities and Exchange Commission reprimand her if she were to be accused? Would it mean the end of her career in the oil business?

Darias was stunned at her disclosure, knowing he'd have to act quickly because of the looming proposal application deadline.

"Ary, if all this is true, you have to behave as though everything is normal. You can't alert Joseph or Dwayne in any way, or let them know you've spoken to me. I've suspected Larsen of more than a few dishonest deals for some time now, but I could never pin him to any one in particular."

"What do you mean?"

"Listen, it's a well-known fact that Joseph is a brilliant business man, but unfortunately, he's let greed and power get in the way of honesty and reason. I knew when I met him years ago that his aspirations soared higher than that of Vice President of someone else's firm. Joseph sees himself as President and CEO of NPI or possibly, Larsen Oil, Inc."

"Are you saying he wants to take over NPI?"

"Perhaps, but I doubt it. For Joseph, winning BP wouldn't be just an enormous feather in his cap to a start-up firm, it would be like getting the whole bird all at once."

"So he'd use me thinking I'd get crucial information from you so that he knows how to structure the winning bid!"

"That's right."

"Why, that…"

"Careful young lady, remember, you don't know any of this and really, neither do I. That's something we'll have to find out."

"What about Dwayne? Shouldn't he play a role in exposing Joseph? He is after all the one who told me all this."

"Oh, he'll get his chance," Darias said, slightly grinning.

"There's something I don't understand though. Why

would Joseph deceive G? I thought the two of them were like brothers."

"Honey, it's all a part of the game, just like you are."

"Me?"

"Yes, you. Think of yourself as 'victory dice,' something powerful, rich men can either brag about having, or use it to gain even more."

Hearing those words from Darias made her feel even more exploited. How could she have let this happen. She was the one who was supposed to use men for what she needed, when she needed it, not the other way around. She was ready for revenge.

"Darias, tell me what I need to do."

CHAPTER 73

S HE wanted nothing more than to feel the warm trickle of water beading down her back from the shower, especially in light of all she'd been through the night before.

Stepping out from the shower, she was still exhausted, but managed to choose an outfit of skinny jeans, a cashmere sweater and her favorite ballerina flats for the 90-minute trip out to Long Island to visit her mother.

Checking her wallet for cash, she grabbed her keys from the foyer table, locked the door to the apartment and walked slowly down and around the corridor to the elevator, which would take her to the private parking garage.

Once inside her car, she turned on the heat to take the chill out of the air and away from her body. The streets were strangely abandoned for a Saturday morning, but she was grateful for the solitude of the roadway. She inserted a '*Six Weeks to Arabic Business Language*' CD, the one she'd bought after accepting the position at NPI, hoping for the opportunity to travel to the Middle East. But instead of repeating, *wein al matar* –'where is the airport?' her thoughts, without warning, turned to her father. Why she still cared so deeply was not logical, yet she could never find it in her heart to hate him. Ironically, she felt she was the person she'd become because of him, and was uncertain whether her life would have been any different had he stayed.

But one thing she knew for sure, Sonya and Marcus would have been much better off had he remained. They needed his strength, his protection, and his guidance. She needed his love and approval—approval of the right man, the right job, the right decisions. Bruce would have certainly found a husband candidate for his precious daughter by now—someone strong, ambitious, intelligent and wealthy—someone who would have helped to secure his little girl's personal and financial future. Someone, she thought, like Dwayne Hargis.

Childhood memories kept her company throughout the entire drive to Brookstone. Turning into the driveway, she noticed Marcus' car missing. She checked herself in the rear-view mirror and fingered through her hair before getting out.

Immediately after entering the house, her attention was drawn upstairs. She listened to the movement coming from Sonya's bedroom.

"Mama, it's me. Are you okay?"

Sonya walked out her bathroom dressed in a pink, satin nightgown and robe ensemble. She checked herself in the vanity mirror and leaned over the banister to greet her daughter.

"Good morning, Ary. I'm a little weak, but otherwise, I feel fine. I wanted to get washed up and grab a cup of tea."

"You look beautiful, mama," she said as she reached the top, "but should you even be up and about on your own?"

"Honey, I feel much better this morning," she answered, walking over to a cozy settee.

"I don't think you should try and do so much so soon," she said, crossing over to her mother's bed. "Where's Marcus?"

"I don't know, I only remember seeing him right before I fell asleep. And when I woke up around one or one-thirty this morning, he was gone."

Ary exploded. "Again! He left you alone? Why, that pathetic…"

"Ary, stop it! We don't know where he's gone or why. And besides, I don't recall seeing your innocent face when I woke up either. Where were *you* last night? Couldn't you stay away from your men for one evening?"

"What are you saying? You have no idea where I was last night or who I was with?"

"You're right, I don't. But what I do know is that when I woke up, neither you nor your brother were anywhere to be found."

Ary was shocked at her mother's animosity.

"I expected more from you Ariel. I didn't think *you'd* let your unbridled relationships dictate the loyalty you'd once held for your family.

"Now my devotion to this family is being questioned?" She got up from her mother's bed and walked toward the door.

"Mama, maybe it's about time you realized who was responsible for your lapse into mental trauma."

"Don't bother. It all came rushing painfully back to me this morning. I remember Marcus talking about wanting to marry a girl who's related to his father's partner," she admitted, carefully rising from her seat. "I guess none of you can imagine the mental and physical anguish I've suffered for so long. Him with his white fiancée, you with your white lovers, all of whom could only mean trouble and heartbreak."

"Mama please. I don't need a lecture from you or anybody else about men and relationships. I know what I'm doing, even if you think I don't. I'm feeding them what they usually dish out. And to be quite honest mama, maybe you should have been just a little bit stronger with daddy and Marcus. Maybe at least one of them would still be around!" she yelled.

"How dare you talk to me that way. How dare you accuse me as the reason your father left or that your brother is engaged to marry that woman. I never asked you to try and complete the missing pieces to our family puzzle, Ary, you took on that role from the time you were a young child. That's what your father loved about you—strong, loving, caring. You were the father and husband he wanted to be—but in reality—he was suffocating in his own role. But it's not my fault he chose me to help him live a staged lie. What is it that you're looking for Ary, really? Are you looking for true love or are you trying to find the man you feel abandoned you? What is it that's been absent from your life? Ask yourself that question, Ariel Marie Alexander."

"Do you even hear yourself, mama. Why don't you ask *yourself* that question? What are you looking for? Are you waiting for him to come running back into your arms? Or is it that you feel there'll never be anyone else? As far as me, mama, I've excelled in every facet of my life so far—in education and business. I became the husband when daddy left you with two teenage kids to raise and the sister who tried to be a father to a brother who had more problems than either one of us has ever had the guts to discuss. I did it because I thought when he first left us, you'd fall apart—that you couldn't handle it. I couldn't stand by and let our family suffer the shame and stigmatism society places on you for having an *imperfect* family, especially us, black and upper middle class! I know you always told us what other people thought didn't matter, but mama, it sure seemed to matter to you." She took one long breath and continued.

"When daddy left, you told people that he left because the

two of you had grown apart. Mama that's what other people do. They fabricate bullshit stories like that so that they won't lose their social standing. We're proud black women, women of color. We cuss out our children, husbands and lovers when they hurt us. Hell, we might even slap them once in a while. We'd tell anyone who'd listen, 'my man left 'cause he preferred to take it in the ass.'"

"Stop it Ary!" she demanded. "How dare you disrespect me! Who are you? I don't even recognize you anymore!"

"I'm the little girl who once had a storybook life with parents who loved her and raised her to be responsible for her actions and decisions. But then her parents turned out to be liars. Yes, you mama. You knew daddy was having an affair and you were miserable, but you chose to live the life of the helpless suburban housewife who turns the other cheek to save face. Marcus and I knew that after we went to bed, daddy went into the guest room to sleep. Why didn't you confront him? Was it because you didn't want to lose the big house? Or was it because you wanted Marcus and I to remain in our little social club? The snobs in that organization treated us like fourth-class citizens because we no longer fit the profile of the perfect, black family—a woman without a husband, children without a father, a son who needed weekly therapy and no more fancy vacations to brag about at dinner parties. I'm sure there was more than one meeting on how to tactfully kick the Alexander's out of all those organizations."

"That's enough, I said!" She walked around her daughter and headed downstairs. Ary followed.

"I adored my father, or who I thought was my father. When he left, I didn't know what to think or how to feel, so I thought and felt nothing—for five fucking years! I pretended to be happy, strong and supportive, when in reality, I needed someone to hug me and tell me that one day, everything would be right again. I only wished that *you* had been that person, mama."

"I tried to be there for you Ary, for you and Marcus. I tried to believe that it wasn't me that drove him from our bed and our home. But it's much easier for some than others. No matter what I did, I couldn't help but think of him. I still loved him for a long time afterwards, and I wanted more than anything for him to return and tell me he'd made a terrible mistake. I would have forgiven him for that. I would have gone to counseling. I would have done anything at that point to keep our family together, anything. But he never said it. He never did."

Sonya broke down and cried. She had never talked so candidly about her feelings for Bruce since he'd left, especially not to her daughter. She sat on the sofa with both hands covering her face and eyes, tears streaming down to the floor. She cried not only for herself but for her daughter, who, she felt, was paving a dangerous road of self-destruction and she felt helpless in stopping it. She cried because she'd never let any other man in her life since Bruce left, and she was shattered and lonely.

Once an example for her children, she felt frail and powerless. She blamed him long ago for turning her world and her life upside down, and she faulted herself for allowing it.

Ary sat in a chair across from her mother, offering no immediate consolation. Then she spoke, slow and soft.

"When daddy came back, I didn't know him. All he did was try and justify his relationship with Matthew."

"Don't mention that name to me anymore!" Sonya shouted.

"Mama, for God's sake, after all these years, just accept it.

He's accepted it and risked a hell of a lot in doing so. Coming out was more important to him than saving his marriage and keeping his family together. And if being at peace with yourself is worth giving up some of what you have, then mama, maybe we should try it too."

Ary got up and walked to the front door. She put her hand on the brass door handle and paused, turning back towards her mother. She watched the matriarch cry before carefully pulling her up to her feet. She held her in her arms and whispered, "I've always been there for you mama, and I'll never leave you when you need me the most. But I have a life too, a life you may not think is perfect, but none-the-less, it's the life I have to live. I've done things that I may not be proud of and I've hurt people who wanted nothing more than to love me. Maybe it was because I didn't think I deserved to be loved, or that if I gave in to someone else's feelings for me, they would sooner or later leave too. I don't know—I don't have all the answers mama. I just want to try and move on. I want to have children one day and be married to a man who adores me. And I'll pray that he won't abandon me for another woman, or man. But if he does, I hope that I've learned enough about life that you take the good with the bad and come out surviving."

She pressed her cheek against her mother's head and walked out the door. As she reached her car, Ary turned toward the house and whispered, "God keep her until I return."

CHAPTER 74

DWAYNE punched his new pillows—careful not to rip them—remembering it was because of his fight with Ary that he had to replace them. He questioned why she hadn't shown up at the restaurant, or fully believed his story. Was it actually possible that she could be in on it too? He needed to talk to someone he could trust. The question was, who was that person?

He thought of calling an ex-girlfriend at BP but quickly discarded the idea after remembering the nasty breakup. He considered calling G to gauge whether or not he suspected Joseph of any wrongdoing. But quickly tossed aside that idea, not wanting G's antennae to go up before he had a chance to corroborate the story and possibly save his job.

Dwayne spread his arms over the cold surface of the granite counter top, contemplating his options. He felt his only hope was in convincing Ary that Joseph was out to destroy her, then let her decide which was more important—a relationship with an immoral VP or her prized career in the oil industry.

CHAPTER 75

MARCUS found a tight space several blocks away and decided to take it. It was Saturday morning and most people preferred to sleep in, leaving parking at a premium. He walked along the pavement, conscious of the City's morning stillness. As he entered the building, a doorman greeted him and asked for the name of the person he was visiting.

"Caroline Grant," he answered, somberly.

He could hear Caroline's faint voice over the intercom. His pulsing heart served as a reminder of how difficult this conversation would be.

"Apartment 12-P, sir," the doorman directed.

"I already...thank you," he said, without further explanation. Approaching the twelfth floor, Marcus reconsidered, wondering if it was too late to change his mind. The elevator stopped, and framed by the opening doors she stood,, waiting, her eyes filled with tears.

"Baby, I've made some terrible mistakes," Marcus said, taking her in his arms.

"Please give me a chance to explain everything to you." Caroline looked up into his troubled eyes and knew, no matter what he had to say, she'd already forgiven him.

CHAPTER 76

MARCUS lay his head on Caroline's lap as they sat on the living room sofa. He spoke softly as she listened with the patience he'd come to love. He recounted his happy childhood up to the moment of initially suspecting his father's homosexuality and told her the truth about his mother's recent medical situation and the guilt he carried around because of it. She stroked his soft hair, he held onto her bare legs. The tears welled in his eyes as he continued to unburden while hers streamed down her chiseled cheekbones.

As Marcus drew quiet, Caroline bent over his ear and asked in a hushed tone, "Marcus, are you unsure about us getting married because of who I'm related to or because you're not sure of who you are? Because I can help sort through the difficulty of the first uncertainty, but unfortunately, the second part has to be worked out by you. And as hard as it would be for me to pull back, I love you too much not too."

He looked into her marble blue eyes and confessed, "Caroline, I have undeniably strong feelings for you and there is no one else I'd rather spend the rest of my life with. But I don't want to make the same mistake my father made and ruin the lives of his family because he wasn't sure. I love you and I don't want to hurt you, but neither do I want to alienate my family, we've been through too much together. So I'll ask you to wait for me, but I'll understand if you can't."

Caroline rubbed his back in a circular motion and stared at her family portrait, the one she'd recently had reframed.

CHAPTER 77

ARY hoped she was doing the right thing. She'd realized she couldn't just stand by and let everything fall apart. She stood squarely behind a casually dressed man waiting for the door buzzer. She blew out her cheeks and waited. He turned and looked over his shoulder.

"Thanks for holding the door. I really didn't feel like searching for my keys," she said, arresting any further suspicions he may have had.

She met him again at the elevator, but deemed she wanted no further conversation once it arrived. "Oh, I should really check my mail. I'll catch the next one."

"You sure? I don't mind holding it."

"Please, go on and thank you." She'd needed a moment alone to think things through before going upstairs. She paced the lobby, then turned hastily to make her way back to the approaching elevator. As the doors opened, a man spilled out in an obvious hurry.

"Dwayne!"

"Ary! What are you doing here?"

"I had to come and talk to you. I had to find out if there was any truth in what you'd said."

"Ary, I waited for you in the restaurant. We could have put a stop to this. But you insist on playing these idiotic games. I've warned you. Now I know I can't rely on you for shit, so I give up," he bluffed.

"My coming here isn't proof enough that I *want* to believe you, that I need your help as well as you needing mine?"

"Listen, I'm tired of counting on you for anything, except of course, winning NPI business."

"What else are you supposed to count on me for Dwayne?" she yelled, causing residents to turn and glance at the feuding couple.

"I care about you Ary," he said, through gritted teeth. "I care about what happens to you, but you're either too stubborn, too blind or too stupid to realize it. You want to continue living in your little dream world, believing that Joseph would willingly share the brass ring. Well, I'm here to tell you that Joseph does nothing without a reason." Scratching his head, he continued. "Even G can't see through him. I'm sure Marguerite has tried to inform him on more than one occasion, but all G sees is the almighty dollar and the brother he never had. But in this industry, green and red don't mix. Somebody always comes up short."

He turned to walk away.

"Dwayne, I can't help the way you feel about me, but I can help save our jobs," she called, stopping him in his tracks. "Can we please go upstairs and talk?"

Dwayne thought about the last time the two of them were in his apartment and hesitated before replying. With his back to her, he closed his eyes and imagined the rhythm of her soft, naked body dancing against his muscular frame. Slowly turning around, he searched her face, desperately wanting to believe her. "I was on my way to the office, but I think this is more important."

As they neared the opening doors of the elevator, Ary reached for his arm and said, "Dwayne, you're okay with this right? I mean, the last time I was here, the day didn't exactly end on a memorable note."

"C'mon," he said pulling her through the closing doors. "This time, I can promise you it'll be different."

Dwayne's house was a mess—a far cry from the immaculate dwelling she'd seen as his guest more than a month before. Clothes were flung across the floor and sofa, an empty pizza box sat in the middle of the coffee table and a half empty bottle of Chivas Regal lay on the floor beside his recliner.

"Yeah, you weren't kidding when you said it would be different," she joked.

"Hey, my cleaning service doesn't come on weekends."

"Maybe you should consider it!" she laughed.

He chuckled—something he hadn't done in more days than he cared to remember.

"Dwayne," she said, moving closer to him. "I have a friend that I trust, his name is Darias Woolfolk, a Sr. Vice President at BP and he's willing to help. I just need to know that you won't back away from this once I get involved. I have too much to lose if what you've accused Joseph of is untrue."

"Are you kidding me, Ary? I think you have your wires crossed here. I called *you* about this, remember? I tracked *you* down, not the other way around! And for the record, I know Darias, not personally, but I know about his professional background."

"Alright, simmer down tiger. I'm not trying to discredit you or what you know. Conspiracy is not something I encounter on a daily basis."

"Yeah, me neither," he agreed, drawing in a deep breath. "I'm gonna make a pot of coffee first. Can I get you anything?"

"Coffee sounds good, right now, thanks."

As Dwayne walked into the kitchen, Ary looked in the direction of the bedroom, briefly reminiscing their night of passion. She pictured his strong, raven-hued body entwined with hers, gently kissing and touching her erogenous zones. The combination of dim lights, soft music, his scent, desire, and vulnerability, came rushing back, all too easily.

They sat at the kitchen table for hours, sipping decaffeinated coffee and discussing a carefully agreed upon strategy of once Joseph's plan had been firmly established, and shared with her, he would be the one to expose him and stand prepared to weather any repercussions from G, or other managers at the firm. Dwayne convinced her that she'd have more to lose than he would. "I can always find another job in the industry, especially with the reputation I've built for myself."

"I'm drained and in no mood to argue with that," she said, yawning. "But before I go, I simply have to at least try and clean up, just a little bit. You never know when you might run into other uninvited guests in the lobby," she teased. Rolling up the sleeves of her sweater, she set to work, picking up empty cartons, wiping down the coffee table and folding clothes. Watching her movements, Dwayne's unrestrained thoughts barely contained the puckish grin on his usually serious face.

"What can I do?" he asked.

"Relax and prepare for the challenges we'll have to face."

"Ok, I think I can manage that," he said, retreating to his desk in the bedroom.

After one and a half hours, she'd finished her self-assigned tasks.

"Hey, I'm all done," she called from the living room. "Is there anything else I can help you with before I leave?"

His heart hammered against his chest at the mere possibilities of answers to her question.

"No," he answered, as he strolled into the room. "I appreciate everything you've done for me today, I really do. So, I'll see you on Monday."

"No problem. Actually, cleaning helped take my mind off things."

"I'll walk you to the elevator."

"I can see myself out. I don't want to break your concentration." But it was already too late for that. His concentration was broken the minute she stepped into his life. "Keep doing what you're doing. I…"

Before she could finish her sentence, Dwayne's lips were firmly planted against her mouth. She pushed back, studying, once again, the bold features of his rugged face, gazing into the depths of his dark, brown eyes. He panicked, fearing rejection. She rushed over to the front door, then turned back, cautiously, looking at him. He tried to interpret the puzzled expression on her face that said nothing, but spoke volumes.

"Ary, don't go, not yet. I need you."

Walking slowly towards him, she whispered, "I think I need you more."

CHAPTER 78

"**M**ICHELLE, call Ary and tell her to clear her calendar from Tuesday through Friday. I'll need her to accompany me on the trip to the West Coast."

"Yes, Mr. Larsen."

Ary arrived early on this chilly Monday morning, stopping first in the ladies room to straighten out her hair. As she checked her makeup in the mirror, thoughts of all the tasks facing her already packed work week, flooded her mind, but were suddenly halted as the bathroom door swung open.

"Good morning Ms. Alexander."

"Morning, Michelle. How are you?"

"Fine, thank you. I left a message for you on your voice-mail and in your email."

"Ok…" Ary answered suspiciously, waiting for further explanation.

"Mr. Larsen would like for you to clear your calendar and go with him to L.A. on Tuesday."

"Of what week?"

"This week, tomorrow through Friday. If you have any questions, you should speak with him." She disappeared into an open stall.

"Alright, thanks." Ary scrolled through her BlackBerry. There was a crucial meeting with Standard Oil tomorrow and a presentation for Dwayne the following afternoon. She didn't want to put either of them off, but felt she had no choice.

A nauseous feeling came over her as she walked down the corridor to Joseph's office, but she knew she'd have to appear composed.

"Hello Joseph, you wanted to see me?"

"Come in, Ary. Listen, I'll need you to go with me to L.A. tomorrow for a meeting with our west coast partners and join me in a negotiations and strategy seminar on Wednesday. I attend it every year, and always learn something new and useful."

"Tomorrow? Well, I…"

"Drop whatever it is you have scheduled for those days. This takes precedence. Michelle will give you the details. Plan to stay until Friday. By the way, how was your weekend? I tried calling your house and BlackBerry on Saturday but… struck out."

"Hectic—with my mother coming home and all."

"I understand. So, I'm looking forward to our trip out west."

"So am I."

"Oh, by the way, your only excuse for not going would be that G needs you, no one else. Understood?"

Ary stared at him before answering. "I don't think anything will get in the way."

"Great. I'll see you on the plane tomorrow morning."

She trembled on the way back to her cubicle, leaning on her desk for support. She needed to talk to Dwayne, but didn't want to risk Joseph seeing the two of them together.

She now firmly believed Joseph was going forward with his plans. She picked up her briefcase and headed for the door.

There was little time to sort out all the details that were now
swimming through her mind.

CHAPTER 79

ARY and Joseph arrived at LAX and walked immediately down to baggage claim. There had been few words passed between them during the flight. Ary pretended to sleep for the first hour while Joseph typed feverishly on his laptop. One hour prior to landing, he nudged her, suggesting a glass of wine. She declined. He drank alone.

"You weren't very talkative on the plane. Is something wrong?"

"No," she answered sharply, never taking her eyes off the baggage conveyor belt. "I guess I'm still recovering from my weekend at my mother's."

Pointing to a passing bag, she said, "that's mine, the Burberry." Joseph bent down to retrieve it, blindly handing it to her after spotting his own leather Gucci. He checked it for bruises.

"They treat your bags like garbage," he complained. She was indifferent, dreading what lay ahead and the time she'd have to spend with him.

"What hotel are we staying at?" she asked, walking awkwardly alongside him.

"The 'W'," he answered, brusquely.

Stopping dead in her tracks and tightly grabbing his arm, she gasped.

"What is it?" he asked, his brow furled.

"I'm not sure." A look of shock was written over her face. She continued. "I thought I saw someone I knew."

Who she saw were Bruce and Matthew at curbside, climbing into a waiting Lincoln Town Car. They were in L.A. for the National Bar Association's convention. Bruce placed his hand on Matthew's lower back as he entered the limo near where Joseph and Ary stood.

"Who was it?"

"I made a mistake. It wasn't the person I thought I knew."

"There's our guy." Joseph took her hand and lead her to the waiting Mercedes.

"Hey, you haven't been yourself since we left New York," he observed as they settled in for the ride.

"I'm fine," she answered, without facing him.

"You're sure now? Because I have news that calls for your full attention and concerted cooperation."

"What do you mean?"

"We have a stop to make before going to the hotel. There's someone I want you to meet, someone very special to me. We've been friends for a long time and share a passion for wealth, women and finance."

A sudden chill washed over her body that not even the warmth of the California sun could penetrate.

"His name is Lawrence Finney, my West Coast business partner. We launched a small firm almost two years ago. The company is similar to NPI in that our commodity is oil, but we've taken it a step further and ventured into drilling and exploration."

Ary was stunned to hear the actual words spilling so easily from his lips.

"Our little enterprise might only be considered a nuisance

in the eyes of the so-called giants in the industry today, but very soon Ary, we'll be a force to be reckoned with. The major players in the States will be begging to partner with us and invest in our dream, realizing the unbelievable amounts of money to be made. Lawrence and I will turn this industry on its head and at the same time have the Saudis waiting in line to negotiate with us. Right now, I have people set up in the Middle East, just waiting for our cue. The time has finally come, Ary. The time is right!"

Every logical question entered her mind: *conflict of interest with NPI, stealing company secrets for the purpose of aiding and abetting the competition, and abusing industry standards,* just for starters. She said nothing, summoning every particle of strength in her body to restrain the rage welling inside. Having quickly determined that the smartest way to protect herself and her job was to pretend to go along with his plans, she began mentally constructing her defense while he appeared calm and decisive, divulging even more details. After a while, she interrupted. "Joseph, I have to admit, I'm shocked. I'd actually envisioned you as the next President of NPI, not the one trying to run G out of it."

"Listen sweetheart, loyalty gets boring after six or seven years, and as G always said, the only thing that matters is how much it adds to the company's bottom line."

"What happened to *'as long as it's perceived as legal?'*"

"That only works for people with limited vision, and the key word there was *'perceived.'* I want you to work with me Ary, reap the benefits of infinite wealth. You might argue that you've enjoyed relative fame and some fortune at NPI, but honey, it'll pale in comparison to what you stand to earn with my company."

"What are you saying Joseph, you want me to quit NPI and work with you and your partner? And when would all this happen? I'm guessing before we go back to work for a firm we're out to destroy?"

"Well, time is definitely *not* on our side. What I'd need you to do immediately is to find out exactly what's required for a BP win. My firm *has* to come out on top, outdo the competition on this one. We need the funding from BP to begin off shore drilling. That revenue stream is the down payment I'll need for crews and construction. But there can't be any screw-ups, we *have* to win that account!"

"Is that where I come in, because of my friendship with Darias?"

"Ary, I've known Darias for a long time. We began as cordial competitors, but as time went on and contracts won, that affability deteriorated down to nothing less than a sincere loathing for one another. So, to answer your question, yes, that's where you come in. I need you to gain classified information from him so that we can submit the winning bid. And there would be nothing Darias or anyone else at BP could do about it once they found out it was my little company that won."

Her mind raced at warp speed. *'Keep your cool'* she thought, *'just stay calm, this is more serious than anything I could have imagined.'* She smiled cunningly and said, "I'll set up a meeting with Darias as soon as we return."

CHAPTER 80

"**YES.** I mean no. I mean I knew she was going, but I didn't realize it was this week. I must have gotten my dates mixed up. I'm sorry, G. I'll call the client today."

The truth was, he'd lied to keep from looking foolish. Ary left him an email Tuesday morning before she left with Joseph and explained that she would be attending a class and would call after settling in at the hotel. She never did.

"They may be small Dwayne," G said, standing in Dwayne's office doorway, but they're just as important as the big accounts."

"I know, sir. I'm right on it. I know Ary pushed the meeting back a day because of her class with Joseph," he lied again.

"A class, with Joseph? I wasn't aware. Anyway, take care of it Dwayne and I want to hear back from you within the hour," G admonished.

"Yes, G, of course."

He blew out a deep breath and glanced at his watch as G turned to leave.

Dwayne rushed around to Joseph's office and asked Michelle where Joseph and Ary were staying in California. Upon strict instructions from her boss on who should be given information, she questioned his need to know. His agitation grew apparent in his tone.

"What do you mean, '*why do I need to know*?' I asked you a question about my boss and my subordinate?"

"Mr. Hargis, I'd be more than happy to send Mr. Larsen an email for you," she answered, looking up at him, smiling, making him even more irate.

"I don't need you to *send anything* to Mr. Larsen, I can do that blindfolded," he said, straddling both hands over her desk. "Which class are they attending? he asked, with obvious frustration. "Can you at least tell me that?"

"No sir, I can't, because I don't know. Is there anything else I can help you with?"

Dwayne was infuriated. What was really going on? Michelle had covered for him so many times in the past, only this time, it involved someone he was in love with. This was not the plan they'd discussed over the weekend. He knew he had to regroup before phoning the client and calm down before continuing his conversation with Michelle. He didn't want to arouse any further suspicion. Wiping his brow, he stepped back from Michelle's desk and apologized. "I'm sorry for screaming at you. We're all under a lot of pressure this time of the year. I'll just have to wait until they return."

"Yes sir."

As he left the area, Michelle kept a watchful eye on him. She felt anxious. For seven years, she'd hidden her true feelings for Joseph, secretly hoping he'd fall in love with her. But she'd meant nothing more to him than what she was paid to do. She pulled out a file from her desk drawer, flipped through the pages and began typing.

CHAPTER 81

"SO, nothing happened?" Dwayne questioned Ary after she returned and met him at his house on Saturday afternoon. "What was the point of him suddenly whisking you off to the Coast if he didn't plan to clue you in on whatever it is he intends to do?"

"He told me very little," she lied. "Nothing that would make anyone suspicious." She wasn't sure if this was the right time to divulge the information she'd learned just a few days before or if she should be the one to expose Joseph. Should she wait for his next move or talk to G or Darias first. Right now, her mind was a ball of mass confusion and she still had to face her mother and brother.

CHAPTER 82

AFTER Ary left his apartment, Dwayne stared at the walls for an hour. *Should I have told her how I feel? What would she say?* he wondered. "I can pretty much answer any question G or Joseph could ever throw at me, but this one, I don't have a clue."

He waved a hand across his hair and determined it was time for a cut. He'd take a trip up to Harlem to see if his barber could fit him in today. After going into the bathroom and lathering up to shave, his nagging thoughts prevented him from concentrating and he nicked his chin.

"Ouch, damn. How could I have let this happen? I was doing just fine before she came on the scene. Now look at me—an absolute wreck who can't even shave without something going wrong. I can't get her out of my mind and I'm afraid something or someone will take her away from me. But this time I'm not gonna let Joseph Larsen intercept this play."

CHAPTER 83

"HELLO, mama," Ary said, with slight hesitations. "Did the nurse show up? I called the agency and requested they send someone out to look after you."

"Yes, Ary she did, and I called the agency and told them not to send anyone else after Friday. I can manage on my own," she stated firmly.

"Mama, why did you do that? You know you're going to need help and I just can't be there the entire time. You know how demanding my job is, and the commute from Long Island just wouldn't be feasible with the hours I keep."

"Ary, I don't need or want strangers in my house. Everyday I'm feeling stronger and God willing, I'll be able to get through this. And please tell your brother for me, that I hold no grudges against him. He doesn't have to run and hide every time he thinks I might remember what happened that night. He deserves to be happy with whomever he chooses. It's not for me to say who he should or shouldn't marry. It is not my life to lead."

"You're quite a woman mama, and I love you for it. I don't think you gave yourself enough credit when it came to raising me. You always said that even though daddy was gone most of the time, when he was home, he spent most of his time nurturing me, ingraining his values on the one person who was more likely to embrace them. But mama, you always had a quiet strength, and your preference was to remain in the background while we all shined as bright as we could. But if anyone had ever taken the time to look deep inside, they would have seen that your star shone brightest, off in the distance, day and night, protecting your family and watching us flourish."

Ary reflected on her own professional dilemma and hoped she'd find answers in her mother's unspoken wisdom.

"I've struggled lately mama, looking inside myself, trying to uncover that elusive strength. I'm sure you must have passed *some* of it down to me," she chuckled.

"But what I found was, it's not as simple as just wanting it to be there—it's more like something inside of you that grows throughout your lifetime."

Sonya smiled, knowing that although her daughter had a long road to travel through life, maybe she would avoid some of the extremely painful bumps and bruises she'd encountered along the way.

"So, Ariel, will I see you before the sun sets?"

"I'd love to end my evening with you. How 'bout we eat at your favorite seafood restaurant on the pier, the one where the dolphins can be seen off in the distance."

"I'd like that, very much."

"I'll be there in a couple of hours."

"I'll be waiting."

"I love you, mama."

"I love you too, baby."

CHAPTER 84

THE workweek was filled with meetings, proposals and presentations put off from the prior week. Dwayne and Ary had visited Standard Oil together. He'd complimented her on her ability to smooth over some of the rough edges the client might have been feeling for having been rescheduled. They were confident that NPI's proposal would beat out the competition and assured that a decision would be made by next Friday. The couple talked about business in the taxi on the way back to the office. He was reluctant to inquire about Joseph's plans again, especially after she'd said she knew very little, but decided, against his better judgment to press on for any morsel of information that might be vital to his allegations.

"Ary listen. I know you said Joseph didn't say much while you were in L.A. but I'm still puzzled. I know what I heard him say on the phone about you being the perfect one to help carry out his operation. Then one day, without warning, you're off to the West coast, and nothing happens! Well, maybe it would be easier to remember if I painted you a picture," he continued. You see, SKG is out of the game because its president had an affair with BP's present CEO's wife, some years ago. And now that some of the members of the old cartel have retired, any contract favors that haven't been paid back yet, won't be. So SKG knows they can kiss what would have been a gift horse, goodbye. And as I told you before, Joseph knows Morgan

Reynolds relationship with her uncle can't help him anymore, so you're the bait!"

Ary turned a heated red, but held her words until he finished.

"You're the clear shot to BP. The fact that he wants me off as lead of the strategy team causes me to believe that he doesn't want NPI taking home the trophy. He knows how entrenched I am with the key players over there and he damn sure knows I can win it for NPI. But Joseph is also smart enough to know that as senior marketing analyst, I'm obligated to update not only him on a daily basis with a contract like this one at stake, but also G and Marguerite, whereas you're only obligated to update him and me—and he would instruct you not to communicate with me so that he could give them useless information and a false sense of security," he finished, taking a much-needed breath. "So in the end, Joseph would use your relationship with Darias to obtain the critical information needed to undercut NPI's initial and final bids. But the only thing I haven't worked out is how he'll explain to G that he wants me to be in the background after he'd fought so hard to get me on it at their meeting. So, this is what I came up with over the weekend. What do you think?"

Looking almost through him, she said, "I think you have too much time on your hands. I told you, I'm not sure what he's up too, but I do know winning BP would be good for all of us at NPI. I also told you that Darius is willing to help if I needed him, but I just can't imagine that Joseph would throw away everything he's worked so hard for to venture out on a limb. But I'll keep my eyes and ears opened and let you know what I find out."

"I noticed you didn't comment when I mentioned your

having a '*relationship*' with Darias. Can I assume that there *is* something to it?"

"I think you've already assumed a helluva lot, Dwayne. My private life is just that—private. I've never questioned what you do or who you see privately, it's none of my business."

"Well, would you consider this your business, Ary, I'm in love with you. I don't know how or when it happened," he yelled, causing the taxi driver to peek at them through his rear-view mirror, "but I am, I love you and it kills me to see that bastard using you and possibly destroying your—our careers. So, for whatever it's worth, I had to tell you and I hope you're not offended by it." He sat back in his seat, preparing himself for the rebuff.

She stared into his eyes. He'd put his feelings out in the open and deserved a reply. The taxi pulled up in front of the atrium entrance and announced the cost of the fare. Ary's concentration was momentarily sidetracked by his thick Caribbean accent. Dwayne placed ten dollars in the tray while she clumsily reached for the door handle, pushing it open with the heel of her shoe, running into the building, leaving him standing curbside as she escaped. Bob noticed her running and manually opened the security gate. The doors of a waiting elevator closed just as she entered, providing a moment of much needed solitude. Her eyes, filling with tears, visually displayed the confusion she felt within. *Why now?* she wondered. *What was I supposed to say?*

As the doors opened on the eleventh floor, Ary, with her head lowered, walked straight into Joseph, who was waiting to go up to the 14th floor corporate library . "Hey, what happened? What's the matter?" She couldn't answer, she could only weep on his shoulder. He placed his arm around her shoulders as he led her down the hallway. Dwayne exited another elevator soon afterwards and noticed the couple as they turned in the direction of Joseph's office.

"Dwayne," Ann called, breaking his concentration. "Is everything ok with Ary? Is it her mother?"

Looking somber, he answered. "No, I think it was something I said."

CHAPTER 85

JOSEPH persuaded Ary to take a few days off. Get an early start to the weekend, he'd suggested. She would need to be at the top of her game next week and his immediate task was to pull Dwayne off the BP account.

CHAPTER 86

"I don't know Joseph," G said, reluctantly. "I'm not sure I agree with you on this one, buddy. I know she has talent, the likes of which we haven't seen in this industry for some time—but BP? You know how important this account is to NPI. Winning would literally put us in the same league as the SKG's of the world. I can't afford to lose. And I'm disappointed that Dwayne confessed to you his conflict of interest because of his on again/off again relationship with the girl at BP, but I respect him for stepping aside so as not to hurt our chances. He's still an asset to our firm. Maybe I'll speak to him."

"I wouldn't suggest it, G. At least, not now. You know how private he is. He doesn't want you to think less of him or worry that he's a liability in any way. So I'd ask you to trust me on this, let me handle it. I'd put Ary up front with our expertise following closely behind."

"Well, I'll want daily updates from you Joseph, and I'll have Marguerite sit in on meetings as well. Once Dwayne has pulled himself together, and hopefully that will be soon, I want to see him. Maybe there's something else going on in his life that I can help him through. As long as I've known him, he's never let relationships stand in the way of business. And you of all people know how I feel about our people Joseph."

"I know, G."

"I think I've heard enough about BP for one day, unless we hit an impasse."

"Believe me G, nothing is going to happen, I promise you. BP means more to me that any account I've ever worked on and I'd be more than willing to put my career on the line to win." G smiled, convinced that Joseph was as sincere and reliable now as he'd been for the past seven years.

CHAPTER 87

JOSEPH called Dwayne into his office and instructed him to shut the door. He shared with him the conversation he'd had with G about removing him from the BP strategy team.

"Joseph, why do you insist on doing this? I just can't believe this is good for the company. Making Ary the lead and taking me off *altogether*! I'm sorry, I'm gonna have to speak to G. I can't let you do this!" he yelled.

"I wouldn't do that if I were you. Even though we'd made a deal not to inform G about our original plan, I had to renege and make him aware of a few subtle changes to the strategy. And I must say my friend, he's quite upset that you would let a personal relationship get in the way of such a substantial client."

"What? What the hell are you talking about?"

"G is questioning your ability to manage your accounts Dwayne—without getting romantically involved. But don't worry, I convinced him that that kind of thinking was overkill. I assured him that by working from home for a few days and regrouping, you'd be more amenable to *helping* Ary obtain the business rather than leading the charge. And listen Dwayne, when all this is said and done, there still might be a chance that I can wriggle a promotion out of this for you if you're willing to fully cooperate. So go and enjoy your long weekend and I'll see you in the office on Monday. Let's keep in touch."

Joseph pushed the button on his speakerphone. "Michelle I'm all done here, what's next on my agenda?"

Dwayne stormed out of Joseph's office and headed in the direction of G's suite. He noticed Marguerite approaching at the same time. G's assistant noticed the savage glare in his eyes and became uneasy.

"May I help you Mr. Hargis?" she asked, cautiously.

Marguerite interrupted before he could respond. "Dwayne, whatever it is, it'll have to wait. I've been trying to see G since this morning and I'm not about to relinquish my time for any reason." She pushed opened the door and quickly closed it before G could notice anyone else standing there.

Dwayne hustled back to his office, stuffed his briefcase with customer files and headed toward the elevators. Ann was on the receiving end of a contemptuous stare after inquiring whether she should forward his calls.

Normally it's not such an offensive question, she whispered under her breath.

CHAPTER 88

MARCUS paced around the lobby of his sister's building, smiling as residents came and went, even offering a friendly 'hello' to strangers. The sweat under his arms was spilling through to his t-shirt. It had been over an hour since he'd arrived at Ary's condo. The sun had retired for the evening, leaving behind a satiny blue night sky to provide a backdrop for thousands of shimmering stars.

This is a nice place to live, he thought, walking outside and observing the majesty of the George Washington Bridge spanning the mighty Hudson River. Swept away by the beauty, he almost missed his sister as she rushed through the lobby racing toward the elevator.

"Hey!" he yelled through the door chasing after her.

"Marcus? What are you doing here? I wasn't expecting you."

"I'm sorry for just showing up at your doorstep, but I'd told you before I had some things to work out and that it might take me some time."

"Well, it's good to see you," she smiled. "Come on upstairs. I think I have a bottle of wine we can share."

Memories of her always being there for him as a child flooded his mind as they rode up to the 26th floor. Once inside, Marcus made himself at home on her sofa and waited for his big sister to open the wine before he opened his heart. "Cheers!" she said, handing him a chilled glass.

Ary sat on the arm of the loveseat, crossed her legs and rested her chin across her knuckles. She watched as Marcus lowered his head and began revealing the phone conversation he'd heard between Bruce and Matthew, admitting how fear prevented him from confiding in her or their mother.

She slid down into the center of the seat, wondering at first, if he were being completely honest. But as he continued, any doubts were quickly halted.

"Marcus, why didn't you at least tell mama? Maybe she could have done something...confronted him..."

"And what would that have done, Ary? Convince him to stay? Transform him back into a heterosexual? It wouldn't have done a damn thing!" he shouted. "It was me who went through the rest of his teen years wondering if and when it would be my turn to come out."

"But I don't get it, Marcus. The therapist said you were ok with it."

"I told the therapist what I thought she wanted to hear, what mama needed to hear. But now, now I can't marry the woman I love because I don't know who the hell I am–straight, gay, bi, I don't know!" he cried out. "I always wanted his approval, Ary. But he never made me feel like he was proud to have me as his son. When it came to sports, I was nothing more than an athletic disappointment in his eyes. And as far as academics, I don't think he ever expected me to make it out of junior high school without a road map. I have *always* felt like the Alexander failure!"

"Whaaat," she dragged. "Marcus, I'm so sorry. I never really understood the extent of your pain."

"No one did. Ary, not only did you have the love of mama, you had the love and adoration of the head of the house, the king of the castle, the breadwinner, the social guru, the well-known, incredibly successful, international business attorney, Bruce Raymond Alexander. Me, I had mama protecting her little boy at every turn, trying desperately to make up for dad's shortcomings when it came to raising his less-than-perfect son. Maybe she should have just let things be. Maybe I would have grown into my manhood. But as it turns out, the amazing part of all of this is, and I didn't realize it until recently, was that it wasn't me he disliked, it was himself. The honorable Bruce Alexander couldn't face his own demons, so he shifted them onto me. They had been destroying him for years and the only way to conquer them was to prove that he was this masculine wonder who excelled in everything he ever attempted to do. You reminded him of all that he wanted to continue being, until the mental cost became too great. And when that happened, he didn't give a shit about his faithful wife, his flourishing daughter and certainly not his disappointing son. Hell, I'm convinced he didn't care if I survived or died."

"How can you say that about daddy? He loved you the only way he knew how. No one is perfect, Marcus, none of us. I don't know what a male child needs from his father, but this much I can tell you, daddy gave up a lot for us, more than we could possibly ever understand. We could never fully know what he'd been going through." Marcus turned away and faced the window.

"I don't think people just turn gay one day, Marcus. This is something I'm sure he'd been struggling with for years, pretending to be straight to protect us until it became unbear-able, until he found someone who could love and accept him for who he truly was. I don't condone what he did and the way he did it—as a matter of fact, I hated him for it. But we have to be fair Marcus. We're all adults. And ultimately, we have to take responsibility for who we are now, and what we do."

He turned again to face his sister. "My life had been characterized by depression and unfulfilled relationships—until I met Caroline, someone I know I'm in love with, but afraid to commit to because I don't want to destroy her life or any children we might have."

Marcus met her stare with profound sadness as she walked slowly over to him, knelt down and whispered in his ear. "I never understood the depth of your suffering until today, Marcus. Please forgive me for being blind. I love you now more than ever."

CHAPTER 89

DWAYNE decided to drive around the city to help eliminate the escalating frustration from his conversation with Joseph. But after getting stuck in mid-day traffic, parked his sports car in a public garage and walked off the remaining anger. He ended up in Central Park and sat on a bench until dusk, watching couples stroll hand in hand, young families pushing carriages, and men throwing and kicking balls in Sheep's Meadow. He saw senior citizens attempting to jog themselves back into good health and Baby Boomers proving that they still were. At thirty-three, Dwayne felt something missing from his life, a wife, a family he could adore, a rambunctious son to play ball with, a beautiful daughter to take pride in and a small fluffy dog who'd grab onto his legs as he walked through the front door from a long, hard day at work. He'd told Ary how he felt. Her response was to run into the arms of another man. He'd asked himself how many times a man could make mistakes before he'd start to learn from them. Falling in love with a former prostitute, fathering a child he rarely ever saw, and now he'd found himself in love with a woman who seemed to be intent on making him pay for every pain and injustice she'd ever experienced in life. It was pure madness, all of it. His job was on the line and he was unsure of how to save it. Clients were depending on him and he was too distraught to care. Thoughts of Ary tortured him, yet he couldn't walk away.

It was probably a good time to become religious, he'd thought, seek divine answers, but he didn't have the luxury of time to wait. He had to do something.

CHAPTER 90

JOSEPH casually walked the four blocks to the 'Ale House,' a local pub frequented by oil executives. The day's stresses had turned out to be more than he'd anticipated and he wanted to clear his thoughts with a double dry Martini before going home. He sat at the cherry wood circular bar where the bartender greeted him by name and offered 'the usual.' Joseph was not in a conversational mood and answered with a curt nod of his head then locked his fingers together and placed his elbows on the edge of the bar. A Giants game glared above the wall of liquors over the counter. Joseph displayed no interest, even after the barkeep delivered his drink and suggested how well the team was finally performing. He twirled a finger inside the tonic before gulping it down, shivering as it traveled through his body. "I probably should have eaten today before tackling one of those," he wisecracked, mostly to himself. He tapped a finger on the bar for a second round and lowered his head in deep thought until he heard someone call his name.

"Joseph Larsen. It's been a while, how are you sir?"

Joseph looked to his left and saw Darias sitting a couple of barstools away.

"Well, well. Darias Woolfolk. Hey man, don't you have better things to do on a Friday night than hang out at a tavern?" he laughed.

"I should be asking you that question, Larsen. You're the

one with the bevy of beauties on his arm at every oilman's affair," he countered, smiling.

"Well, I guess you could say I'm on hiatus, focusing more on a little contract I heard is up for grabs." Both men shared a forced laugh.

"Yeah well, I think the entire industry must be focused on that. That's all anyone talks about anymore. You know, there are more important issues than how to beat out the competition and score the BP account, isn't there?" Darius questioned.

"No, Woolfolk," Joseph laughed, "there isn't."

"Well, since I work for that little jewel, I'd have to say I agree with you."

"Hey, can I freshen up your drink without BP considering it a bribe?"

"That would cost you much more than a drink, man." Darias moved over one seat. Joseph signaled for two refills.

"Hey Larsen, let me ask you a question. Everybody knows you're next in line at NPI, but really, are you willing to wait the innumerable years for G to step down and retire before assuming the President's role?"

"I don't think I know what you mean."

"C'mon man. The buzz around town is that you're either now being, or soon will be solicited by other national and international firms. What gives Larsen? I think I'm way better at the game than you," he laughed. "The real question is, will G let you get away that easily? And your new kid, Ary Alexander, I hear she's being heralded as the female 'Joseph Larsen.' What's in the water over there? There's even talk of Dwayne Hargis being wooed to jump ship for even more money than what G dishes out for his oil superstars."

Joseph planted a rigid stare on Darias, testing his

genuineness, trying to read his facial expression through his own waning consciousness. Could any of what Darias said be true? And if so, why hadn't he heard about it?

"Well, it's all very flattering," he stumbled, "but I can tell you, there's no truth to it. With all my contacts, I would have at least gotten an inkling of this so-called *buzz*. And you of all people, Woolfolk, know that rumors in this business are par-for-the-course. And as far as me taking over at NPI and having to work with Marguerite Armstead on a daily basis, I'd rather be eaten alive by sharks," he laughed. Joseph was too inebriated to remember Darias' past relationship with Marguerite. "Before I'd ever consider taking over someone else's dream, I'd make my own come true."

Bingo! Darias thought.

"I have no intention of unseating G and running his empire. No one could run NPI like he does, neither would he allow it. G's business philosophy is written in stone, and his dedication to NPI is im-im-mutable," he stammered. "It just works—for him. Besides, he's been good to me. But as far as Hargis and Ary go, I don't know what plans they have or who's trying to '*woo*' them." Joseph raised his hand to gain the attention of the bartender. "A final round for us, my good man."

"And afterwards Larsen, may I offer you a ride home, that is, if your driver isn't here already."

"That won't be necessary," Joseph snapped. "Are you in-in-sin-u-ating that I'm drunk, Woolfolk?" The bartender's concern was evident, but was eased after Darias gave him a reassuring eye that he would be responsible for getting Joseph home safely.

"Of course not, but my driver is standing by and he could just as easily drop you off."

"Maybe. And to answer any questions you might have Woolfolk, Ary will be on the BP strategy team, presenting the proposal next week. And she *is* as good as they say."

"What about Hargis? Is he still on? That guy is one helluva marketing talent. You know, he use to date one of ours at BP a while ago and now I hear he's dating Ary." Joseph's facial muscles tightened. "There's no truth to that," he said, slurring, "no truth at all!"

"So she's free? And *you* have no interest?" he inquired, innocently.

Joseph's head was spinning circles from the effects of the alcohol.

"The truth is, Woolfolk, I did have an interest, but no more. Not after she mentioned her attraction to you."

"Me?"

"Didn't the two of you have dinner a Saturday or two ago?"

Unaware of Joseph's intentional trap, he answered truthfully.

"Dinner? No. The last time I saw her was at the Polo Club. Listen, I'll be frank with you man. I am attracted to her, but right now is not the time to pursue a relationship because of the contract. However, I do plan on asking her out afterwards—if there's no truth to the rumors."

Joseph could barely suppress his rage. *Why would she lie to me after I'd revealed my plans?* He believed she might even expose him to G. Ary would have to answer to him tonight. "Hey Woolfolk, I think I'll take you up on your car offer."

CHAPTER 91

DARIAS dropped Joseph off at home and offered to escort him upstairs. He declined, stumbling past the doorman into the elevator. Darias smirked, shaking his head as he left the posh building. He thought about Ary and how he'd love to spend the rest of the evening with her. But his candid discussion with Joseph wouldn't allow it—at least, not tonight.

Joseph collapsed onto his bed and tried to remember what he'd talked about with Darias. The attempt proved to be futile. The only dialogue he could recall was Darias' intention of dating Ary and the rumors of Dwayne already beating him to it. In his present state of mind, he felt betrayed. Pulling himself up out of bed, he walked jaggedly through the hallway, falling against walls and closet doors, finally stumbling into the kitchen where he attempted to make a cup of instant coffee, but not before scalding his right hand from the mug of hot, micro waved water.

"Shit! Damn!" he screamed, throwing the mug and its contents into the sink. Shards of glass flew everywhere, lodging a visible splinter in the palm of his burning hand.

"What the hell is going on here?" he yelled, tearing multiple sheets of paper towels from the roller to catch the flowing blood.

"Somebody's gonna have to pay for this!" he shouted, pounding his wounded hand on the counter.

"Ahhhh! Idiot!" he bellowed. "That's right, Joseph Larsen, you're an idiot for trusting her. Trusting is for losers. You've never trusted anyone. Life's not about trust. When you trust—you lose." Joseph wandered unsteadily to the bathroom, hoping to find medicated relief for his burn and tweezers for his splinter. He found neither. He washed his hand with cold water, washing away the blood and squeezing back the pain as he pulled the splintered glass out with his teeth. Catching a glimpse of himself in the mirror, he muttered, "I'll bub… buzzz the con…con…cierge and have him call a car for me. I think I need to pay her a visit."

CHAPTER 92

ARY yawned as she threw the cotton blanket, lying across the back of the sofa over her body. Although the TV was on and the volume loud enough to be heard, none of it registered. Her thoughts centered on Marcus and her family until Dwayne's dramatic taxi revelations crept in. *How dare he tell me that*, she thought. He had no right, especially with the way he'd treated her in the past.

She'd come to NPI to make money, not find the man of her dreams or make hordes of new friends. She rarely had time to socialize with her old ones.

Suddenly, the apartment buzzer screamed louder than the voices in her head.

Looking at the digital clock on the lamp table, she wondered, *who the hell could that be at this hour?* She ran over to the wall panel.

"Who is it?"

"Ary, it's me, Dwayne Hargis. I know it's late and I apologize a thousand times over, but I had to talk to you. I've been driving around for hours…"

"Dwayne!" she interrupted. "It's eleven o'clock…at night. Are you sure this can't wait until Monday? I'm dressed for bed and I'm really tired."

"Ary, ordinarily I'd say yes, it could wait. But what I have to say is very *out* of the ordinary. I have to talk to you about what happened today…please." Ary leaned her cheek against the metal plate and closed her eyes. Her arms and legs went limp, barely able to support her body.

"Ok. Give me a minute to pull myself together."

She ran into the bathroom, sprayed mint flavored mouthwash on her tongue and fingered through her hair. Dwayne paced nervously in the vestibule, waiting for the buzzer. His attention was briefly interrupted by the sound of an idling car outside the apartment entrance. A black limo with dark privacy windows was parked out front. He couldn't tell if anyone was inside or if the driver was picking up a late night passenger.

Ary paused at the panel before pressing the '*door open*' button and tightened up the satin robe she'd pulled on from behind the bathroom door.

Startled from the grating sound of the buzzer, he quickly reached for the heavy door handle and raced toward the elevators. The driver of the car opened the back door and a tall unsteady figure emerged.

Joseph ambled slowly and carefully into the building scowling after confirming that who he saw, really was Dwayne. He stood fixed in front of the door, unaware and not caring that residents had to maneuver themselves around him to get inside. With his right hand wrapped awkwardly in an ace bandage, Joseph reached to push the intercom button. But with squinted eyes and a tense stance, he decided it would be best to handle this situation soberly. He returned to the car and to the driver who dutifully held the door open and inquired, "Where to sir?"

Joseph answered through gritted teeth, "Take me home."

CHAPTER 93

ARY stood behind the partially opened door. "Dwayne, what could it possibly be that couldn't wait until Monday?"

"Ary, I didn't mean to upset you today. This is not like me at all. I'm all out of character and that only leads me to believe that what my old man said to me when I was younger, was true."

"And what was that?"

"May I come in? Or should I just stand out here and tell you?"

"I'm sorry. I'm really exhausted. Come in. Now what was it that your father told you, Dwayne?"

He walked into the middle of the living room. The moonlight flowing through the blinds seemed to cast a graceful glow around her. It took him a few seconds to respond.

"He told me, I'd know. I'd know when the right woman came along. Ary, my mind and thoughts are so jumbled, I don't even recall driving over the Bridge to get here—but I did, I came. And I need to try and explain who I am and what I feel for you."

Every bit of strength she'd regained began emptying from her body.

"Dwayne, are you trying to tell me that you're in love with me? We haven't even known each other for a year yet. These things take time."

"Ary, what we've been through together some couples never experience in two lifetimes, let alone one. I know it hasn't been easy working for me, but that's how I've succeeded in this industry. And I can see that same quality in you. Ary, you've held up under the most extreme circumstances, both personal and professional. You've held your own in meetings with the most racist, corporate meatheads in the industry and had them eating out of your hand. You've won the respect of hard-nosed businessmen who found it difficult, at best, to even communicate with an intelligent black man. Never in their wildest dreams did they think they'd be heeding the advice of an equally talented and erudite black woman, telling them what's best for their company. But it's not only your sharp skills or professionalism I'm impressed with, I love you for who you are—the good and the challenging," he said with a smile. "And if you don't want to pursue the incident with Joseph, I'll understand and continue checking up on him alone. All I want is a chance, an equal chance. And if you decide that it's not me you want, then I'll graciously step aside and chalk it up as an unforgettable loss."

Ary walked over to him and held his hands. She saw the sincerity in his eyes and felt the power of his words penetrating her heart. He pulled her close to his heaving chest and wrapped his solid arms around her waist. His hands directed her buttocks into his expanding manhood and listened as she moaned. He closed his eyes and imagined Heaven feeling like this. Ary's hands slowly stroked his back, dipping in and out of the groove. Her head, buried deep in his chest, moved rhythmically from the pulse of his beating heart. Dwayne inhaled her essence and dreamed of a place where there was no male competition, no personal battles to conquer, and no impossible obstacles to climb over or break through. He dreamed of a perfect life with her.

"There are things I need to tell you about myself," he whispered, shattering the majestic spell. Reluctantly, she obliged and reentered the universe, however, still unwilling to disconnect from his mystical grip.

"Ary," he said, holding her face in his hands, "We all have a past, some of which we'd like to keep hidden away in a closet forever, but you need to be aware of mine—it might help you in making a decision."

"I don't want to make any decisions right now, I just want to be held safely in your arms," she whispered, never taking her eyes from his.

"Ary, please listen to what I have to say, and keep in mind what you once told me—that no one is perfect."

He pulled her gently down to the floor, positioning her back to his chest while guiding her head to rest in the hollow of his neck. He began disclosing his very private life. Although she'd already known, she listened with the intensity of a sequestered juror. Somehow, with it coming from his lips, it all seemed more real, more accurate. For the first time, she felt they shared something in common—pain, love and disillusionment. Time passed quickly, but Dwayne was in no hurry to release her. Instead, he reached for a throw pillow on the sofa and placed it behind his head, thinking, *this is the way it should always be.*

CHAPTER 94

"**Y**OU wanted to see me Joseph?"

"Yes, please come in. Have a seat." He wondered how she got past his assistant without being announced.

"No, thank you. What can I do for you?"

He stood up and walked around the desk to close the door. "Let me get right to the point. I've not been satisfied with the performance of our friend, Dwayne Hargis, and I for one, am extremely disappointed. After all, it was me who fought for him to lead the BP account strategy. I'm sure you recall that meeting."

Now, he had her undivided attention. "Why the change of heart, Joseph? I thought he was your number one *boy.*"

"He was. But ever since Ary Alexander came on board, his concentration has not been, shall we say, focused. And you of all people know how G feels about office romances," he sneered. "And quite honestly, Marguerite, I've even noticed a change in G. The way he behaves in meetings when Ary's presenting. I'm sure it must be somewhat disturbing for…some of the staff."

"What's your point, Joseph?" she asked, annoyingly.

"Well, with a client like BP looming above our heads, NPI really can't afford to have a gushing school boy at the helm. And with the ego that he has, I know he wouldn't stand for playing second fiddle to any man, or woman. So regrettably, this might this be the perfect time to sever our ties."

"All because of BP? G wouldn't hear of it. And why the sudden impulse to get rid of someone you've been fighting to keep in the spotlight for the past two or three years? Did he steal away one of your prized fillies, Joseph?"

"Now Marguerite, how long have you known me?" he asked, placing his elbows on the desk and folding his hands beneath his chin. "You know I don't have any problems in that department. Hell, I could have even had you if G hadn't beaten me to the punch," he laughed.

"That is highly unlikely," she countered.

"Nevertheless, I feel that Dwayne is getting, how shall I put it…a little too ambitious, if you know what I mean?"

"Uh huh. But why now, Joseph? Who's going to take over the lead on the BP strategy at this late hour? We can't afford to fail. You know what this means to G. This win will put him where he dreamed of being five years *down* the road. Are you sure about this? Have you talked it over with G?"

"You must know that G had to unexpectedly go to Europe, and from there he's making a stop in South America—he won't return for the next six or seven days. So all of his meetings will be pushed back a week, and both you and I have experienced what that's like—our own calendars get tossed out the window. We spoke before he left. G trusts me, and knows I wouldn't do something so drastic if I didn't feel it was for the good of the company. So, to that end, we're covered. And as far as the lead goes, I've chosen Ary Alexander with Mike Castellano as her backup."

"You have totally lost your mind, Joseph Larsen. That bitch may have all of you pussy whipped and acting like eighth grade schoolboy's in love, but I will have none of it, especially when it involves the lifeblood of this firm."

"Settle down, sweetheart. I've thought it all through. I'll help Ary every step of the way."

"Just like you've done for Dwayne Hargis I'm sure. I knew he couldn't have achieved those milestones on his own. Those people are simply not that capable when it comes to this business."

"As I was saying. With me behind her, and her relationship with a certain Mr. Darias Woolfolk, we're sure to win. And with a major windfall like that, there's sure to be rewards. And the reward I know you've been waiting for is the one that'll get Ary Alexander out of G's kingdom." Joseph sat comfortably in his chair and pushed back towards the window. "Have I at least piqued your interest Ms. Armstead?"

"I didn't know she was his type, but keep talking. How would winning BP take her out of the picture? If anything, he'd want her to stay and maybe even offer her a promotion."

"I happened to run into an old oil friend on Friday night at the local pub who has a strong interest in her coming to work for them," he lied, convincingly. "They're willing to pay her top dollar *right now*—so just imagine how valuable she'll be to every firm in the industry after she scores BP. There'll be offers even she can't refuse. So I'll get what I want by getting rid of Dwayne Hargis, and you'll get to keep your man and never have to worry your pretty little brunette head about him losing interest, because of a younger model."

Marguerite took a moment to absorb this astounding news. She studied Joseph's face for any signs of false claims and considered what this would finally mean for her plans with G.

"I'll prep Castellano," she said.

"And I'll take care of business on my end."

Michelle buzzed Joseph on the speakerphone to remind him of two afternoon off-site meetings and his usual five o'clock managerial conference.

"Thank you sweetheart, and please get Dwayne Hargis on the line. Tell him I need to see him now!"

Michelle frowned before replying. She wasn't in the mood for his playfulness. All the pet names and perpetual promises of pay raises suddenly lost their amusing appeal. Her subtle efforts to attract him had gone unnoticed for far too long. She had come to realize that Joseph would never see her as more than a secretary, his faithful assistant, and it was time to move on. Her best friend, an attractive executive assistant at a large technology firm ended her career after marrying the CEO after only three years, even though Michelle thought of herself as the more attractive one.

"Mr. Hargis is on his way over, sir."

"Thank you. Oh, and get Human Resources on the line, they're going to need to make a few changes in the org chart," he mocked.

Dwayne tried to contrive an excuse not to meet with Joseph, but Michelle assured him that Joseph would not take no for an answer. He went over every account in his head to make sure that all was in order and that he was on top of Ary's proposal progress for BP. *What now?* he wondered in frustration.

He took the long route to Joseph's office. Michelle ushered him in immediately.

"Good morning," he offered.

"Please close the door and have a seat. Listen, I don't know how to say this any other way than to come right out and say it. Lately your performance has been less than stellar and you know our policy at NPI, we expect nothing short of perfection from our high-level managers. And frankly, Dwayne, I've seen better in the last three or four months from some of the mailroom guys. At least I've been receiving all of my mail, unopened! I'm not about to try and guess what the cause might be and truthfully, unlike G, I really don't give a shit. The only thing I do care about, however, is the success and profitability of this firm, nothing else, and I won't sit idly by and watch you, destroy it."

"What!" Dwayne yelled, rising from his chair. "Destroy this company? What the hell are you talking about Joseph?"

"Sit down, Dwayne! How dare you come into my office yelling like a madman!"

"How dare you accuse me of destroying this company when it's you Joseph, preparing to take it down. And I may not have all the answers yet, but when I do, so will G."

"I don't think you'll have enough time to figure anything out Dwayne Hargis—your days at NPI are over," Joseph said, tapping his watch.

"Fuck you, Joseph Larsen."

"Thanks for making my decision easier, Dwayne. So, should I consider that a resignation, or do I need to fire you? I'm sorry, everything suddenly got lost in translation," he laughed.

Dwayne stormed out of the office racing towards Ary's cubical where he found her on the phone with a client. He stopped, looked inside and said loudly, "I hope for our sake, you had nothing to do with this." Puzzled, she hastened the phone conversation to an end and ran after him. "Dwayne, stop, what's wrong? Stop, please." She followed him into his office and shut the door where he began emptying out his drawers at a frenetic pace. "What are you doing? Where are you going? We have a meeting in an hour," she reminded him.

"*We* don't have a meeting, *you* have a meeting. There will be no more NPI meetings for me. Your boy just fired me, or I quit. I don't know what just happened, and I really don't give a shit. At this point it really doesn't matter."

"Quit? Fired? What are you talking about? I don't understand!"

"Listen, this thing is about to explode and he needs me out of the picture. With G gone until who knows when and Joseph only having a few more days to do whatever it is he's planning to do, things are moving faster than I even anticipated. And I'm not sure who all the players are, but one thing's for sure, I'm in the way," he surmised, stuffing papers into his briefcase. "Hey, when it's all over, be sure and tell G that good 'ole Dwayne Hargis tried to save his little company from his trusted brother, Joseph. And it wasn't just for the sake of G's company, nope, it was 'cause I enjoyed making tons of money. But what I failed to realize was that there's always a hefty price to pay for success. I guess it's just that country-boy upbringing that prevents you from distinguishing good from evil, huh, Ary? So be careful while you're here and remember what I told you before, I love you and I'll protect you, at any cost." Dwayne crossed the room and bolted out the door, causing her to step back to avoid a collision. Ary held her hands up to her flushed face and stood in his office in apparent shock, not sure if she should run after him or go straight to Joseph.

Was this my fault? she wondered. *This wasn't supposed to happen.*

Ary ran towards Joseph's office and found Michelle sitting at her desk as if everything were normal.

She has to know something. How can she keep working when this company and everyone working for it is falling apart?

"Michelle, I need to see Joseph," she demanded, out of breath.

"I'm sorry, but he's not in his office. Is there something I can help you with?"

Ary turned away without a response and ran down the hallway, yelling as she approached the receptionist desk.

"Ann, did Mr. Hargis leave yet?"

"Ary, what's going on around here? Mr. Hargis turned in his badge and was escorted out by security, What's happening?"

"Ann please," she begged, tears falling down her cheeks. "Did he say anything?"

"No honey, he didn't."

At that moment, she noticed Joseph coming out of the office of the VP of Human Resources.

"Joseph," she screamed. "We need to talk."

"Please lower your voice, Ms. Alexander, this is a respectable place of business—even more so in the last twenty minutes or so," he smirked. Meet me in my office.

"What have you done?" she shouted, following him down the corridor.

"Michelle, hold all my calls," he ordered, as he entered his office suite. He slammed the door shut and turned to face Ary.

"Now you listen to me. Dwayne Hargis is out of our hair. All I need you to do is be honest with me!" he yelled. "You told me you'd had dinner with Darias more than a week ago, yet lo and behold, when I brought it up to him, he was clueless. Where were you? With that nig…"

"Go on. Why don't you say it. Isn't that how you really feel about us. Dwayne was right. All I could ever do for you was to fuck you."

"You know that's a damned lie. I have plans for us. But with him in the way, I couldn't focus on what I needed to do, always wondering if you were with him on the weekends we weren't together. Ary, it's all coming together, soon, very soon. You just have to follow through on what you'd promised."

"I don't want any part of you or your ill-fated plans," she cried.

"Ary, calm down, you're just upset because I let your little friend go. Don't worry, he'll find another job, he'll make out ok." Joseph walked over to her and held her arms down by her side. Looking deep into her terrified eyes.

"Listen to me, we're both under tremendous pressure right now. Take the rest of the day off. Here," he offered, reaching into his wallet. "Take my credit card, go shopping, have a spa treatment. We'll talk later."

She wrestled away from him. "You've gone too far, Joseph. You didn't have to fire him. Dwayne is a good person, he didn't deserve it."

"Who does, Ary? This world is not meant for the 'good.' They're the ones who always end up finishing last, remember? Now, don't be too upset and do something you might regret. I'd hate to have to spill the dirt on another friend of yours, Mr. Darias Woolfolk, and inform his CEO that he's romantically involved with one of the bidders of the contract and that possibly some insider information could have been mentioned during a night of pillow talk," he said, grinning. "All those years it took him to climb the ladder to VP would be quickly flushed down the toilet. Uh, uh, uh. That wouldn't put you in a very good light either, now would it? Seems like everybody you care about gets hurt in some way Ary. Let's see, mom, brother, Dwayne, Darias. Whadup wit dat?" he said, amusing himself.

"You monster!" she screamed, fleeing his office. She made it to her cubical, grabbed her purse and ran towards the elevator. Ann could only stare as she disappeared into the opening doors of the car.

CHAPTER 95

ARY ran past the guards in the lobby and headed for the garage. Searching frantically for the keys buried in her purse, the entire contents spilled onto the pavement. "Damn, damn," she cried, hurling the empty bag to the ground. Feeling helpless, defeated, and guilty, she slid down near the front of her car and wept. She watched powerlessly as her lipstick, gloss and make-up stick rolled into the path of an oncoming car. The shattered fragments she thought, symbolized the feeling in her heart. As she swung her legs around, underneath her, the heels from her pumps punctured a gaping hole in her stockings.

With her mind snarled in emotion and her body afflicted with grief, she pushed around to the side of her car, hoping that no one could see her sitting on the cold pavement of the garage floor. But after a few minutes, she heard a commotion a few spaces down and crawled around, on her knees, to get a better look—it was Marguerite and Bob. Ary moved back just enough, so as not to be discovered.

"Why didn't you call mother to let her know you were coming last weekend so that I could have made alternate plans. You know we have an arrangement. Why do you insist on trying to be a part of my life, Robert? What if G was with me? I'd have to explain mother's affair with your father!"

"Marguerite, I apologize. I just happened to be upstate fishing with a friend and thought it'd be nice to introduce him to mama. I wasn't thinking about whose weekend it was. I'm sorry I put you in a bad light, but truthfully, I really don't think Mr. G would care one way or the other 'bout who your mama is."

"Well, I'm not taking that chance. Can't you understand that this is *my* future you're toying with? I love G and he loves me, but there is still a huge segment of society who doesn't accept mixing of the races. Look at mother or my father as examples. If G knew I had even one drop of black blood in me, our relationship would be finished. So I'm asking you again, please abide by our agreement—I don't know you and you don't know me—we just happen to have the same mother."

"Yeah, a half-black mother who loved my black daddy, but wasn't allowed to marry him back then. Marguerite, this is the twenty-first century, people don't care who or what you are or where you come from if they really love you. And if you ever opened up your eyes, you'd see how your arrangement has hurt mama all these years—never being able to have both her children in her life at the same time."

"Listen Robert, I'm happy, mother's happy and I'd suggest you find your own happiness. It was because of you that my British father left mama and caused me to lose contact with him for years and you also interfered in my relationship with a man who's now a Vice President of a prestigious oil firm," she lied. "I will not stand idly by and let you come between G and me. I won't! I'll have you relieved of your guard duties downstairs before I'd let that happen," she threatened. "Look, we're not getting any younger, and my chances of marrying someone like G gets slimmer each time he hires some new babe out of the woods. I'd like to be able to introduce him to mother as my fiancé in the very near future. So please, stay away from her house on the days I'm scheduled to be there and stay away from me." She continued, taking on a false, sympathetic tone. "Robert, whether you know it or not, that's how she wants it too. Now, please, let's not go changing the rules."

Marguerite got into her dark gray Jaguar and drove off. Bob stood in the now empty space with his head bowed. Ary didn't know she could feel any worse than she did, but now her aching heart, was broken. Bob, walking in Ary's direction, noticed a checkbook and makeup mirror on the ground. She flinched, hearing his approaching footsteps and pressed her back against the cold steel of the car. Upon closer inspection, he saw the pocketbook and the mournful oil protégé sitting nearby.

"Good Lord, Miss Ary, what happened?" He knelt down beside her.

"It's Joseph Larsen. He's fired Dwayne and now he's threatening me with Darias, and I don't know what to do—how to stop him," she recounted, speaking as though Bob were familiar with NPI's unfolding drama.

"C'mon young lady, let me take you inside. You need to calm down."

"No, I can't go back there right now!" she cried, looking into his eyes. "I need to go home. I'll be ok as soon as I get home."

"Well, I certainly can't let you drive in this condition." He looked down at his watch and came up with a solution. "I'll take lunch now and drive you home myself."

"I can't let you do that. I live across the bridge, in Jersey. You'll never make it back in time." She rose slowly, collecting the salvageable articles from her purse. "I'm fine, really, I can make it home," she said, trying to assure him. "Bob, I overheard the conversation between you and Marguerite." His eyes grew wide.

"You have to promise me you won't say a word, Miss Ary. That's between me and her, just like she said, everybody's happy with the way things are. Now, c'mon, sit in my office for a little while before you get on the road, just until you feel better." Reluctantly, she agreed and followed him to a metal chair in the guard's cramped office space. Entranced by the multitude of intrusive monitors that watched people as they filed in and out of the Phillips building, on different office floors, Ary was oblivious when Bob appeared with a hot cup of coffee then excused himself to speak with another guard. Drawing a deep breath before sipping the hot brew, she'd settled back in her chair and once again focused on the monitors. She was drawn to the one displaying what looked like the eleventh floor elevator bank of NPI and was startled when she noticed the Human Resources VP hand over a folder to a laughing Joseph. She placed the cup awkwardly on the edge of the desk, jumped to her feet and rushed out the door. This time, she made it to her car without incident. Speeding through the dimly lit garage, she laid on the horn, shouting epithets after the huge automatic garage doors took too long to rise. The chassis of her car barely missed the speed bump outside the garage exit when she revved the engine and accelerated into oncoming traffic. Ignoring all posted signs, Ary made illegal right turns on red and blocked busy intersections. Finally, she made her way onto the West Side Highway and headed uptown, with the Bridge in full view. She prayed there'd be no traffic, or accidents over the expanse and exhaled as she passed the sign welcoming visitors to the Garden State.

"I'm home," she cried, wiping tears from her eyes and turning into the condo's underground garage, "I'm home."

CHAPTER 96

ARY unlocked the front door and rushed through it. Without taking off her shoes, she sat on the floor in the living room, near the spot where Dwayne held her safely in his arms. She wanted to recapture that feeling of being protected by someone who cared—someone who admitted to loving her. Instead, all she felt now was agony and despair.

How could this be? she wondered, leaning against the sofa that held his scent from days before. Her mind drifted. *Could she love him? Could she trust another man, most of whom held a contemptible track record in her life?* She needed to tell him that this was not her doing. She dialed his home number only to have it ring incessantly. Giving up, she placed the receiver clumsily back in its cradle, unaware that it sat slightly off base, preventing any incoming calls. She rose from the floor and walked slowly into her bedroom, stopping near the closet doors and slid down to the wooden floor. Her eyes welled with tears. Life had proven itself overwhelming. With all that she'd accomplished, at this moment, none of it mattered, she felt like an absolute failure—alienated from the people who claimed to love her, a stranger inside her own body.

"I've tried and done everything I possibly could have to make you proud of me—except now I realize, I've never done any of it for me. But now it's my turn to take total control—not owing anything to anyone. No more family responsibilities to mama, Marcus, or to you, daddy." She sobbed uncontrollably. Pulling herself up from the floor with the help of a door handle, she walked down the hallway into the bathroom and opened the medicine cabinet. She took out two bottles of prescription drugs—one filled with painkillers she'd received after a minor surgery, the other, a medication containing codeine for when she had the flu. She searched further back and discovered a bottle of unopened acetaminophen caplets.

She wondered which drugs would cause the least amount of pain. She only wanted to go to sleep and wake up in a more peaceful, safe and understanding world. This one was cold, calculating and self-absorbed. She took all three bottles, along with a cup of water back to her bedroom and sat on the edge of the bed. She no longer felt strong, she was exhausted. *How could I have been so naïve? The only thing I proved was that I was never really the one in charge of anything,* she thought.

Still, she would never apologize for trying. Neither would she admit to, or ask forgiveness for all the iniquities others had accused her of during her lifetime—her fierce determination, her illicit male relationships, even her family loyalty had been questioned by her own mother. The continuous flow of tears aided her feelings of sorrow.

My only regret will be forfeiting the chance to bring life into this world. Never having the responsibility of caring for my own flesh and blood. I think I would have made a good mother, she smiled, beneath the tears. *At the very least I would have taught my daughter to be responsible for her own happiness first, before taking on the monumental, nearly impossible task of everyone else's. It wouldn't have mattered how strong or successful she was, or that her family didn't turn out to be perfect—it wouldn't have been her fault. And she wouldn't have to spend her life trying to fix them or marry the wealthiest or most powerful man—like I wanted to do, only one that truly loved and respected her. But now, it's too late. I ruined that for you too.*

She took off her shoes and centered herself in the neatly made bed.

I really do love you mama, and you too, Marcus. I think you both know that. Daddy, you left a void in my heart that I've tried to fill with men who reminded me of the man you were—but they could never measure up to you in my head and I've grown tired of searching. I don't know if I love you anymore, and I hope that's ok. I've tried to make peace with that and accept it. I know you loved me once and I'm grateful to have experienced that love at all.

Ary swallowed a handful of prescriptive drugs and lay down in the middle of her bed. Now, if anyone wanted to judge her actions, she wouldn't be around to hear it. Wanting so much to end the pain, she slowly drifted to sleep.

Dwayne tried calling her after Ann reached him on his cell phone expressing her concerns. This time, Ann didn't care if she was meddling in Ary's personal life. Everything at NPI was coming apart at the seams. After calling her house and getting a constant busy signal, he contacted Marcus through Caroline and urged him to get there as quickly as he could. The men drove up within minutes of each other to the entrance of her condominium, and at the same time, ran from their cars yelling, *"Emergency!"* to a woman opening the lobby door. They ran into the elevator and down the hallway to her home. They found the door partially opened and hurried inside.

"Ary, Ary, where are you?" Dwayne shouted. Running into her bedroom, he found her sleeping. He grabbed her wrist, checked her pulse and gently shook her. Turning to Marcus, he yelled, "Call 911, now!" Marcus was terrified at the thought of losing his sister, Dwayne knew he wasn't going to.

The ambulance came within a matter of minutes, rushing her to the hospital emergency room where doctors pumped her stomach and revived her. After several hours in recovery, Dwayne assumed full responsibility, signing the release documents and offering to take her home. Ary obliged under the condition that no one at NPI be notified and that no one try and prevent her from returning to work the next day. The troubled men looked at each other, then unwittingly agreed. Ary had been given a second chance. She knew she had to use it to mend her world, torn apart by years of denial and confusion. It would be her last attempt to finding real happiness—the kind she felt had eluded her for so long.

CHAPTER 97

WALKING past Dwayne's closed office door, she felt a sudden hollowness inside. She glanced at her watch—it was seven-forty-five in the morning. Normally at this hour, he would have been working ardently on a proposal or preparing a contract or presentation. She paused and said quietly, "I'll make it up to you, I promise."

Not exactly sure what she'd do or who she could talk to, she sat stoically at her desk and turned on the PC to check for messages. Joseph had scheduled a two o'clock meeting with her. It was marked *urgent*.

I have to do something now, she thought.

Ary dialed Ann's extension and told her it was imperative that she contact G without Marguerite or Joseph's knowledge. Ann assured her that she could track him down without raising anyone's suspicion.

She walked around to Joseph's office. There was no sign of Michelle, but his door was slightly opened. She backed away and hurried to her cube. A flashing red light on her telephone signaled a waiting message—it was Darias, telling her to call him on his cell phone, ASAP.

Ary went into the ladies room, checking to make sure all the stalls were empty. She returned Darias' call from her cell, speaking softly.

"Darias, it's Ary."

"I tried calling you at home late last night and about an hour ago. Is everything ok?"

She panicked, hoping he hadn't gotten wind of her attempted suicide yesterday.

"Yes, I'm fine. I fell asleep early last night," she lied, "and didn't wake up until this morning. I needed to come in early to prepare for a presentation."

"Ary listen. I have a package for you. It contains false numbers that you'll want to pass on to Joseph for the BP proposal. He questioned me about a dinner with you last week, catching me off guard. You should be aware."

"Believe me, I was made well aware. He thinks I was with Dwayne, and fired him."

"Holy shit, that was fast!"

"What?"

"Nothing. Listen, you have to convince him that you got these figures from me somehow, maybe, over the weekend, and that they're the ones to go with. At the same time, you have to conduct business as usual as far as the actual NPI proposal goes. And remember—all the preliminary bidding responses are due on Friday. We don't have much time. I'll leave the envelope at the visitor's desk downstairs in the lobby. There's no need for you to come upstairs to my office."

"Thank you, I'm on my way."

She grabbed her purse from her cubicle and walked down the hall toward the reception area.

"Ann, I'll be back. If you get hold of the information I need before I return, call me on my cell, it's extremely important."

"Not to worry. You'll have it as soon as I get it."

Ary read over the bogus numbers as she headed back to the

office in a taxi. They looked very convincing and were similar to the actual numbers she'd discussed with Dwayne, with a few obvious gaffes in the estimated time of project completion and incremental cost increases during the four-year contract. She would doctor them up, so that Joseph wouldn't be able to spot them so easily.

As she entered the building, looking around, Bob was noticeably missing. Ary questioned the guard posted at his usual station. She was told that he'd been let go as of last evening. Ary raced into the elevators and ran towards Ann after reaching her floor. But before she could ask if there was any information, Ann handed her a note with G's private cell phone number as well as the hotel and satellite office numbers. It also contained an email address for emergencies.

Ary raced around the counter and hugged her.

"I love you for this."

"Be careful honey," she said, as affectionately as any mother.

Ary spent the rest of the morning and afternoon preparing two initial proposals—a forged one for Joseph and the authentic one for G. She gathered the notes she'd gotten from Dwayne, the information she'd gleaned from Darius as well as her own facts and findings, to come up with a document she was sure would put NPI at the top of a short list of contenders for a final submission.

Joseph stood outside his office door chatting with Michelle. As Ary approached, he looked at his watch and commented, "Hey, right on time. Come in, please."

"Here's the information you need. I met with Darias yesterday...and last night. Inside this envelope are the figures you'll want to present to BP on Friday as an initial offering. I've included my supporting notes for your reference only."

Joseph took the package from her and sat at his desk. He immediately flipped through the document until he reached the financial summary. His eyes moved swiftly across and down the page. Looking up at her, he said, "These numbers are very close to the ones I'd calculated in my head. You're a treasure, Ary." He walked over to a corner of his office and placed the document in a fax machine, and pushed the '*send*' button.

"Will there be anything else? I really need to get started on the Standard Oil proposal."

Returning to his seat, he urged her to wait a moment. His cell phone rang.

"I agree, I think the estimate is perfect. I know we'll come in lower so proceed as we discussed and I'll see you late Friday. What's that? Yes, maybe I'll bring her out to the Coast with me on Friday," he said, winking at her. "Anyway man, get ready for the ride of your life—this is only the beginning." He ended the call laughing.

Ary felt nauseous.

"Well, I think this calls for a celebration! The Standard Oil proposal can wait until tomorrow, love. How about a private dinner party for two at my place? How's seven o'clock?"

Ary had to think quickly. She glanced at her watch. That would give her just a few hours to make crucial decisions without any mistakes. "Seven sounds fine. Should I bring anything?"

"Everything I need is standing right before my eyes."

She squeezed out an insincere seductress smile. "I won't be late."

"And you won't be sorry. And after tonight, I guarantee

you'll forget all about Dwayne Hargis," he said, wearing a deceptive smile.

Ary walked past Michelle, who by now was engrossed in her final evening's obligations. As she headed to her desk, Marguerite appeared, coming out of a manager's office. Ary's heart thumped.

"Good evening, Marguerite."

"Annie," she said, cynically.

"It's Ary."

Not for too much longer, Marguerite thought, smiling. "I'm so sorry Ary. And it's such a *common* name to have to remember."

Ary continued down the corridor. She wanted so much to question her about Bob, but decided to quell the surging emotions and resurface them in a revealing document to G. She went up to the fourteenth floor library, sat down at an available computer station and began typing a letter:

Dear G:

This is probably one of the toughest business assignments I've ever had to tackle, and unfortunately it involves the one company that I have the most admiration and respect for, NPI...."

Ary's letter detailed everything she knew about Joseph's plan to undercut NPI's bid for the BP contract and siphon the actual information to his company in L.A. She outlined the role he wanted her to play in gaining insider information from Darias, to the title she would hold in his new firm. She chronicled Dwayne's sudden dismissal and Marguerite's true identity. Ary wasn't sure if Marguerite had anything to do with the firing of Bob, but she mentioned the conversation she'd overheard in the garage and the one she shared with the friendly guard.

G, I don't know if any of this would have taken place had I not come to work for NPI, somehow I feel responsible. Before I resign, I wanted to do all that was possible to save the company that gave me the opportunity to learn the business, to grow as a professional and to prosper as quickly as I have. The authentic BP proposal will be left with your assistant, marked 'Confidential' and a copy will be sent to you as an attachment in this email. Please know that I have the utmost respect for you as a business leader and a person, and I pray that you can find it in your heart to forgive me for the trouble I've caused.

Sincerely and Regrettably,
Ariel 'Ary' Alexander

Ary read the letter several times before hitting the '*send mail*' key. She agonized over the consequences, but was resigned to accept the worst. She'd lost everything she'd worked so hard to accomplish.

CHAPTER 98

G read the email over and over again in astonishment. He sat in his European office and wondered if this was some kind of sick joke. He made several phone calls to L.A. to substantiate Ary's claim of Joseph's company and contacted NPI's Human Resources VP to find out if Dwayne was indeed fired by Joseph. After twenty minutes of tense waiting, he was told about the oil firm founded by Joseph and a partner and the news of Dwayne's unjustifiable termination added insult to injury. G contacted the building security guard supervisor and inquired about Bob's discharge, and was informed of Marguerite's request that a trustworthy, non person of color replace him—he was livid!

He opened the email attachment, read over the proposal and placed a call to Connie, making sure Ary had indeed left an original copy as she'd said. He then called Darias Woolfolk before calling a friend on the Board of BP and asked about Ary's role in getting forged information from him to pass on to Joseph. It was all true. G was outraged. He called Connie again and had her cancel the second leg of his trip to South America and prepared to leave Italy on his private jet within two hours.

Placing a call to his Administrative Vice President at NPI, he instructed him to get as much information as possible on Joseph's company and have a document prepared and waiting for him in his office by morning. He thought about contacting the SEC and OPEC, but decided to hold off until every piece of evidence could be validated. Joseph and Marguerite would pay dearly for their betrayal.

G arrived on U.S. soil in the early morning hours on Wednesday. His car was ready and waiting to whisk him off to NPI, but this time, it would be different. He wouldn't have Joseph standing in the corridor, welcoming him back from a successful trip or Marguerite waiting for him to summon her to his office for their own personal rendition of a business merger. No one expected his return today.

Ary informed Joseph of her appointment with a client and suggested that he go to the office without her. The night had been demoralizing, but she'd convinced herself that it was for the good of everyone involved and the only way to prevail in her quest to expose Joseph and his vulgar plot. He'd spent the better part of the evening on the phone with his partner— going over the financials and the proposal. Everything seemed to be in perfect order. So as not to arouse any suspicion, he and Ary discussed how they would eventually leave NPI—and move to L.A. G would surely understand and offer his bless-ings. She pretended to be in agreement with his plans and excited about using her professional skills and contacts for the firm. Joseph left her with specific instructions on submitting the NPI proposal to BP on Friday. She was to meet with Mike Castellano in the afternoon, insert his suggestions and findings into the document, pass it by Marguerite and leave a copy with Connie to be forwarded to G tomorrow.

G walked into his office and found a large white envelope marked 'Confidential' in the center of his desk and another from his Administrative Vice President. He hesitated before opening either one. Taking a deep breath, he opened the one from Ary and found a copy of the letter she had emailed him and the original proposal for BP. The second envelope contained a document outlining the short history of Joseph's firm and its principals—Ary's name was not on the list. He also found a CD on his desk, with a note inside. The note read:

Dear Mr. Gicardi,

Although I don't profess to know what is or has been taking place in the last few months, I do know that something isn't right. I hope that you find the information in this CD useful. I've loved him for years and I hope one day he can find it in his heart to forgive me. Please consider this my immediate resignation.

Sincerely,
Michelle

The clearly audible voices on the CD were of Joseph and Marguerite discussing Dwayne's removal and Mike Castellano's new role on the BP strategy team. G's muscles grew tense as he sent his fist into the back of his chair. The recording ended before Joseph's final meeting with Dwayne.

G called his driver and told him to bring the car to the front of the building in five minutes. He was to take him downtown ASAP. It was six forty-five a.m.

Marguerite had finished dressing and was putting the final touches of makeup on her flawless face. Thoughts of her conversation with Joseph were still dancing in her head. Never in her wildest dreams had she imagined Dwayne being fired from NPI, and by Joseph of all people. And the unexpected bonus of getting rid of Ary soon after, caused goose bumps to appear on her well-toned arms. With Bob now gone, Marguerite felt more relieved than she had in months. Although Joseph would remain at the firm, she felt he was more of an annoyance than a threat—someone she could put up with until a suitable replacement could be found.

As she walked into the kitchen to make her morning coffee, the noise of the door buzzer startled her. "My God, who could that be at this hour?" She pressed the intercom button. "Yes Manny, what is it?"

"It's Mr. Gicardi, Ms. Armstead," he said cautiously, reacting to her brusque tone.

"G? Manny, let him in."

Marguerite rushed to the bathroom and checked her hair. She smoothed out her clothes and ran to the foyer to open the door. G walked quickly down the corridor to her condo. She stood in the doorway smiling.

"Honey, I wasn't expecting you. What a delightful early morning surprise." She threw her arms around his neck as he entered. He looked at her, stone-faced. "G, what's the matter? Baby, what's wrong?" she said, backing away. "Why are you back from Italy so soon?" Without acknowledging her, he walked over to the sofa and casually began taking off his raincoat.

"Marguerite, I know about your scheme with Joseph and your secret family connection to Bob," he announced. Her body went limp, as if the bones had suddenly escaped her flesh. Turning to face her, he continued his attestation. "I trusted you and believed in who I thought you were. I foolishly believed what we had would last forever. I was wrong," he shouted. "You were the one person I thought I could confide in, about anything!" he yelled. "And here it is, I don't even know your real identity. You've even accused me of having an inappropriate interest in Ary Alexander—so you planned to get her out of the picture—someone who's brought in more revenue to this firm than anyone I can remember in our short history— someone who's capable of helping to seat NPI on its rightful throne, next to all the oil heavyweights—but you wanted her out regardless of her professional contributions. I'd suspected that you didn't care for minorities, not knowing that you were a minority yourself. But even still, I never thought of you as an outright racist. What were you thinking Marguerite? Did you think I was a racist too? I'm done with you and you're finished at NPI."

"G, please. How could you do this to me? I never intended to hurt you or NPI. So many times I wanted to explain it all— but I didn't know how. I didn't know if you'd understand or accept me. Then Ary came to NPI and you, along with every other man in the industry, seemed to be mesmerized by her. G, she's young, talented and beautiful. I felt like I was losing control of my life and you," she cried. "G, I love you. There's never been anyone who made me feel the way you do. It's been nothing less than a living hell not being able to tell the world that I loved you. I've wanted nothing more than to lie next to you every night, hold you in my arms, make love with you and tell you about my family," she screamed, tearing off her blouse, causing the buttons to fly across the room.

"Don't do it," he yelled.

"Please G, don't leave me. Let me explain." Her crying became uncontrollable. "I'll do anything," she begged.

"If you can renounce your own brother, what else are you capable of hiding?" he asked, gritting his teeth.

She didn't hear him. The thought of losing him caused her

to abandon all sense of reason. "Take me G, please—I'll do whatever you want." She struggled to get out of her pants.

"I don't want you any longer. I don't know who you are."

"Don't say that," she pleaded. "I want you back."

"I pity you and everything you once stood for. There was a time when I felt you owned the world. You even had me, me!" he shouted, "eating from the palms of your lying hands." She fell into a chair, her head drooped towards the floor.

"Now look at you. For God's sake Marguerite, pick yourself up and go on with your miserable, misguided life and stay the hell out of mine." He reached for his coat lying neatly across the arm of the sofa. She grabbed his arm. He glared fiercely at her, no longer recognizing the woman he'd at one time loved, and jerked himself away from her feeble clutch.

"I don't ever want to see you near my company again." As he left the apartment, slamming the door behind him, she fell to her knees, fervently screaming his name and begging his forgiveness.

It was too late.

G walked into the reception area of his company, complimented Ann on her dress and headed for Joseph's office. An office temp sat at Michelle's desk. He took a deep breath.

"Good morning. I'm John G. Gicardi, President and CEO of this company and I'd like to speak with my *former* Vice President, Joseph H. Larsen."

The young woman stared at G before answering. "Of course, Mr. Gicardi, please go in."

G walked into Joseph's office and found him sitting stunned at his desk. He'd heard G's announcement and realized the game was over.

"I'm sorry G. I'm really sorry."

"Save it Joseph. There's nothing more to discuss. I've put up with your shit for more than seven years for the sake of money and how did you want to repay me? By destroying my company. You're done. Not only at NPI, but in the industry. When I'm finished with you Joseph Larsen, there won't be an oil firm willing to let you come within a foot of their premises. Get the fuck out of my sight." There were guards waiting in the hallway to escort him out.

CHAPTER 99

ARY drove in the right lane of the Long Island Expressway. Traffic was light heading south. She glanced at the throng of cars going in the opposite direction and sighed. Thick clouds above appeared to break up as the steady rain changed over to a light drizzle. She reached for the *Arabic* CD, sitting on the passenger seat and popped it into the player.

Maybe I'll get the opportunity to go there with my next job, she thought.

It all seemed like a dream—the first day at NPI, flying off to Paris and winning an impressive contract, romantic rendezvous' and working for someone who in the beginning, she vehemently disliked, but now felt a puzzling passion. The sun was starting to shine through the fast moving clouds. She reached for her sunglasses and repeated the words after the speaker on the CD and smiled for the first time in a long while.

CHAPTER 100

"I think you should go after this woman Dwayne. I don't ever recall seeing you this confused since I met you. Now, is this short enough or do you want a little more off the top? I tried to tell you those midtown business folks can eat you alive! Specially a country boy like yourself. I know you done well in the past but now it's time to put all that talent to work for a *black* firm. There must be one at least out there that'll appreciate you."

He maneuvered the mirror. "Thanks for the vote of confidence Ricky, and my hair looks just fine. And hey, I haven't given up on her yet. You know, before I start searching for a new job, maybe I'll take a trip to the Mediterranean. I've been itching to get over there, although, I had planned on the firm footin' the bill somehow," he laughed.

"Sounds like a vacation for two, Ricky said. Ask her, you never know what she might say. Listen handsome, life is too short not to pursue the one you love. I should know—I've pursued duzzens of 'em." Every man and woman in the salon burst out in laughter.

"You're absolutely right, Ricky. I'm gonna call her and ask her to go with me."

"What *call* her? Boy, go *find* that girl. Take her to one of those fancy restaurants rich people go to and charm her into going. Am I the last romantic fool left on earth?" Ricky asked, scanning the patrons for an *'amen.'* "Wit all them degrees, seems like I still have to tell y'all every little thing."

Dwayne turned around and shook his head. "You're a dying breed, Ricky. May you live a hundred more years." Dwayne reached for his wallet and pulled out a fifty dollar bill. "Keep the extra for the advice."

"Hey handsome, when am I gonna get the chance to meet this special girl?"

Dwayne winked and walked towards the door. "As soon as I know she's mine. I'll see you in a couple of weeks…before I, we, go on vacation."

Dwayne sat in his car and checked his BlackBerry voice-mail. There was one from G and another from Ary.

"Dwayne, it's G, call me. Everything will be straightened out—I guarantee it. If you still believe in NPI and want to continue your career with a firm you've contributed so much too, I'd be honored to have you back. Please call me on my cell."

His heart raced. He called Ary at work, but was told she'd taken the day off. He called her house, there was no answer. He scrolled through his list of contacts, hoping he hadn't deleted her cell number in a fit of anger.

"Ary, it's me, Dwayne. I have good news, but I'd rather tell you about it in person. Where are you?"

"I'm on my way to see my mother. Can it wait until tomorrow?"

"No. Would you mind if I met you there?"

Ary scratched her brow and smiled, then gave him her mother's address to Brookstone.

Marcus called Sonya early that morning, asking her if he

could come over to apologize for all the trouble he'd caused and to offer a final explanation. She assured her son that none was needed.

"Marcus, do you love her?"

"Yes mama, I do. But it's important that I know I'll still have you and Ary in my life."

"Honey don't worry, you'll always have me. I'm not too old to learn. I've wasted so many years. I finally understand that Bruce is happy with Matthew and they've built a life together. When he left, it didn't necessarily mean that he rejected us as a family, it only proved how important it was to be able to find the peace within yourself before you attempted to share it with anyone else."

"Thank you mama. I love you and I'm on my way. I'll see you soon."

Bruce was in New York on a business trip, but instead of leaving the same day as he usually did, he drove to the beach house. He rented a car and drove out towards Long Island... he wanted to be near the ocean. He called Matthew and left a message for him at work saying that he'd decided to stay on the east coast for an extra day or two and that he could reach him at the beach house. For an unexplained reason, it felt good driving along the expressway. Memories of he, Sonya and the kids entered his thoughts as he passed familiar landmarks.

The green overhead signpost showed 'Brookstone' one mile away. His attention was abruptly diverted. The Hamptons exit was much farther. He exited at Brookstone.

Ary's cell phone rang as she exited the expressway. He must be lost, she thought, thinking it was Dwayne.

"Where are you?" she asked, playfully.

"Ary, everything's going to be alright here. I had to call and tell you. Oh, I'm sorry, you were obviously expecting another call."

"Oh my God G. I'm so sorry about everything, but I hope I was able to help NPI. Listen, I hope to see you once in a while in the field, after I find another job. And please know how grateful I am for all that you and NPI gave me."

"Ary, about that letter of resignation, I never really accepted it, and I'd like to make you an offer that would be extremely difficult to refuse."

She smiled. "Well, I *was* going into the office tomorrow to clean out my desk. But I'd be willing to put that on hold until we had a chance to discuss that offer," she teased.

"I'll see you in the morning Ms. Alexander."

"Goodbye G." Ary could barely contain her emotions.

As she turned onto her mother's street, she noticed an unfamiliar car parked in the driveway. She drove in slowly and noticed a casually dressed man wearing a hat, standing in the doorway hugging a smiling Sonya. She tried to identify him from her car, but couldn't. As she opened her door to get out, Marcus drove up beside her. He walked over and kissed her on the cheek.

"I didn't know you were coming Marcus."

"I didn't expect to see you either."

"Was mama expecting company?" she inquired.

"Not that I was aware of," Marcus answered curiously.

As they walked up to the house, the stranger turned around. Ary stopped dead in her tracks, held tightly onto Marcus' arm and said, "Marcus, forgiveness really is life's true love."